My Friends the Miss Boyds

Jane Duncan

MY FRIENDS THE MISS BOYDS

with a new Afterword,
'Jane Duncan Remembered'

Millrace
Revivals

My Friends the Miss Boyds,
Jane Duncan Centenary Edition,
published in Great Britain in 2010 by
Millrace
2a Leafield Road, Disley
Cheshire SK12 2JF
www.millracebooks.co.uk

First published by Macmillan & Co, London, 1959

ISBN: 978-1-902173-31-3

by
RW

Jane Duncan,
1910–1976

Jane Duncan made publishing history in the late 1950s when, as an unknown Scottish writer, she had a sequence of seven novels accepted by Macmillan. She had written them secretly while living in Jamaica, hiding the manuscripts in her linen-cupboard. The first to appear in print, and an instant success, was *My Friends the Miss Boyds*. Its setting is the coastal countryside of the Black Isle and the hilltop croft near Cromarty which Jane Duncan regarded as her 'real home'. This was where her grandparents lived and where she spent her childhood holidays. Her 'away home' was a series of police stations in the Glasgow area, where she lived with her policeman father Duncan, her mother Janet, and later her stepmother.

Jane Duncan was born Elizabeth Jane Cameron in Renton, Dunbartonshire in 1910. She was educated at Lenzie Academy and Glasgow University, where she read English Literature, before going to England to work as a 'secretary-companion-general-dogsbody'* in the 1930s. At the start of the Second World War, she joined the WAAF, was commissioned and posted to Photographic Intelligence. After the war, working near Glasgow, she met and fell in love with Sandy Clapperton, a Scottish engineer, and accompanied him to Jamaica in 1949. It was when he became terminally ill that money worries drove her to seek a publisher for the novels in the cupboard.

Sandy died in 1958 and Jane Duncan, returning to Britain in time for the publication of *My Friends the Miss Boyds,* suddenly found herself the centre of media attention. She retreated to the Black Isle to make her home with her uncle George in Jemimaville. There, in between gardening, cooking and entertaining, she wrote over twenty more books, including another twelve in the internationally successful *My Friends* series and several books for children. Her brother Jock and his wife and four children were frequent visitors in the school holidays (see 'Jane Duncan Remembered', page 269) and eager fans would often turn up on the doorstep.

Jane Duncan died at home in 1976 and is buried in Kirkmichael churchyard. This new edition of *My Friends the Miss Boyds* has been published to celebrate the centenary of her birth.

*Quotations are from Jane Duncan: *Letter from Reachfar*, London, Macmillan, 1975.

I arrived at Rose Cottage on the 18th January and these five months so many things have happened that there's been no time to write this. The Boyds is out—published 7th May— and is a best-seller, bless its heart.

Jane Duncan's diary
Jemimaville, 18th June 1959

Part I

y Friend Monica has a small daughter called Janet-Lydia, known to her intimate friends as Jay-ell, who between the ages of four and five worried her parents a good deal by her preoccupation with the word 'house'. Jay-ell refused to accept a great number of words common in the English language, and replaced them by 'house' words of her own construction. A matchbox was a 'matches house', a handbag a 'money house' inside which there might be a 'lipstick house', the stable was a 'horse house', and the cutlery drawers of the sideboard were 'spoon houses'. The principle seemed to be that any container for anything was a 'house', so that a book was a 'story house', which led to the complication of a 'story houses' house' for bookshelf, and Jay-ell would invite you, if she liked you, to 'let a story out of its house' for her at bedtime, and at the end would say: 'Finished now. Put it back in the house for next time.' With which you had to close the book.

'She must be made to stop it,' Monica would say. 'Drives me mad—it's so unnatural. You'd think I had been frightened by a house before she was born!'

Shortly after she was five Jay-ell 'stopped it', and began to refer to stables, matchboxes and handbags like everyone else, but it is my private belief that she has never really 'stopped it' at all, that she never will 'stop it' and that in the private part of her mind she will still, as a very, very old woman, use the word 'house' in a thousand unorthodox ways. Thought language can be entirely different from the language spoken aloud between two people—the words can have different meanings, different connotations, significances entirely personal to the mind that is using them. 'House' for Jay-ell has a thought meaning, probably, that she may never disclose to another person, partly because she may be shy of disclosing it and partly because she may never be completely aware that it has a special thought-meaning for her at all.

I am fortunate enough to be a partner in a marriage in which, in slang parlance, 'anything goes'—by which I mean that there are not, between my husband and myself, any concealments of deed or feeling, any restrictions of thought or speech, any guardedness of opinion or expression, and one day, after I had described something as 'old-maidish', he said to me: 'Just what do you mean by old maid, old-maidish? You apply it in so many ways, to so many different things, that it certainly doesn't have the conventional meaning for you, and I'm starting to wonder if you know yourself what you mean by it.'

I could not answer this question straight away, any more than could Jay-ell, at the age of four, have told you in concise terms what significance the word 'house' had for her, and, very much as Jay-ell might have done, I stared at my husband, waved my hands about in a gormless way and said: 'Oh, *you* know—just old-maidish!' The more basic a thing is, the more difficult it is to describe or explain. My dictionary, which is a very good one, deals with the unlikely word 'bdellometer' (look it up for yourself) in four lines, but requires no less than eighty-four lines to deal with the word 'be' and another thirty-three lines to deal with 'be-' used as a prefix. 'Old-maidish,' occupying as it does a basic place in my thought structure, was, therefore, difficult for me to explain, and it took me a long time to decide precisely, for my own information, what the word connotes for me.

This word is one that, for me, has become a victim of transference of meaning—it is a displaced person of a word. In my mind it is not descriptive of an unmarried woman, or of any woman at all. No. For me it is descriptive of the ugly, spiteful things that 'They'—that monster that is always speaking out of turn and usually thoughtlessly and cruelly—say about unmarried women. In other words, 'They', in its remarks about unmarried women, is what I call 'old-maidish'. The word conjures up for me a thoughtless social attitude, a cruel mental climate and a lack of human kindness that are utterly repugnant to me in their smug complacency, their inhuman cruelty and their mindless and heartless insensitivity. The 'old-maidish' remark is, for me, the smug or cruel or scornful or patronising comment, made out of sheer malice, where no effort at understanding has been made, and its main characteristic is that it should, in human decency, have been left unsaid.

This story that I am going to tell you about My Friends the Misses Boyd will show you, I hope, why the term 'old maid' has such a thought structure in my mind, for the phrase is tied up inextricably with things I saw and heard and felt at an age when the perceptions are still groping among the wonders of the great world and yet, when an impression is received, it is very sharp and indelible.

At the time when the events which I shall try to describe took place I did not know what I thought about the Misses Boyd or the community in which they and I lived. Now, forty years later, I know what I think of the community, although the Misses Boyd remain, as all human beings do, an unsolved mystery.

And now, if the gentleman who is setting this up for printing will kindly let us have a row of asterisks to denote a gap in time—just here, thank you—

*   *   *   *   *

—I will begin my story.

In my young days there was a class of women known as 'old maids', or, if you like, once upon a time there was a class of women known as 'old maids', for now, in the late 1950s, the very name has about it the fairytale atmosphere that hangs about poor swineherds, princesses and other romantic figures that are dying away in our mundane times. Mark you, in the days when old maids still existed they were regarded by the general run of people as the very opposite of romantic, but that is part of the general short-sightedness that is part of the character of every age. There is always a prevailing belief that to be romantic or interesting in any way at all a thing or a person has to be unusual or different, but, in my opinion, this is a mistaken belief. The commonest, most everyday thing becomes interesting and even romantic if you take the time to look into it.

Now I, probably, would never have thought of looking into the question of the Miss Boyds at all—and although 'the Misses Boyd' may be more correct, they will be referred to throughout this story as 'the Miss Boyds'—but for the fact that I happened to be born in the year 1910 at Reachfar in Ross-shire, which is a quiet unhurried part of Britain which gives people time for looking into things, and I happen to be by nature a bit of a looker-in to what are probably unconsidered trifles to other people. At least, that is the sort of person that people tell me I am. For myself, I do not agree. My own contention is that, left to myself, there are dozens of things I would never have looked into at all had they not been thrust upon me as, we are told, some people have Greatness thrust upon them. The time when the Miss Boyds were first thrust upon me was the year 1918, the place was my home, Reachfar, and I was eight years old, which is where this story really starts.

As this story deals mostly with things that happened when I was between eight and nine years old, and the happenings are told as I saw them and understood them, I may as well tell you now that I was no infant prodigy. You will not find in this chronicle any startling revelations of an unusually brilliant child mind surveying its world, or anything of that sort. No. In sober fact, I think I was rather a slow-witted child although what was known as 'clever at the school'. This may be because I did not have any of the kindergarten play-therapy practised on me which is so common nowadays, for in my family there was no money to spare for 'toys and such-like capers'. I do not mean that we lived in dire poverty—far from it—but the view taken was that a normal child would play, anyhow, and that it was no more necessary to provide things for it to play with than it was to provide special equipment to make the lambs, calves and foals skip about the fields. The way to deal with a child, my family thought, was to stop it playing to excess and try to turn its energies into sensible, useful channels. My family found this quite difficult enough, without providing any special playing equipment. I cut a piece of the plough reins to make a skipping-rope and skipped when I was supposed to be cleaning the hen house; and I dressed Chickabird, my pet hen, in my grandmother's sun-bonnet and let her walk about the yard in it, so that my uncle said: 'It made a fair ruination of the Ould Leddy's bonnet but you couldna but laugh when she wasna looking.'

5

The women of the tight little community of the village down on the shore of the Firth used to ask me periodically if I 'never thought long up on that hill with no other bairns to play with', and when they asked me such questions I used to think to myself that the village people in general must be weak-minded. I had never 'thought long', wearied or felt bored in my life. I am now of the opinion, in my maturity, that there was indeed a weakness in the reasoning of the village women when they said there were no other 'bairns' at Reachfar, for youth of mind has little relation to years of age, and I had two companions at home, then, in Tom and George—the former our handyman and the latter my uncle who did not like the title of 'uncle'—who had never lost their youth of mind, and now, forty years later, have still not lost it.

Instead of being given toys, then, I was given animals, which carried with them a responsibility from me to them. My nurse-maid was my dog Fly, and as soon as I could carry her dish I had to feed her myself every dinner-time. I had Chickabird, my hen (really a series of hens), who hatched a flock of chickens each spring—I had to attend to their going out, their coming in and their feeding. I had a pet lamb every year—I had to see that he was fed and kept out of mischief and see that he was safely in the Little Fieldie with his triangular wooden collar on before I left for school. Someone once gave me an albino rabbit in a hutch which I did not like very much—although white, it was part of the family of vermin which Fly, Angus my ferret and I killed all the time. I neglected to keep it clean, and my father took it up to the moor and set it free. If a thing was mine I had to look after it or it was mine no longer.

I had, too, opportunities to earn pennies to put in Mr Foster's bank in the village that they might save and multiply in case I did well enough at school to be able to 'go on to the Higher Eddication'. My grandfather would pay a halfpenny per half-dozen for rabbits, a penny a tail for rats and twopence a tail for moles (he had a particular hatred for moles) if Fly, Angus and I would catch them. I would be given a setting of duck or turkey eggs and a mother hen in the spring and be allowed to sell the production in the village at Christmas if I looked after them and got them good and fat—the food for them was free. But if I neglected them, even for a day, they were put with the general flock and I had lost the trouble and work I had put into them as well as all prospect of the money for them. My father, my uncle and Tom would pay twopence a week each to have their working boots cleaned for six days of the week—cleaning materials were free. But that was sixpence for eighteen pairs of boots, which would be turned back to me if the job was not up to standard with the words: 'Do it right or don't do it at all!'

Although there was no money to spare for 'toys and non-sense', there was always enough for plenty of books and writing materials, wool for knitting and cloth and thread for sewing, and my young aunt, in secret, would pay a farthing-for-small and a halfpenny-for-big for darning the holes in the heavy woollen socks that our menfolk wore. These occupations were all largely winter ones, for we were out-of-doors and busy as long as it was light in the fine weather, but the reading and writing went on on Sundays all through the year. The reading and writing had the approval of one and all as a pastime and every one of my family took an interest in it. Reading, writing and 'the areeth-*met*-ic' were, you see, the basis of that Tremendous Thing, 'the Higher Eddication', which was now open to people of only average ability even, and at small cost. This was a modern miracle, and, as such, put the reading, writing and areeth*met*ic on the level of the holy things, like going to church, psalm-singing, Bible-reading and other practices which were permissible on the Lord's Sabbath Day. Money spent on a 'useless toy' would have been a Sinful Waste, but money spent on books, paper, pencils and the material of 'the Eddication' was of the same character as money put into the collection plate at church on Sunday. It was money dedicated to a God of whom nothing but good could come. Until this day and age no child born on the harsh ground of Reachfar had had what my grandmother called a 'right chance', but the millennium was now here, and 'the Bairn', as I was called mostly, was to have that 'chance' which had been withheld from her forebears. As I have said, I was not a brilliant child, but from my earliest days I was aware of my opportunity, was grateful to my family for it, and repaid them by trying, even at eight years old, to maintain the standards they had set for me.

This then, in 1918, was the background of my life at our croft of Reachfar—in modern agricultural terms, our marginal smallholding of Reachfar—the home of my family, where lived, in order of seniority of age, my grandfather, my grandmother, Tom, my father, my Uncle George, my mother, my Aunt Kate and me, but, as you may know, age has nothing to do with command, and the Reachfar strength was commanded, in the main, by my grandmother, who, strangely, could be brought to question and sometimes even overruled only by the most unexpected members of my family, namely, my gentle, delicate, dark-haired mother with the beautiful soft eyes, and my tall, silent, white-bearded, eagle-nosed grandfather.

Reachfar was a busy place. My father and my uncle, at that time, did not work our own land, for my father was grieve—a sort of farm manager—to Sir Torquil Daviot of Poyntdale, our neighbour on the north march, and my uncle was grieve to Mr Macintosh of Dinchory Farm, our neighbour on the west march. My grandfather, who was about sixty-five, and Tom, who was about fifty (I think), worked the ground of Reachfar, and my grandmother and my aunt did the milking, the churning, the cooking, the baking, the cleaning and hen- and pig-feeding and a thousand other things. My delicate mother did the sewing, the light weeding in the flower garden, most of the letter-writing to the members of the family overseas, and generally kept the peace. I did What I Was Told, mostly, and when I did not I got into Bother. As I remember it all, Bother in a variety of different forms caught up with me fairly often.

I am now quite an old woman, but a thing I have never come to understand is how Bother can catch up with one out of a clear blue sky, as it were, in a most unexpected way, and how it is usually generated into one's ambient atmosphere through somebody or something with whom or with which one did not realise that one had any connection at all. For instance, the Miss Boyds, whom I did not even know when I turned eight years old, were destined to cause me Bother in what My Friend Martha would call No Ordinary Quantity at one time and another during my life.

At the end of June 1918 my school, which was the village school at our village of Achcraggan, down on the shore of the Firth, 'came out' for the summer holidays. I liked school very much, but I also liked my home at Reachfar, and I looked forward to being at home for the holidays, because I had so many things to do. I had all sorts of special places to visit, like the newt pool in the old quarry, Donald the Trout's pool in the Reachfar Burn, the pond in the moor where the double buttercups grew, the Waving Tree to climb and the Thinking Place to crawl into.

In addition to these things, I had a certain amount of reading to do; a poem or two to write; probably, if the feeling came over me, rabbits, rats and moles to catch; and, of course, I would have to do the million-and-one errands that my grandmother was always requiring to have done. At the age of eight I was sure that there was no other person in the Whole Wide World with so many errands needing doing as my grandmother.

Usually for the first few days of the holidays her requirement for errands to be done was less great, but not this holiday apparently, for after Prize Day on Friday she allowed only Saturday and then Sunday to elapse—and Sunday did not count because errands never got done on Sundays—and at six o'clock breakfast on Monday morning she said: 'Oh, and Janet—don't you go off hiding in some hole this morning. I want you to run down to the Miss Boyds with that butter and eggs they asked for.'

'I don't know any Miss Boyds, Granny,' I said, knowing as I said it that it was within an inch of being a Back Answer.

'Then you'll never be younger to learn,' said my father in a voice that indicated that I had come too close to giving a Back Answer at that. 'Just you be here when Granny needs you, Janet,' and he and my uncle went off to work.

In silence I mixed the oatmeal, salt and water and went off up the yard with Fly to feed Chickabird and her chickens, and, when out of earshot of the house, I told Fly and Chickabird, in so far as I could find the words, just what I thought of the Miss Boyds. Not that I knew much about them. In fact, now that I came face to face with them in my mind, while outwardly I was face to face with Fly's intelligent golden eyes and enquiring cocked ears, all I knew about the Miss Boyds was that there were several of them, known collectively as 'the Miss Boyds', and that they lived in a biggish house, inside a wall, down in Achcraggan, and that this house was called 'the Miss Boyds'. So after I had used up my two 'swear words' and had said 'Och, *poop* to the Miss Boyds' and 'Ach, *dirt* on the Miss Boyds' several times, Fly seemed to lose interest, so I left her and went to sit on top of the moor gate and apply my swear words to butter and eggs and errands in general.

All the way to Achcraggan, I thought. It was nearly four miles there and nearly another four back and all right for a sensible purpose like school, but a Bother to do for the sake of these Miss Boyds. And butter and eggs! Just about the worst basketful a person ever had to carry! The slightest jolt and an egg would crack, the slightest knock and the thistle print on the butter would be blurred in outline. And on a *Monday!* Why couldn't the Miss Boyds have had their butter and eggs delivered on Friday when Tom went down with the trap to deliver butter and eggs to the dominie, the minister and Miss Tulloch's shop? Poop to the Miss Boyds!

'See anything of Dick and Betsy, Janet?' Tom asked, coming to the gate and starting to fill his pipe.

'They were west there in the whins a little ago,' I said, and stood up on the second-top bar of the gate. 'Betsy! Cah-up! Dick, cah-up!'

The two big Clydesdales came through the heather and between the trees towards us, their shiny necks arching, their manes tossing after their fine summer night spent among the fir trees of the Home Moor. Tom swung the gate open with me on the bar, and as Betsy came through she stopped and looked along her side as much as to say: 'All right—climb on', and I caught her springy mane and climbed on to her broad back. Dick tossed his head, did a little dance on his big hairy feet, gave a sprightly nicker and cavorted his way down the yard to the water trough, pretending to be dying of thirst and then blowing about at the surface of the water and not drinking at all.

Tom gave him a slap on his shiny hip. 'Be off to the stable with your capers!' he said. 'A day at the hay will take some of the steam off ye!'

'Ach, Tom!' I was finally disgusted. 'You're not going to start leading the hay?'

'Aye, we are that.'

'But, Tom, I have to go to the Miss Boyds! Who will tramp the stack?'

'Granda and I will chust have to manage, I doubt,' said Tom.

By this time Dick had cavorted his way past the stable door, through the gap between the granary and the cartshed and was racing down the road, mane and tail flying, head tossing drunkenly in the summer morning breeze.

'Dang it!' said Tom. 'A person would hardly believe that that ould devil would caper like that and him six year-old come the back-end.' He took off his old tweed hat and handed it to me when he had lifted me down from Betsy's back. 'Here—take this and go and get me a little oats from the barn. Oats! The ould devil!'

Betsy, the orderly creature, went to her stall in the stable and began to champ away at her breakfast that lay in her manger while Tom and I went out to the north side of the steading. Dick, having come to a closed gate a hundred yards down the road, was now dancing back uphill, for it was a fine morning and Dick did not want to go anywhere in particular—he merely wanted to dance a little. He was really a law-abiding, hard-working person, but some mornings are dancing mornings.

'Come, lad,' said Tom in seductive tones, holding out the hatful of oats. Dick came close in, blew on the oats, savoured their smell and took himself a smart fouetté or two round the rim of the midden. 'Come, there's a clever fellow,' said Tom, when Dick paused to look back at us. Dick remembered the seduction of that smell, looked at the old hat which always held something good when offered to him, resisted temptation, tossed his head, bent down gracefully and bit a little at something on his off foreleg and then looked away west at Ben Wyvis, as if contemplating a trip to a far country. '*Bonnie* lad!' said Tom, in the oily tones of the traitor. 'Janet, look at Dick, the bonnie, clever fellow!'

Almost against his own will Dick stepped daintily round the smooth grass edge of the midden towards the hat, and then, the smell getting the upper hand of him, plunged his muzzle into the oats. But the rope halter in Tom's other hand was quicker than the plunge of that greedy muzzle.

'Ye ould boogger!' said Tom and looked down at me. 'Here, carry the hat, and not a word to your granny about me saying that word to Dick.'

'Oh no, Tom,' I said in solemn promise, while I with the hat, Dick with his muzzle *in* the hat and Tom holding the halter made our way to Dick's stall in the stable. I led the hat to the manger and transferred Dick's muzzle from oats as bait to oats for breakfast, while Tom tied the rope of the halter to the hayrack.

'He'll do now,' said Tom, sitting down on the chest at the end of the stalls. 'Let them eat in peace and then we'll put the harness on them. A person is always the better of a little peace before the harness.'

This, dear reader, is how I was brought up, surrounded by

'persons', some two-legged, some four-legged, some having skin, some hide, some wool, some feathers, but all 'persons', and comments of the higher philosophical nature were part of the lives of these persons and me.

'Tom, who is the Miss Boyds?'

'That three ould maids that's come to live for good now in that housie down near the Manse at Achcraggan,' said Tom.

'But, Tom, what *about* them?'

'About them?' said Tom thoughtfully. 'Well, now, I don't know that I know very much *about* them. Their father was ould Andra Boyd, the unctioneer o' Inverness, as big a rascal as ever sold a pig.'

I knew that what Tom called an 'unctioneer' was really an 'auctioneer', the big fat man with the red face that stood at the high desk in the sale ring and said: 'Now, gentlemen, here's a nice lot. Six stirks put in by Sandison, Reachfar. You all know Reachfar, and you never saw a bad beast come off it yet. Well, gentlemen, who'll give me a start? What-am-I-bid-what-am-I-bid? Twenty-five? You are making chokes, Mr Anderson! Thirty, Mr Donaldson? Come, now! Thirty-five? Forty? Forty-five? Thank you, Mr Crombie—that's fine for a start. Where are the gentlemen who *know* a cattle beast? Fifty? Thank *you*—'

And as the heads nodded and fingers were raised on all sides of him, his sharp little eyes saw everything and the voice spoke more and more rapidly until, as the bidding slowed down, it became softer in tone, insinuating, as the 'unction' flowed into it.

'Now *then*, gentlemen, I see one or two here who know better than let this lot go past them! Come now—guineas, Sir Alex? Thank you! Well, you local gentlemen, is Sir Alex to get to take this lot away west the country there? Five more, Mr Crombie? Thank you!'

There would be a glance towards where we sat, a nod from whichever man of my family was at the sale that day, and the hammer would fall. All 'unctioneers' were reputed to be rascals, so, so far, Tom had not told me much about the Miss Boyds.

'Aye, ould Andra made a lot o' money one way and another,' Tom continued, 'and he built that housie down at Achcraggan there, and the wife and the bairns used to be coming to it for the holidays in the summertime. Then the second wife used to come too—she was a terrible silly craitur, the second wife, I mind.'

'Tom, people *don't* have two wives!' I protested. 'They can't. It's against the law. My mother said so when I was reading about Bluebeard.'

'It is not against the law if they'll be having them chust the one at a time,' said Tom. 'You see, with ould Andra it was this way: he got married and him and his first wife had three lassies and then the wife died. And then, a good whilie later, he got married to another wife and dang it if she didna have *another* three lassies!'

'But that makes *six* Miss Boyds!' I said.

'Aye, there's six o' them right enough, but it's only the three old ones that's down bye at the Miss Boyds, mostly. The younger ones is all working in this shoppie they have in Inverness, I think. Aye, they have quite a bittie money among them.' Tom rose from the chest and put his pipe in his pocket. 'Well, it's time I got them yoked,' he said, and took Betsy's big collar down from its wooden peg on the wall.

'Janet!' came the voice of my grandmother. 'Janet!'

'Here I am, Granny.' I ran along the yard to the house. 'Poop to the Miss Boyds!' I thought once more.

'Come through here till I brush your hair,' said my mother.

15

I followed her into her room on the ground floor. This was almost Too Much. It was the holidays, I had already brushed and plaited my hair that morning, and even although I did not make a very good job of it, I was not, after all, going to school. I was only going on an errand to these Miss Boyds. My mother undid the pigtails, brushed the hair, re-parted it right into two halves from the middle of my forehead to the middle of my nape, re-plaited each half and tied my school ribbons on the ends.

'What's that on your kimono?' she asked.

My 'kim-*oh*-no' was the calico dress, of which I had half a dozen, made like a sack with holes for my head and arms to go through and a belt tied round the middle. In summer I wore this and a pair of calico knickers underneath and nothing else. In winter I wore my 'kim-*oh*-no' on top of my woollen skirts and jerseys when I was at home.

'Some of Dick's slobbers,' I said. 'Tom and me had quite a caper catching him this morning.'

'Tom and *I*,' she said. 'Run up to your room and put on a clean one, but wash your hands first.'

When I had done What I Was Told, I said: 'Mother, who are the Miss Boyds?'

I do not know when I discovered—but it was fairly early in life—that if you made enquiries round all the members of my family on a subject you could often end up with quite a lot of information, and some of it contradictory, which was very interesting, and being committed to the Miss Boyds this morning, in any case, I might as well find as much interest as possible in them.

'They are three very nice ladies who live in Achcraggan,' said my mother.

'Tom says they are old maids.'

'Maybe they are, but you and Tom mustn't gossip. Now, go out to the milk-house and get the basket from Granny and off you go.'

In addition to giving me the basket, my grandmother gave me a lot of instructions—to be careful this way and that way, to go 'straight' to the Miss Boyds, and to mind my manners when I got there, and off I went.

*　　*　　*　　*　　*

Once I was on my way down the hill I felt better. It was a beautiful day, and on a beautiful day it did not very much matter what you were doing as long as you were out in it. When you were carrying butter and eggs the thing to do was to look 'far'. If you looked 'near', you might see all sorts of things that would cause you to put the basket down and have an even 'nearer' look, and, once you did that, you were no longer 'going straight', time simply disappeared, and when you returned to the basket the butter would be melting. I had a long experience of the tribulations that followed on 'not going straight' when doing an errand. So I looked 'far' as I went on a long north-easterly slant by moor and field paths down to Achcraggan, which was a little huddle of reddish houses around the crescent of a bay, with, on its east side, round a secondary little bay within the bay, a huddle of whitewashed houses which was the 'Fisher Town'.

The ships of the Fleet were lying in the Firth, swinging round on the tide, and the morning mail train to Wick was running along the north shore of the Firth like a little black caterpillar, giving off a plume as long as itself of white smoke. I wondered what a train was like when you were really close to it, for I had never seen a train nearer than this one was now. Probably, I thought, it would be bigger and longer than even Poyntdale's 'string' of six pairs of horses and carts when they were all lined up nose to tail when the coal boat came in to Achcraggan.

It was a wonderful thing when the coal boat came in, but it did not come until after the harvest and just before the winter, but *everybody* went to the coal boat. Poyntdale's 'string', of course, was the big sight of the day, and always made me want to burst with pride because my father was responsible for it, although the horses and carts belonged to Sir Torquil Daviot. The big Clydesdales would be shining to the last hair, their manes and tails plaited and tied with golden straw, their harness glittering, their carts bright blue with red wheels and every cart with its brass plate gleaming the words 'Sir Torquil Daviot, Poyntdale'. The next biggest string at the pier would be the five pairs whose brass plates said 'Wm Macintosh, Dinchory', for which my uncle was responsible; but the best string of all, to my mind, was one of the smallest, the three carts behind Dick, Betsy and Dulcie, which were as smart as any with their brass plates saying 'Sandison, Reachfar' and were driven by my grandfather, Tom and me. That was what had happened last year. Before last year my grandfather had always managed two of the Reachfar carts, while Tom handled Dick, who never came down to the 'County Road' if it could be avoided, for he was a 'hill person' and did not like the sea and boats and a lot of strange people and horses all round him. Then last year Dulcie, the lighter mare who was used for the trap for church and for the smaller cart, was new, and none of us knew what *she* might feel about the coal boat either. So Tom said: 'We'll put the bairn on Betsy's back and she'll stand like a lamb. You'll see.' My family was inclined to argue a little, but they 'saw'. Betsy was the best-behaved horse person on the pier.

Dominie Stevenson, the schoolmaster, always declared a special two-day holiday when the coal boat came in—unless the 'tattie holidays' were on, in which case we got a two-day extension. He did this because he was a clever man, who could always recognise a force greater than himself. None of the boys would come to school while the coal boat was in if they could help it; if forced to come to school they would learn nothing, and the girls were very little better. And if the 'tattie holidays' were on, nobody would dig and gather potatoes while the coal boat was in either. In addition, Dominie Stevenson loved beyond anything a convivial dram, and a convivial dram with a visitor from the big world outside was even better, so when the coal boat was in he, the doctor, Captain Robertson of Seamuir, my grandfather, Sir Torquil and a few other cronies formed a nucleus round the plush-covered table in the parlour of the Plough, at the head of which sat the captain of the boat, and round which eddied and flowed a vast number of more temporary visitors, such as my father, my uncle and all the farmers and crofters who had carts at the boat.

The coal boat did not bring coal alone. Indeed, it was one of these miracles of country organisation, in which, probably, Sir Torquil had been the leading brain. The boat was a little tramp steamer, which was chartered for this trip to Achcraggan each year, her main cargo being the coal for the community, but she also carried the winter stocks for the grocer and general merchant, who was Miss Tulloch; for the drapery and general warehouse, who was Mrs Gilchrist, and for the ironmonger and seed merchant, who was Mr Dickson. In addition to this she would have some barrels and cases of bottles for the Plough Inn; maybe a new binder or some other piece of equipment for one of the farms; and one time she brought a beautiful brass bedstead, with the mattress, pillows and blankets done up in a waterproof bale, which was a present to old Granny Macintosh from her son who was doing very well in the police force in Glasgow. The great thing about the coal boat was that you never knew just *what* she might bring, and the men who sailed her were an adventure in themselves, with their outlandish tongues that spoke in the accents of Aberdeen and Glasgow, while some of them were even *Englishmen*, and all of them with their rakish caps and their faces and hair salted by the sea.

Although the boat only stayed in Achcraggan for three or four days, the work connected with her went on for about a week or ten days. The 'clean' cargo, like Granny Macintosh's bed, was taken off first, and delivered amid much jollification and with a horde of children running alongside to Granny's cottage by one of the bright clean carts with its proud horse in shining harness, and then the driver of the cart would give Granny's daughter Jean a 'bit hand' to set the bed up and lift Granny, in her clean nightgown, mutch and shawl, into it. Then everybody would have a 'droppie tea', and the small boys, who were now all 'holding the horse' outside, would get scones and jam. Something like the bed occupied one man, one yoke and a dozen small boys for a whole morning, but in the meantime the other carts would be carrying the stocks for the shops. This was almost as leisurely as the business of the bed, for Miss Tulloch, Mrs Gilchrist and Mr Dickson would all be dispensing some kind of hospitality to the men who delivered their goods. Tom and I usually made the delivery to Miss Tulloch, and she always had a big dram and water biscuits and a big hunk of cheese for Tom, and my portion was a big cube-shaped box of fancy biscuits, to sit beside on the counter, dig into and eat as many as I pleased, while some were also put in a bag to take away. And the horses had the broken biscuits that she had been saving for them for the last month or so.

As soon as the clean cargo had been removed from the pier the coal would start 'coming out' and the excitement really set in, for the principle was to get as much coal as possible out into the carts and the 'dump' on the pier while the boat was riding on the high tide, for the time would come when, amid much shouting, she would blow her whistle and rush out to deeper water, to lie there and wait for the tide to fill again. The coal boat was a flighty difficult female who was understood only by her captain and the men who sailed in her, and we land people with our horses and carts could not understand her mysterious sea-going needs and tantrums at all. Nor, apparently, could she understand *us*, and the effects that her capers might have on us.

A year or two ago she chose the very moment when Johnnie Greycairn's horse was right alongside her to blow her flighty whistle. Greycairn is a sheep croft, away in the hills, higher even than the marginal land of Reachfar, and Johnnie had only one little hairy horse and a small cart, but, as I said, everybody came to the coal boat, so Johnnie and his horse were there, although everyone knew that, in the end, one of Sir Torquil's big strong horses would have to haul the few hundredweights of coal up to Greycairn, while Johnnie's horse Diamond would act as a trace over the worst parts of the road. Diamond, being a very wild, remote, sheep-croft person, had his poor head in enough of a muddle seeing all these people and horses round him while chains rattled and coal dust flew, so when the boat blew her shrill whistle right in his ears he reared high in the air, shook off his master and dashed down the pier, dived off the end into the deep water, cart and all. Fortunately my Uncle George and some of the fishermen from the Fisher Town who were there were strong swimmers, and there was a throwing off of boots and coats and a dozen men were in the water around the struggling Diamond. The fishermen were as terrified of Diamond as Diamond was of the coal boat's whistle, and would not have gone near him even on land, and Diamond, lashing his well-shod hooves about in the water, was no swimming companion for anyone, but, directed by my father from the pier, the fishermen supported the cart and tried to shove it shoreward against the tide while my uncle, with the help of his big clasp-knife, got Diamond free of his yoke. Suddenly a mighty cheer went up as Diamond and my uncle began to swim away westwards, leaving the fishermen with the cart; all the boys began to run westwards along the beach abreast of the man and horse in the water, whooping like Indians, and Johnnie Greycairn was dancing up and down on the pier shaking his fists at the coal boat and shouting: 'Poor Dye-mon! It's west at Inverness he'll be with the fright that's in him before Geordie catches him!' But even as Johnnie shouted, George was leading Diamond, still shuddering with fright, up the sand, and calling: 'Come, Johnnie! Leave your cart and take Diamond home', which Johnnie did, but not before he had told the coal boat and her crew what he and Diamond, individually and collectively, thought of them.

Oh yes. The coal boat was a great institution, and anything could happen when she came in. The first day of her visit was always the best, though. Once the coal started coming out, the men worked hard at the loading to keep the horses moving in a continuous stream on the little, narrow, slippery, stone pier, and everybody and everything—men, children, horses and carts—became grimed with coal-dust. On the second day there was no proud setting off with horses and carts groomed and shining to the last hair and brass trimming, the big horses stepping lively and tossing their heads in front of the empty carts whose weight they did not feel. No. On the second day the carts were loaded on the outward journey with bags of potatoes, bags of oats and barley or wood from Sir Torquil's sawmill, and every horse had a pull on his collar. Mind you, in spite of the hard work there was always a certain amount of fun.

Hughie Paterson, from the little croft of Seabrae, which lay above the big farm of Seamuir, had a big grey mare which he had bought, as Tom put it, 'for half-nothing' because she had been badly broken to harness and was not 'guaranteed for work'. She was a handsome animal, as good in appearance as any at the coal boat, her name was Pearl and she was a character to be reckoned with. Pearl was in no way vicious—she never thought of rearing, kicking, bolting or biting or other horse protests at injustice. No. When it came into Pearl's big head that she had had enough of work for the present she simply refused to move. This idea invariably came into her head when her cart had been filled with coal and she was politely requested by her soi-disant master, Hughie Seabrae, to move off with it. Pearl would give him a blank look of sheer insolence, blow through her nostrils, stare out over the Firth and not move an inch. Every man on the pier prided himself on his horsemanship, and certain ones, like Sir Torquil, my father and my uncle, were reputed to be able to 'do anything with a horse'. They would all try all their tricks on Pearl. The hatful of oats would be held a foot from her nose, they would cajole and flatter her with all sorts of encouraging words and noises, and, as a final resort, they would threaten her with a whip (after one had been fetched from the back shed of the Plough, for no driver of working horses in our part of the country at that time would have been seen dead with a whip in his hand). Pearl would not move, or else, in the middle of some man's speech to her, she would give him a scornful, disgusted look and march away with her load, leaving him looking a fool in mid-word, to be followed by his infuriated: 'Ye bliddy, thrawn, ould bitch!' for she made it obvious to all that she had moved merely because she felt like it and not because of anything that had been said to her.

All the time that these efforts with Pearl were going on the children would be laying bets on who could get her to move, and the men would be arguing among themselves and at the threat of the whip Hughie Seabrae would start to dance up and down and shout: 'Don't be coorse on her! If you'll be at her with the wheep it's sit *doon* she'll do!' But one memorable day, Sir Torquil, exasperated, *did* tap Pearl on the rump with a piece of rope. Hughie Seabrae's promise came true. Pearl sat down on her well-fed behind, with a hideous rending of wood as she broke both trams of her cart, and stared at Sir Torquil as if to say: '*Now* try and move me!' Work had to stop altogether for half an hour until Pearl chose to rise and march off with great dignity, up the pier, with the pieces of broken trams hanging from her harness.

In a contrary sort of way all of us, who were so proud of our intelligent, hard-working, 'guaranteed' horses, had a special pride in Pearl. She was a symbol of the freedom of the individual to entertain his own views and indulge his own whims. She was not mischievous like our big Dick from Reachfar, who, if he thought he was being kept waiting in one place for too long or was bored in any way, would start stamping his big feet, tossing his head with a jingling of harness and nickering until he had infected every horse on the pier and had them all capering too. Pearl was not like that. Pearl lived unto herself and would pull a load to oblige when she felt like it, but when she did not feel like it no power in heaven or on earth would make her do it. Secretly everyone admired her for her stolid independence of spirit, although, at the coal boat, it could be the limit of exasperation both for the landsmen and the crew of the boat, for the coal boat was always in a hurry, and what with the time lost on the turn of the tides, there was no time to spare to indulge Pearl's temperament.

I never could understand why the coal boat was always in such a hurry. My family was always scornful of people who were in a hurry, and I had been brought up to believe that there was something disgraceful in it. I knew that you had to 'step smart', of course, and not 'waste time' and not 'dally' and 'look businesslike', but all these things were quite different from being in a hurry.

'Get up in time in the morning,' my grandmother said, 'and you won't be running in a hurry all day.'

'Get off to church in time,' said my father, 'and not be hurrying at the last minute like Teenie Ferguson.'

But the coal boat was always in a hurry, in her every puff and whistle and rattle of her chains, and I asked my father why this was.

'It's because of the war,' he said. 'Before the war, when you were too little to mind on her, she had more time. But with the war, she has a lot more places to go, so she is always in a hurry. Indeed, but for Sir Torquil, I doubt if we would be getting any coal at all these days.'

The war was a very peculiar thing. People talked about it a great deal, and always in phrases like: 'because of the war' and 'to, with, by and from the war' and in a sighing way of 'before the war' and in a sad way of 'at or in the war'. The war did hundreds of dreadful things, far worse things than making the coal boat be in a hurry, so I asked Tom about it, and he told me what it was and where it was, but he could not tell me how or why it was. Nobody could. It was a thing even more mysterious than the tide that swung the big ships round in the Firth on their buoys, for Dominie Stevenson could make you understand the pull of the moon on the sea, and, although it was miraculous, you had to believe it. But even the moon, which controlled the tides, and the sun, which could ripen the corn, could do nothing about the war, apparently. In the end I asked my mother if God made the war, and she said a very queer thing. She said: 'No. I think the war is one of the few things that people have made for themselves and it is nothing for them to be proud of.'

At the end of a week or ten days, long after the coal boat had sailed away and we children were back at school, the last load of coal would have been carted away from the dump at the pier and my father and my uncle would sigh with relief at suppertime in the evening.

'Lord, but it's me that hates the coal!' George would say. 'And the stour and the dirt and a-all. Got your horses cleaned up yet, Duncan?'

'Och, aye,' my father would reply. 'But it makes the devil of a mess of the carts and harness. Still, it's by for another year.'

'I feel as clarty as Jock Skinner,' George would say, scratching at himself, and we would all laugh.

It was not possible, we all knew, for my big, fresh-skinned uncle or any of my family or any of the men who worked on the land of Poyntdale or anywhere to be 'as clarty as Jock Skinner'. Jock Skinner was a native of the Fisher Town, but he did not go to sea like the others. Jock Skinner was what was called a 'dealer', which was reckoned to be an even more rascally occupation than that of 'unctioneer'. He lived at a seaside croft at the east end of the Fisher Town, with his clarty, shrill-voiced wife and a gang of unruly children who were always having to be 'whipped in' to school by the whipper-in, whose official title was 'School Board Officer'. All around the untidy house and its overgrown garden there were heaps of old iron, and torn sacks hung over every sagging fence, while hens were scratching and pigs were grunting round the door, to which, periodically, Bella Skinner would come with a basin and hurl out a dollop of potato peelings, fish guts or other refuse, regardless of the youngest child who would be crawling there among the pigs.

Jock had a flat cart and two shabby little horses, which were yoked to the cart turn about, and when not yoked fed themselves as best they could, mostly by breaking through into the pastures of Captain Robertson of Seamuir. With his cart and his horse, with his poaching lurcher dog running under the axle of the cart, Jock roamed the country, 'dealing'. When the fishermen made a good catch Jock would be at the pier with his cart, buy a load of fish and drive madly off with them 'west the country', where he sold them at excessive prices, and on his return trip the next day he would call at all the farms and crofts and exchange cups and saucers and bowls for rabbit-skins and rags, in the intervals concealing in his cart the rabbits which his dog killed and carried to him. Back in Achcraggan, he would exchange the cost of the haulage of some beer from Dingwall for drink at the Plough, and the haulage of some grocery commodity for tobacco at Miss Tulloch's, and then he and Bella would be seen sitting at the gable of their house, smoking their clay pipes and drinking whisky and beer out of cracked teacups with no handles.

Jock Skinner, people would tell you, 'had done very well out of the war', particularly with the fruits of his poaching and thieving, for the big ships that came into the Firth had a constant demand for fresh food of almost any kind, and how, as Tom said, 'would the decent hard-working sailors be knowing that Jock Skinner was thieving the most that he was selling to them'? Reachfar was too far from the beaten track to suffer a great deal from Jock's depredations, but my father and my uncle, whose charges of Poyntdale and Dinchory both had fields bounded by the County Road, lost turnips by the cartload, and on one occasion two of the Poyntdale calves disappeared without trace. There was a big to-do about this, and the people of Achcraggan said it would be nearly justifiable to 'send west for the policeman', but this disgrace was avoided by my father borrowing Sir Torquil's riding crop in the evening, going to Jock's croft and 'putting the fear of God in him'. I never had explained to me, precisely, the connection between Sir Torquil's riding crop and the fear of God that came into Jock, but certainly neither livestock nor turnips disappeared after that from Poyntdale or Dinchory.

One of Jock Skinner's more honest bits of 'dealing', however, was his coal-merchant's business which he operated from the dump on the pier. Among the farm people like ourselves it was considered a disgrace to buy coal from Jock Skinner—we bought our coal 'direct', which meant that we made payment for it to Sir Torquil, who 'backed' the entire boatload. Let it not be thought, though, that we burned only coal. Far from it. The coal, at Reachfar, the whole two tons of it which we bought per year, was a treasured luxury, and every black stone of it was put on to the fire, with pride, by hand. Our main fuel was wood from the moor, and the coal was used only to put heart into the fire for a specially skilled piece of baking or on a particularly cold winter night, and to burn too much, so that we 'ran out' before the boat came again, and had to have recourse to Jock Skinner, coal merchant, would have been, in our eyes, a deep disgrace. Decent people, people 'of any standing', did *not* buy coal from Jock Skinner. The church, the Manse, the doctor's house, the school, the schoolhouse, the smithy, the few merchants and the people of the village, the farms and the 'Big Hoose' of Poyntdale, all had their coal direct from the boat, delivered by the massed farm carts of the district, and then Jock Skinner 'made a deal' with Sir Torquil for what was left in the dump and 'took a gamble' on someone running short—owing to sickness in the house perhaps—so that he could charge them a shocking price, while the fisher folk kept his business alive by buying from him a little at a time, as they could afford it, through the winter.

*   *   *   *   *

In 1918, as I made my way towards Achcraggan and the Miss Boyds with my basket—no, I have not forgotten the Miss Boyds—our district, like most other places, was fast in the grip of a great change, of which I, like most other people, was unaware. Until the war Achcraggan had been a healthy little fishing town of about thirty family boats that brought their catches in to the pier and disposed of them in a dozen ingenious ways. Doctor Mackay, with his trap, setting out on his round, would take a man and a creel of fish out to the limit of his visiting, and the man would sell out his creel on the way back. The mail cart would take away several boxes, all the way to Dingwall. Sir Torquil's coachman, down with the trap for the Big House letters, would pick up the huge supply of haddock or herring for the use of the Big House and, in addition, pick up a man and a creel to drop him in Poyntdale 'farm street' which was a hamlet in itself. And, of course, the brown-faced, sloe-eyed, barefoot Bella Beagle, in her blue-and-white striped petticoat and grey drugget apron, would set off, heavy creel on back, aslant and south-westerly over the face of the hill, on my school route, and take in every croft and shepherd's house on her eighteen-mile round, including Greycairn and Reachfar. Bella Beagle, whose name was really Bella Gunn, but who was known by the name of her family's boat *The Beagle*, just as my grandfather was called 'Reachfar' and I was called 'Janet Reachfar' by the name of our croft, was one of my earliest friends. It was she who taught me to scale, gut and bone a herring with more than the usual proficiency of an amateur, although I never could match the speed and skill of her flying fingers.

Bella was never allowed into the house of Reachfar until she and I had cleaned the fish and handed them over to my grandmother in the white enamel basin, and Bella's creel was never allowed into the house at all. When the scaling, gutting and boning were over, and we had given the refuse to the pigs, and we had washed our hands in the outside wash-house with the carbolic soap, we were allowed to come in, and Bella was paid for her fish and given a large bowl of broth from the pot and a large oatcake and butter. Fish, although a help on the menu, were 'dirty, stinking brutes'.

Then, when Bella had finished her soup and had called down a blessing on the house for it, we went outside and I helped her to hoist the heavy creel on her back and then walked along the yard and round to open the north gate for her. Bella, who a short time ago had been up to the elbows in fish refuse, would pick her way daintily through the hen droppings of the yard, step carefully round the stable drain and turn away her head from the midden behind the steading. Farm animals, although necessary, were 'dirty, stinking brutes'.

I have never, later in my life, been so aware of the gulf fixed between two races of people as I was of the gulf between the land and sea people of Achcraggan. They had nothing in common except the church, and even there, there was a deep-rooted difference. The land people tended to be tall and fair of skin, the sea people short and sallow; the land people were soft and slow of speech, the sea people shrill-voiced and rapid; to the land people fish were repellently dirty and stinking, to the sea people dirt and stink were the main characteristics of farm animals. The two races had nothing in common except their belief in God, and yet here came the deepest difference of all. The sea people claimed that they were God's chosen because His only Son had made His friends among the fisher folk of Galilee. The land people claimed that they were the Lord's chosen because He had put His first created man on earth to live in Eden, a garden. There was nothing to be done about it. The grown men fought over the issue at the Plough; the grown women fought over it in the village shops, and the children fought over it in the school playground. Grown-ups and children could be controlled only by the greater powers vested in the persons of the Reverend Roderick Mackenzie, the minister, and of Dominie Stevenson, the schoolmaster. Civil war simmered always just below the surface of Achcraggan life.

But by 1918 this was dying away, just as the family fishing boats were dying out one by one, swamped by the competition of the bigger boats from the bigger ports; just as the smaller, poorer crofts were becoming merged in the bigger farms as the older people died off. And the process was being accelerated by the war, which had drawn off so many of the younger men, landsmen and fishers alike, leaving on the land only the experts like Mr Macintosh, my father and my uncle and the older men like Sir Torquil, my grandfather and Tom.

And so, looking 'far' at the warships in the Firth and at the cloud shadows drifting over the hills to the north and thinking of the joys of the visit of the coal boat, I made my way, 'stepping lively' and without once putting the basket down or bumping it in any way, to the gate in the red freestone wall that ringed the 'Miss Boyds', to find that the gate was standing wide open, a most unusual sight. But, queerer and queerer, drawn up at the kitchen end of the house was none other than Jock Skinner's shabby little cart and tatty little horse, the whole weighed down with numerous torn, dirty sacks of coal.

'Well!' I thought. 'Out of coal already and it only June of the year and the boat won't be in until October. What a disgrace!'

I went up to the door, covered with blushes of shame for the Miss Boyds. However, the three ladies in the kitchen did not seem to be feeling the slightest disgrace or any need of my blushes. Jock Skinner was drinking tea at the kitchen table, and they were all sitting round chatting to him as if they had nothing better to do.

'Good morning,' I told them severely from the open door, for they were so busy talking that they did not at first see me.

'And who is this pretty girl?' one of them said.

This made me feel more severe than ever, for it was well known that I was not a pretty girl like Jean Macintosh with the reddish-gold curls and the blue eyes.

'I am Janet Sandison from Reachfar,' I said. 'My granny sent me with the butter and eggs.'

They all started flapping and fluttering about like the hens in the hen house when I had to crawl in in the evening and catch a broody for my grandmother.

'But what a long way!'

'And this heavy basket!'

'Poor little thing!'

I was mortally insulted—nothing, But Nothing, connected with Reachfar or the Sandisons was poor—and, to make things worse, Jock Skinner, who had finished eating and was filling his dirty clay pipe, threw his head back and began to laugh like a man gone crazy.

I looked at him, and thought of my grandmother.

'Have you no work to do?' I asked, just as my grandmother would have said it. He got up and slid out of the kitchen with the slithering movement of his own skinny dog. The women watched him go and then stood staring at me. I stared back, and after a moment they all gathered round the basket with their backs to me and I had a good look at them. Two of them were quite old, with grey hair, but the third one was much younger, about the same age as my mother, I thought, and, of course, there was between the older two and the younger one that difference in dress that prevailed in those days and made the difference in age even more marked. They all bore a strong resemblance to one another. They were all tall and thin, with big, beaky noses and long necks, and they all wore steel-rimmed spectacles. I thought them three of the ugliest women I had ever seen, and they made me think of the picture of the Ugly Sisters in my Cinderella book, especially the two older ones. The next most striking thing about them was that they had not the slightest idea what to say to, or do with, me. I was a horrible embarrassment to them, I could feel, and this was an embarrassment to me too, for I had never before met grown-up people who could not control the situation and me along with it. They looked at the things in the basket, they looked at me, they looked back at the basket, they looked at each other, looked at me again and I looked back at them.

'You take the butter and eggs out,' I said at last as kindly and helpfully as I could, 'and give the basket and the napkin back to me to take home to my granny.'

In a frenzied sort of way the two older ones started picking eggs out of the basket and laying them down on the dresser and the table, where they rolled dangerously.

'Would you be putting them in a bowl or something?' I suggested, stopping an egg at the table's edge. All three sprang at a cupboard and came back with three bowls. 'I'll take them out,' I said, for there would be a Big Bother at home if any of these eggs got broken, and they all sat down on three chairs at the table, like the Three Bears, while I unpacked the basket.

'It is very good of you to bring the eggs down for us,' the young one said at last.

I could not think of any reply to this, for it was not 'good' of me at all. I had simply come because I had been Told, but the young one was determined on conversation and tried a new tack.

'Do you know the gentleman who brought the coal, Janet?' she asked.

I appreciated that she was trying to be polite, so I said: 'Yes, but he's not a gentleman. He is Jock Skinner, and he is a dealer, Miss—Miss Boyds,' and then I looked at all three of them, because you have to look at the person you are speaking to and I was telling this to all three of them and they were all Miss Boyds.

They all giggled like anything again, I could not think why, and then the young one said: 'That's Minnie and that's Lizzie'

—she nodded at the two old ones—'and I'm Annie and you are Jannie. Four girls!'

I privately thought they were all crazy, as they sat there nudging one another and giggling.

'No. I am Janet,' I said. 'We are three ladies and one girl.'

There would be more than a Bother if I went home to Reachfar and said I had met three girls called Lizzie, Minnie and Annie Boyd. Did they even want me to get a slap on the bottom with their foolishness? I folded the napkin, put it in the empty basket and said: 'Well, I have to go now.'

They began to flap and flutter again. 'Oh, you don't have to hurry away. Wouldn't you like a biscuit?'

This was more like the thing. 'Yes, please, Miss Annie,' I said, and they all nudged each other and giggled again, but a very nice plate with pink roses on it and four biscuits were produced. I thanked them and began to eat.

'And there's the money for the eggs and butter,' one of the older ones said.

'You don't give the pennies to *me*,' I told her. 'You wait until you see one of my family and give them to *them* or leave them with Miss Tulloch at the shop. I am not allowed to carry the pennies.'

'Oh! Not even one for yourself for carrying the basket?'

I had never heard of anything so ridiculous as this.

'Oh, no!' I said. 'Carrying the basket is Doing What I Am Told. I *have* to do that—I don't get pennies for it.'

They nudged each other again and stared at me in wonder, which made it obvious that they did not know the basic principle of Doing What You Are Told, which is that you do not get anything for doing it, but you get something you do not like at all for *not* doing it. I would have explained this to them in a kindly way, but that Jock Skinner at that moment pushed his ferrety face with its sharp little eyes round the lintel of the door and said: 'Well, leddies, that's your coal! Any time you'll be in need of any little thing, jist gi'e me a call. I'm intirely at yer service. I'm always willing to oblige the leddies!'

He gave a leering smile round the table which turned itself off when it came to me. I went on with my biscuit-eating, and stared at the spot where his face was until the face disappeared, fading out like the face of the Cheshire Cat.

'Just a minute, Mr Skinner!' Miss Lizzie fluttered and ran out to the passage behind the kitchen.

Jock was already whipping up the ragged horse and trundling out of the yard. I pulled open the back door.

'Jock! Wait! Miss Boyd wants you,' I said.

He pulled up the shabby equipage. 'I'm a-always at the service of the leddies!' he said with a leer.

'That's enough of your impudence!' I said to him in my grandmother's voice.

He stopped leering, gave me his skulking weasel's smile and began scratching himself under his jacket with the butt of his whip, and as Miss Lizzie came out of the house with her purse I went inside and left them together. When she came in again after a few moments I said: 'You should buy your coal direct and not from that rascal.' I discovered that they did not know about the coal boat, owing to having come to Achcraggan only for the summer in past times, so I told them I would ask my father to come to see them and make proper arrangements about it, now that they were going to be living here permanently, as had emerged in the course of the conversation.

When you became used to their giggling manner they were really very nice and most generous in the matter of biscuits, but ask questions? In Tom's phrase, they would speir a hole in your hide. Did I go to school? Did I like school? Had I any brothers or sisters? Wasn't it a long, long way to Reachfar? Didn't I get tired with all the walking?

I have always liked questionful conversation, there always having been many questions to which I myself have wanted answers, but the Miss Boyds' questions seemed to me so dull and silly that I thought I would ask them a few. So I enquired if it was correct that there were three more Miss Boyds. Yes, they told me, that was quite correct. They were six girls all told, they said, and had themselves another fit of giggling and nudging.

'Of course,' said Miss Annie when she had got her breath back, 'the Girls are much younger than us,' and off they went into another cackling. I had never been in the presence of so much fluttering, cackling, nudging and Girls in my life.

'And are you *all* going to live here?' I asked.

'Yes, but the Girls will only come down at the weekends, mostly. They have the Business to attend to.'

'What is the Business?'

'Well, we have a shop in Inverness, a drapery.'

'And what are the Girls' names?'

'Iris and Daisy and Violet—Violet's the baby.'

I could not see how a person could be a shopkeeper and a baby both at the same time, but let the matter pass, as I was fascinated with all these floral names which my grandmother would undoubtedly call 'silly and outlandish'. I had always wondered what an 'outlandish' thing or person was really like, and I thought that maybe I knew at last. Could it be that the Miss Boyds were 'outlandish'?

'Will there be plenty of room for you all to sleep?' I asked next, which seemed to me to be a practical, sensible question.

They all giggled like mad again and offered to show me the house. I was delighted. I have always enjoyed being shown anything that anyone has to show me.

One way and another, I spent the whole morning with the Miss Boyds and became quite interested in them, giggles, vases of pampas grass in the parlour and all, and agreed to carry home a letter to my grandmother telling her how much butter and eggs they would like to have each week. I even agreed to make a special delivery to them myself each week, apart from the normal one by the trap on Fridays, but 'not on Wednesdays', I said, 'for that is Tom's and George's and my soldiers' evening'.

In 1915 Lady Lydia—the wife of Sir Torquil—had turned part of the Big House into a convalescent home for wounded soldiers who were well enough to move about on crutches or with their arms in slings, and they roamed about the Poyntdale policies and Home Farm in their light-blue suits and red ties and were all very pleasant and cheerful. On Wednesdays my aunt spent a large part of the day baking scones, which were then packed into big baskets under white cloths, and Tom, George and I drove down in the trap to Poyntdale with them on Wednesday evenings. But although I told the Miss Boyds all about this, I did not tell them about the Big Secret about which no one but Tom, George and I and certain soldiers knew. This was the letter in my kim-*oh*-no pocket which I had to give to a certain soldier when nobody was looking. It was tremendous fun, and very easy to do, for all the soldiers would pull me close and give me a hug and all I had to do was whisper to the chosen one: 'It's in my pocket,' and he would pick out the paper like a flash. I could deliver the letter unbeknownst with Lady Lydia, the Matron or a nurse standing right beside me and the chosen soldier, and Tom said I was 'real clever' at it.

It was about ten years later that my father told me how he used to shudder when Lady Lydia would come up to Reachfar and would say to my grandmother: 'I cannot *think*, Mrs Sandison, how the boys are getting the whisky. Not that I mind, but Matron makes such a fuss and it makes her furious to know that they are getting it against the rules and under her very nose. After all, no one is allowed in the wards except the visitors she passes herself, and the boys are never allowed out without an orderly with them. Can they have some arrangement with that rascal Jock Skinner who comes for the swill, do you think?'

'Och, poor Jock!' my grandmother would say sanctimoniously. 'He's a rogue in many ways, but I wouldn't put *that* on him.'

Matron never found out, however, that the smugglers were George and Tom, on whom she doted, and that I, to whom she was always so kind, was their go-between-in-chief. I am a little irritated even now when I realise that even *I* did not know exactly what I was doing, but feel better when I realise that the cunning of Tom and George was too much for people far cleverer than I shall ever be.

Although I did not tell the Miss Boyds a word about the secret letters, however, they were very, very interested in 'soldiers' evening' and said that they would like to have one too, so I told them that if they had some cakes or something to bring I was sure the soldiers would like to see them some evening, and that they would like the soldiers, and, having arranged their special delivery for Tuesdays, I took my way back to Reachfar.

I reached home in time for dinner at half-past eleven, and after my grandmother had asked where I had been all this time My Friend Tom asked how I had 'got on' with the Miss Boyds, so I told the members of my family who were present all about my morning. No. That is not true. I did not tell them *all*—I reserved my views about the giggles and nudges for private discussion with Tom or George or both.

'But, Janet,' my mother said, 'you must not take orders for butter and eggs like that. Granny may not be able to supply them.'

'Och, the poor craiturs!' said my grandmother. 'I'll manage to give them a little, anyway. The hens are doing very well.'

'Granny, they are *not* poor! They have plenty of pennies in a black purse and a parlour with South American grass in vases and a black clock on the mantelpiece!'

'Never mind that,' said my grandmother. 'Eat your pudding.'

'And Jock Skinner was there and got pennies for coal, so I told them they must get it direct from the boat and not from that rascal.'

'Janet Sandison!' said my grandmother. 'That tongue of yours will be the disgrace of us all!'

'It's your *own* tongue that's in it, Mistress,' said my grandfather. 'If the bairn had never heard it, she wouldn't say it. Now, be done of your blethers and give Tom and me a little more of that pudding.'

During the afternoon, when I went out to help Tom and my grandfather with the hay, there was plenty of time while riding up and down from field to stackyard in Dick's cart to go further into the matter of the Miss Boyds with Tom.

'They are very, very different sort of people, Tom.'

'Are they now? What way would that be, could you be telling me?'

'They don't do any work—no cleaning or baking or anything—just sit there laughing and nudging one another and it the middle of the morning.'

'Och, well, Lady Lydia won't be baking or cleaning in the mornings either.'

'But they are not like Lady Lydia!' I was indignant. 'And they are not like us either, and they are not like the fisher people, or the dominie or the minister. They are just *different*—they are different like Jock Skinner is different.'

Tom was inclined to be scornful. 'Where would the three decent craiturs be like that dirty, twisted rascal?'

'Oh, they are not dirty or clever like him—they are clean and sort of silly—but they are *like* him all the same.'

'Och, away with you!' said Tom. 'W-oah, Dick. And stand *still*, ye capering craitur! The very ould Nick himself is in that beast this day. *Stand* there, now, before I take the wheep to ye!'

Dick had never felt the touch of a whip in his life, but seemed to realise what the dire threat meant and elected to stand still. Tom began to fork the hay up on to the cart while I tramped about packing it, and then my grandfather and Betsy came on to the field and Tom came up on Dick's cart with me while my grandfather forked to us.

Granda was a tall, spare man with white hair and a long white beard, and he lived, much of the time, in a happy, dignified silence. He was a little hard of hearing, but he often pretended to be more deaf than he really was in order not to be bothered with idle chat. He was happy, working easily yet swiftly in the warm sun amid the good smell of the hay, and would stop forking, now and then, to give Tom time to balance the load, and would stand with one gnarled hand on the horse's face, while he looked away across the Firth to the Ben, with his brilliant old eagle's eyes shaded by his old tweed hat.

Families like mine did not run to the keeping of archives and muniment rooms, so I do not know where we originated or when, but I think it must have been out of the soil of Highland Scotland a long time ago. By hearsay, I have been unable to trace us back further than 1800, but my memory of Granda convinces me that he was a product of a long pure-bred line, which is backed by Lady Lydia's dictum—she was the daughter of an English duke who married our local baronet—that 'Reachfar was the handsomest man' she had ever seen.

He had been grieve to 'Old Sir Turk ', a general of the Boer War, when Lady Lydia came to Poyntdale as the bride of the heir, and she never tired of telling of her first meeting with the tall, spare, dark man.

'We were riding,' she would say, her blue eyes looking away into the distant sky, 'and we stopped in a cornfield and Torquil said: "This is Sandison of Reachfar, our grieve." And I looked at him and he said: "It's us that's pleased to welcome you, Your Ladyship," and I just knew it was true and that I hadn't left my home for nothing. I was only twenty-two.' She would smile in the direction of her husband. '*You* didn't convince me about Poyntdale as a new home, Torquil—it took Reachfar to do that.' Granda and Lady Lydia remained a little in love with each other all their lives, and she was one of his sincerest mourners when he died.

The men of the Highlands are very good at this thing of loving reverently and from a distance—the women are not so good at it and have little patience with it, and my grandmother, therefore, kept the situation within bounds although still respecting it in a queer, acid way. 'Och, aye,' she would say. 'Leddy Lydia this and Her Leddyship that, but in the long run it will be "Have ye fed the calves, Mistress?" for where would Reachfar be if the calves didn't get fed? But she's a fine leddy and no mistake and a blessing to all around her.—Janet, for pity's sake don't stand there gawping about you! Did you ever see Leddy Lydia gawping like that? Have you shut in the young turkeys yet?'

Had *she* ever seen Lady Lydia shut in the young turkeys? My grandmother could be aware of dreams although not herself a dreamer and she kept them in their place. My grandfather was a dreamer who yet could recognise the frail fabric of a dream and he also kept the dreams in their place. I have often wished that just one of their descendants could go all out for the dreams and forget about pinning them down, tidily, in their 'place', but that has not happened yet. We are all as mixed in mind as my grandmother and grandfather.

But in us, as I became aware at eight years old, there is nothing of the material that is in the Miss Boyds of this world. The gulf between them and us was as great as that between the fisher people and us, but, in the strange way that a child can know much more than adult people think it can know, I knew that my people had not the respect for the Miss Boyds that they granted to the fisher folk.

*   *   *   *   *

My next visit to the Miss Boyds was on Friday, when Tom, Dulcie and I went down to Achcraggan to the market. Of course, there was not really a market at Achcraggan now—not a sale of animals as there had been when my grandfather was a boy—and 'going to market' meant going down with baskets of butter and eggs, a box of sections of honey, a basket of wild raspberries which I had gathered and several pairs of wood pigeons that Tom had shot. The butter, eggs and honey would be delivered at the houses that had ordered them, and some would be exchanged for our groceries and butcher-meat through accounts that had been going on for years, but the raspberries and pigeons were for Tom's and my Red Cross, and we were both wearing our Red Cross clothes and had our Red Cross box hanging on the front of the trap. My clothes were a miniature nurse's cap and apron made by my mother, and Tom's consisted of a cross of red ribbon sewn to the front of his Saturday second-best tweed bonnet.

The people of Achcraggan were very good about our Red Cross, and would always put something in our box in exchange for our raspberries, rabbits or pigeons or whatever we happened to have, while plenty of people like Sir Torquil or the minister, if we happened to meet them, would put something in the box in exchange for nothing at all. Sometimes, too, a liberty boat would have come ashore with some sailors to let them have a dram at the Plough and 'stretch their legs, poor fellows' as Tom said, and the sailors would put pennies in the box for nothing, too. And then Tom would take the box into the Plough and get some more pennies there. Indeed, nearly every week my father had to take our box down to Lady Lydia to be emptied so that she could buy things for the sick soldiers with the money, for, of course, the Red Cross was really Lady Lydia's and Tom and I just helped her with it in a neighbourly way.

So down Tom and I went to the village on Friday afternoon, both in very good form behind Dulcie, who was spanking along, once we were out on the County Road, as if she thought it a fine thing to be alive, and so it was. Everybody knew us, of course, and stopped to speak to us, and Doctor Mackay reached out of his own trap and put a threepenny piece in the box on the shore road when we were still a mile out of Achcraggan— 'just for luck' he said; and, feeling that it was a good omen, we went gaily on our way, talking all the time as we always did.

'And we have this new call to make the-day, on the Miss Boyds,' said Tom. 'Should we be keeping a pair of Red Crossing pigeons for them, do ye think?'

'Maybe they couldn't pluck them, Tom,' I said. 'They are awful handless-looking, somehow.'

'Maybe you're right,' Tom agreed. 'It's them being from the town, the poor craiturs. People from the town is very inclined to be useless in a lot of ways. They'll be buying their pigeons from a mannie that plucks them all ready for the pot, so they never get a chance to learn a thing for themselves. Aye. We'll chust sell the pigeons as usual, and maybe they'll be putting a penny in the boxie whateffer.'

It was a good Red-Cross-ing day in Achcraggan. Quite a lot of sailors were ashore stretching their legs, and they put pennies in the box in exchange for a try-on of Tom's Red Cross bonnet while Tom tried on their caps with the HMS ribbons on them; and it being summertime, Dominie Stevenson had visitors from the South staying with him and an old gentleman who had a single spectacle for only one eye—a thing I had never seen before—asked me a lot of questions about history and geography and then asked: 'And why does a hen cross the road?'

This was one of Tom's riddles to which I had long known the answer: 'To get to the other side,' so, having answered this, I thought I would try Tom's *other* riddle on him.

'Do you know, sir, why the Prince of Wales wears red braces?'

'Wheesht, now!' said Tom. 'It's time we was going—'

'Just a minute,' the gentleman said. 'No, Janet, I don't. Why?'

'To be holding up his trooser,' I told him.

The gentleman and Dominie Stevenson laughed like anything, and so did Tom, and then the gentleman put a whole half a crown in the box and we drove away to the Miss Boyds.

'We will *not*,' said Tom, staring solemnly ahead as we drove, 'be saying a word at home about speaking chokes with the dominie's chentleman.'

'All right, Tom,' I agreed.

Once, in the course of some Bother at home, my grandmother had said: 'It's that Tom! He has her as fly as a badger.' And although I was not sure what this meant, I had always found it beneficial to take Tom's advice about what to tell at home and what to leave unsaid.

At the Miss Boyds there were no less than five of them, all cackling and fluttering round the cart to the degree that even Dulcie, who came to Achcraggan every Friday or Saturday and every Sunday and was used to strangers, began to show the whites of her eyes and fidget with her feet. Tom got out of the trap and went to her head. 'I'll chust tie the mare to the gate here, leddies,' he said, 'and we'll be taking the basket inside.'

In order to get them away from Dulcie, I handed down the basket and climbed down over the high wheel myself while they all screeched and giggled, far enough away from the mare to be safe themselves, but too near to be comfortable for Dulcie. The old ones had been giggly enough, but the two young ones had to be heard to be believed, and they were young and active and sprightly on their feet into the bargain—they reminded me of the hens at feeding time, running hither and yon and cackling. They all talked at once—a thing which we were never allowed to do at Reachfar—and interrupted each other, and when one was interrupted, she went off into another gale of giggles. The only one of them who was half reasonable at all was Miss Annie, the middle one, who stood in age, rather nondescript, between the two old ones with the shawls and the long black skirts and the two young ones with the 'glad-necked' blouses and hobble skirts. At last we were all in the kitchen, Tom carrying the basket, and there at the sink, if you please, was Jock Skinner.

Tom looked at him. 'Aye, Jock?' he said. 'And what are ye at the-day?'

'I was chust skinning this rabbits for the leddies,' said Jock slyly.

'Iphm,' said Tom and put the basket on the table. 'Ootside would be a better place for that job than making that clart and stink in the house.'

'Have you a bowl for the eggs?' I enquired, while Jock gathered his rabbit refuse into a bucket and took it and himself outside. The Miss Boyds were busy blowing up the fire with a pair of bellows, getting cups and saucers out of a cupboard and getting in each other's way while I unpacked the basket and Tom stood by the window looking awkward. They were very kind. They insisted that we have tea, and the table was spread with an embroidered cloth, and lace doilies were fetched from another room and put on the plates, and the bread and the biscuits were put on the doilies and Tom was made to sit in a padded wicker chair that creaked every time he breathed and told to 'make himself quite at home'.

I was very interested in all these Miss Boyds and amused to watch them flapping round, but even I began to think that the tea would never get ready. And Tom was looking crosser and crosser and more and more impatient, although they were all being so nice to him and nudging him in their giggly way, for he always 'had business' to do at the Plough on market-day while I usually had tea with Miss Tulloch. As time went on, I became very, very worried about Tom. I had never seen him so quiet, not speaking a word at all, just sitting there with his bonnet on one knee while they all fluttered about him with plates of biscuits, and I thought he must be feeling sick. I was going to ask him if he was feeling sick, but with all the Miss Boyds talking you could not get a word in edgewise and I just had to wait until, at long last, we were in the trap and driving away.

'Are you feeling sick, Tom?'

'No, no!' said Tom, in a comforting voice. 'Where would I be feeling sick and it market-day? ... Can ye be eating another tea with Miss Tulloch, do you think?'

'Och, surely,' I said, equally comfortingly. It was quite easy for me, always, to eat two teas.

On the way home, after I had had my second tea and Tom had done 'his business' at the Plough, though, it was not like a usual market-day. Tom was very quiet and did not seem to be interested, even, in talking about how well we had done with our Red Cross that day, so I was quiet too and went over the whole thing in my mind while Dulcie plodded slowly up the steep road from the County Road, through Poyntdale to Reachfar. Everything had been all right, I decided, and quite as usual until we came to the Miss Boyds. It was the Miss Boyds who had spoilt things. Poop to the Miss Boyds!

Even at home, at supper, Tom went on being unusual until my uncle noticed it. Of course, my uncle would just be the one to notice a thing like that. The Big World outside Reachfar thought that my father was far cleverer than his brother, my uncle, but all of us of my family knew that this was not the case. My father was cleverer than my uncle at letter-writing and business—though not at farming—and, of course, my father was a year older which gave him a little more of that thing called experience, but my father would never be as good or as quick as my uncle at noticing when people were not 'in their usual' as Tom was tonight.

'Well,' said my uncle, 'I hear that you and Tom was calling on the Miss Boyds the-day, Janet. … And did they give you a tea-*par*-ty?' My uncle, who did not like to be called 'uncle' but by his name of 'George', was very fond of doing what my grandmother called 'playing the clown', and one of his ways of doing it was to pronounce words in a queer way, like saying 'tea-*par*-ty' with the accent in the middle like that. This was a signal for me to play the clown too, so I said: 'Och, yes, man, George! A proper tea-*par*-ty with lace doilies on the plates an' a-all.'

'Now, now!' said my grandmother. 'None of your lies, Janet!'

My grandmother was always accusing me of telling lies, especially when I said that Fly had 'told' me this or that. I often thought my grandmother was a little too clever when she was so much more certain than other people what was a 'lie' and what was not, for, although Fly could not speak, Fly could still tell me that Bill-the-Post was on Reachfar ground with letters although nobody else could see him or hear him.

''S *not* lies, Granny!' I said now, for it *was* not.

'Gently, Janet,' my mother said. 'Not that tone of voice to Granny. Lace doilies, you said?'

'Yes, and a cloth with coloured flowers sewn on it, too!'

'Mercy on us!' said my aunt.

'And, Tom,' said my clowning uncle, 'did you mind to be lifting your cup like this'—he picked up his own cup with his little finger curled into a question-mark—'and you having your tea with all them nice leddies?'

'Ach, hold your tongue, George, man!' said Tom disgustedly.

'My,' said my uncle, 'but it's me that would like fine to be having my tea with a-all that leddies and the lace table cover and a-all! And me sitting there and them a-all waiting on me and saying Take another droppie tea, George, dear, och, *do* and—'

'And ye can bliddy well be *doing* it next week!' said Tom in a wild-angry voice that made me jump.

'Now, then!' said my grandmother.

'That will do, now, George,' said my father quietly. 'That's enough of your capers.'

'I'll do anything mortal that's needed,' said Tom, looking at my grandfather, 'but back among that lot of cackling ould bitches I will *not* go!'

'That will be a-all right, Tom,' said my grandfather quietly. 'Come over to the fire, man, and take your smoke. . . Did you bring the teebacca the-day, Janet?'

After that, there was a quietness in the house about the Miss Boyds, and even I did not dare to mention them to Tom, for if he had got away with saying 'bliddy' and 'bitch-meaning-a-person' in the house about them, it meant that they were not a subject to be trifled with.

The next day my father and George stayed at home and the first ploughman from Poyntdale came up with his pair of horses and two carts and by the evening we had all the hay in and my father and George were roping the first big stack and we were all so busy that I quite forgot all about the Miss Boyds. Then, it was Sunday, which, especially in summer, was always a very nice day at Reachfar. All of us except one—for one person (who never was I, of course) had to stay at home to look after the dinner and the beasts—went to church in the morning, and then,

50

after dinner, my family had their Sunday Sleep, during which I had to keep quiet, and in the later afternoon Tom and often George and I would go for a Look Round, and quite often we had visitors in the evening. It was not only for all these things that Sunday was a nice day, however. It was nice in having a different feeling from other days, for no one was doing anything very much, so that they had time to talk and did not just say: 'Och, Janet, be off now with your ask-ask-asking!' as they so often said on weekdays. Also, on Sundays, my grandmother had no errands to be done—not even little ones up to the well for a little ice-cold water to pour into the churn—for she did not churn or bake or do anything on Sunday. I was not allowed to do my knitting or sewing—and I was not supposed to dance or sing—on Sunday either, but I was allowed to read and write and, really, you could not want much more than that—'not in ordinary reason, you couldn't', as Tom said.

Church was always enjoyable except for the sermon, which could be tedious and sometimes even a little alarming. On this Sunday my mother, who sometimes was not very well and who always tired easily, was to stay at home and my father was going to stay with her, so my grandmother and my aunt got into Dulcie's trap while the rest of us walked. It was another beautiful day, and I had on my short white Sunday skirt, my white blouse, white socks, black shoes with ankle straps and a white linen bonnet with a wreath of blue cornflowers on it, while my grandmother had my white gloves and black Bible on her knee in the trap.

'Janet, stop hopping like a hen on a hot girdle!' she said as we turned eastwards through Poyntdale on to the County Road. 'That bairn's skirts are too short,' she told no one in particular, giving her feather boa a shake, 'especially hopping and dancing as she's always doing.'

'Ach, the bairn is fine,' said my uncle. 'What would she do with big long skirts walloping round her feet like an old maid?'

My gentle mother controlled my clothes and would not hear of the frills and sashes that my grandmother thought proper for Sunday, nor would she hear of the long skirts and petticoats. At that time I was the only little girl in the district who was really comfortable, who went to church and school in skirts above my knees and socks that came just to my ankles in summer and to my knees in winter.

'Some of the Miss Boyds don't have big skirts, George,' I said, restraining a hop and a skip, 'although they are old maids.'

'We'll not be speaking of that the now,' said George. 'Come on. Here's the County Road—we'll all get up in the trap and give Dulcie a bit canter to herself.'

Once on the smooth tarmacadam of the County Road that wound eastwards beside the sea, Dulcie was only too willing to make with all speed for Achcraggan, to get to the stable behind the Plough and get her nose into her manger, so off we went at a fine pace. As we neared the church we fell in behind a line of traps and governess carts which were coming in from all directions and then there was a general raising of hats by the men and bows from the women as the Poyntdale wagonette came past behind its pair of greys, with Sir Torquil himself driving and Lady Lydia with her house visitors in the back. Lady Lydia was, in my eyes in those days, the most beautiful person I had ever seen, with her golden hair, her big beflowered hats, her soft grey or blue frilly summer dresses and the long white gloves with the row of tiny buttons. None of her visiting lady friends were half as beautiful as Lady Lydia herself, I thought, although my mother and my aunt were often enraptured by the 'up-to-date London' clothes of the visitors.

On a fine summer day like this it was the custom for everyone to gather in the churchyard while the bell pealed overhead and the horses were being stabled by one male member of each group, and Sir Torquil, the doctor and the dominie would go round talking to everyone until the bell stopped, when, led by Sir Torquil, we would all go inside and take our places. On this day Lady Lydia brought the ladies who were staying at Poyntdale over to meet my grandmother where we were standing outside the porch, and they all had pretty dresses and big hats and long gloves, and after my grandmother and my aunt had shaken hands with them Lady Lydia said: 'And this is Janet Sandison—you met her father yesterday, remember?'

The ladies smiled and the first one held out her long-gloved hand; but not being a grown-up person yet, I had to curtsy before shaking hands, and just as I bent my knee the most extraordinary thing happened that had ever happened in all my days of going to church. A troupe of six Miss Boyds, in a fluttering, giggling covey, with more frills and feathers on them than a dozen Lady Lydias, came rushing up the path and into the church, leaving me in mid-curtsy on one side and Lady Lydia and her friends on the other. At the same moment, the big bell stopped and there was the usual silence before the little bell would start its little hurrying ringing, but today it was more than the usual silence—it was deader and longer, as everyone in the churchyard, and even the tombstones, seemed to stare at the door through which the giggling covey had disappeared. 'Yes,' said Lady Lydia's clear voice into the silence, 'this is Janet,' and something in her voice actuated my muscles so that I came up straight again, let go of the sides of my skirt and shook hands with each lady in turn. The normal hum of quiet conversation broke out around the churchyard again and the little hurry-up bell began to ring. Soon we were inside, the Reverend Roderick announced the Twenty-third Psalm, John-the-Smith, who was the precentor, made his tuning-fork go 'Ping-oing!' on the pulpit stairs and we all rose and began to sing.

In church I always listened to a fair amount of the long sermon although I could understand very little of it or our erudite minister's ramblings through the mazes of the moralities and the philosophies, partly because I was amused by the Reverend Roderick's soft Hebridean accent and voice and partly because, when George, Tom and I were alone, we had competitions at 'imitating the minister', which would have caused the wrath of my grandmother and father to burst over our heads had they known of them. Today, when the Reverend Roderick announced his text, it was the one that George and Tom called 'the ould hollow square', the Master Formation, as it were, that the minister fell back upon when at his fighting, Highland best, with his very soul in battle against some colossal, almost overpowering sin.

A deadly hush fell on the congregation as the Reverend Roderick rose, majestic in height, impressive of dark hair and beard and eagle nose, gripped the fronts of his black gown and said: 'At the thirtieth chapter of Profferps you will find these words——' Not a Bible page was turned. From Sir Torquil right down to me the entire congregation knew what was coming. 'There pe three theengs wheech are too wonderful for me, yea, four wheech I know not: the way off an eagle in the air; the way off a serrrpent upon a rock; the way off a ship in the midst off the sea; and the way off a man with a maid.' The deadly silence prevailed. 'Today, I am going chust to speak apout the first two—that pird of prey the eagle and that sympol of a-all evil, the serrrpent.' A sort of inaudible sigh, a sort of invisible movement of relief passed through the church.

With the 'Hollow Square' as a text, the sermon could fight on four sides as it were, and we were all relieved to know that, today, it was not the fourth side, 'the way of a man with a maid', that was coming. The Reverend Roderick had his finger on the pulse of the parish, his ear to its whispering ground, and he knew every young couple who were staying out too late o' nights in the Green Loaning or other idyllic places. Fighting the fourth side of his Hollow Square, he could, without naming any names, do everything in a sermon except consign the couple to the bottomless pit then and there while at the same time bringing the grey heads of their parents in disgrace and sorrow to the grave. Today, however, we realised right away that it was that 'serrrpent the Kaiser' and his 'Cherman eagles' that were 'in for it', and we all settled back in comfort. In principle, we all agreed with the Reverend Roderick that sinners should be chastised and drawn back from the edge of the bottomless pit if possible, but it was more comfortable and relaxing on a warm morning that the sinners should be real enemies and 'them rotten Chermans' at that, instead of, perhaps, young Kate Findlay and the third ploughman from Dinchory. So, while the minister declared that the ways of eagles and serrrpents were beyond his comprehension as well as that of King Solomon, but also declared his faith that they were not beyond the comprehension of the Almighty and would be duly and justly punished for their sins in His Good Time, I gave myself up to contemplation of the Miss Boyds and the probable effect of their behaviour on the temper of my grandmother for the rest of the day.

When church was over we all came out into the sun again

and stood in the churchyard while Tom went to get our trap and George was sent by my grandfather to bring the wagonette round for Sir Torquil, and Lady Lydia came again, with her visitors, to talk to my grandmother, while Sir Torquil talked to my grandfather. The relationship that existed between these people is difficult to describe, for I know of no parallel today or, indeed, at any time in history, although in my childhood it was common enough in Highland Scotland. My people were not part of the Poyntdale tenantry, as were many of the people at church, for they were independent owners of Reachfar, just as Sir Torquil was the owner of Poyntdale. For this reason my father was not an 'employee' of Sir Torquil, as were his ploughmen and cattlemen—he was the son of a neighbour, the neighbour being my grandfather, who, at one time, had 'helped' Sir Torquil's father by acting as grieve of Poyntdale. My grandmother put a point on the whole thing like a tall black exclamation-mark as she stood there in her black Sunday clothes. She was a daughter of the glens of the West, fiercely independent, highly skilled in the arts and crafts of her peasant class, and cleverly cunning enough in veterinary and obstetric matters to have earned the reputation of being a witch, a reputation which she was at pains to foster rather than disclaim. When Lady Lydia and my grandmother held converse in the churchyard, a local throne was speaking to a local throne, and the local populace knew it, stood back and held their peace. I think now, forty years later, that if I had been the local populace I would have looked forward to witnessing a difference of opinion between these thrones, but I also know now, forty years later, that my looking forward would have been in vain. They *had* no major differences of opinion, but, apart from that, if they had had, they were both—in their own estimation—ladies much too great and dignified to stoop to making a raree show of themselves for the hoi polloi. No. Any differences they might have would be settled in strict privacy. In public, thrones would always have the dignity of THRONES, as long as Lady Lydia and my grandmother were their occupants.

'Yuh know-oh, Miz Sandison,' said one of Lady Lydia's visiting ladies, 'Ah think yo' li'l gran'daughter is jus' the cutes' thi-ing!'

It was a beautiful voice, I thought, that sounded as if she were laughing, singing and speaking all at the same time. My grandmother, about six feet tall, counting the feather in her hat, bent an eagle eye on me from away up high.

'She is cute enough, madam,' she said. 'Sometimes a little *too* cute, maybe.'

'Mrs Sandison doesn't mean quite what you mean by "cute", Maddy Lou,' said Lady Lydia.

'But yo' ah-ah cute, huh, Jah-net?' the lady asked.

I smiled at her. 'Please, why is your name Maddy Lou?'

'See, ain't that cute, Lydia, honey? The way she says "Please, why?" ... Mah name is Madeleine Louise de Cambre, sweetie, an' mah frien's say Maddy Lou for short, see?'

'I think that's nice—and cute,' I said. *I* knew, I thought, this lady's meaning of 'cute'.

'Janet!' said my grandmother. 'That will do. There's Tom with the trap. Say Goodbye and go now.'

I made my curtsy. 'Goodbye,' I said, and went away to Tom, followed by the languid trailing voice: 'Wa-al, Ah think it's jus' the cutes' thi-ing Ah've seen in this ol' country!'

Maddy Lou put the Miss Boyds clean out of my head, and I thought about her and practised her voice silently to myself all the way home, where my mother and father came out to meet the trap. My father led Dulcie away to unyoke her while George and Tom went in to change out of their Sunday clothes and my mother took me to her room that my bonnet and gloves might be put away in their box on top of her high wardrobe.

'Mother! There was a *very* bonnie lady at church with Lady Lydia and she spoke like this: Miz Sandison, Ah think yo-oh li'l gran'daughter is jus' the cutes' thi-ing—'

'Janet, you must *not* mimic people. Go and change your skirt and blouse.'

'No mimicking, Mother. It was nice, as if she was singing and laughing as well as speaking.'

'I see. That would be the American lady who is staying at Poyntdale. Run and change. Dinner's ready.'

When I had changed and had come down to the kitchen where the Sunday broth was already in the plates and the Sunday boiled beef was sitting in its ring of turnips and carrots on the dresser, everyone was in place and I slipped into my chair between George and Tom on the 'bairns' side' of the table. My grandfather looked round us all, covered his eyes and said: 'For what we are about to receive, Lord, make us truly thankful. Amen', and then we all began to have our soup.

'Little Clip-Cloots there tells me that Lady Lydia brought her visitors to church,' my mother said.

The Highland description of a gossiping tongue is 'a tongue that would clip cloots', and occasionally I was referred to as 'Clip-Cloots', for, in another Highland phrase, my tongue was reckoned to be 'for ever clapping like a kirk bell'.

'Aye,' my grandmother confirmed. 'One of them was the American leddy—Duncan, what's her name now?'

'Madeleine Louise de Cambre,' I said in the French fashion and singing accents of Maddy Lou. My mother gave me a Look, but Maddy Lou had called me cute and I was away above myself and not to be put down by a Look, even from my mother. I gave tongue with another of the remarks Maddy Lou had made. The Looks now became a concentration and I realised that I Had Gone Too Far, and when I had Gone Too Far one of the best Ways Back was a request for scholastic information, so: 'Madeleine Louise de Cambre—George, I bet you couldn't spell a name like that! Dad, how do you spell it?'

George and Tom, as always, were right on hand and ready to help me. 'Where could your poor crofter of a father be spelling a name like that?' said George.

'And it foreign an' American an' a-all? ' said Tom.

With a tightening of the mouth that did not quite nullify the smile in his eyes, my father looked at the three of us on the bairns' side of the table from his place by my grandfather's right hand. 'That's enough of your capers, the whole three of you,' he told us. 'I saw her name on her luggage when the men brought it from the station.'

'Then spell it for me, Dad.'

'All right.' He spelled the name for me. 'And now, be quiet and eat your soup.'

I did as I Was Told, but although my family could stop a person from talking they could never stop a person from listening, and all adult people should remember that even to cease talking and go into a Trappist silence is not an effective method of stopping a child hearing *some*thing, especially a child brought up in a lonely place, whose whole world is concentrated in the persons of the few people sitting round the Sunday dinner table. I knew every shade of expression on their faces, could interpret every glance of their eyes, could identify to hairbreadth precision the meaning of every inflection of their voices.

There was a little normal conversation about Lady Lydia's guests, and my father told them that Mrs de Cambre was the wife of an 'American diplomatic gentleman' who had come over on 'business connected with the war' and that she and Lady Lydia had gone to the same finishing school as young ladies. He also said that she was 'a very free sort of leddy with no stinking pride about her', very inquisitive about everything about the estate, that one minute you would find her at the sawmill and the next in the hayfield, and that she was already a great favourite about the place. I absorbed all this along with my soup, and then my grandmother went to the dresser to cut the beef while my aunt dished up the potatoes and cabbage from their big pots on the fire.

'And a fine disgrace these silly craiturs made for Achcraggan in front of an American leddy that's come to help us with the war!' my grandmother said vengefully, plunging the fork into the beef.

'How? What happened?' my father asked.

Normally nothing derogatory was ever said about any grown-up person in my hearing, with the exception of two—one was Jock Skinner and the other was Old Hamish the Tinker, and this was because these two were reckoned to be so far beyond the pale that even a child must see their faults, so there was no point in attempted concealment. Jock Skinner and Hamish apart, my family's attitude in my hearing always was that all grown-up people were perfect; and although I knew from their eyes, faces and voices that much of the time they did not believe this to be true, I also knew that that was the belief I was expected to adopt and that no argument I might advance would get a hearing. Children did not—repeat NOT—have derogatory opinions about their elders who were, consequently, their betters. With the exception of that rascal Jock Skinner and that dirty, thieving, old tinker Hamish, of course.

Today, however, things were different. Having served everyone with meat, while my aunt dispensed the vegetables, my grandmother, in the panoply of her second-best skirt and blouse into which she had changed on coming from church, and her black sateen Sunday non-working apron, gave tongue in no uncertain voice about no less than six grown-ups, to wit, the Miss Boyds, and when she had finished with the words '— neither fitness nor decency and that's all about it' there flashed into my mind a vision of My Friend Bella Beagle.

Sometimes I would take myself a walk to Achcraggan to visit Bella at her whitewashed house in the Fisher Town and often she would be sitting at the gable-end, baiting the family nets with mussels from the big enamel basin by her side. Always, when she had baited the last hook, there would be some of the slimy, shelled mussels left over and Bella would pick up the basin, go down to the grass bank at the shore and, with a swinging movement, throw a long stream of mussels high in the air and say: 'There, then, ye deevils!' and with fantastic, swooping skill the big seagulls who sat on every roof of the Fisher Town would fall, screaming, upon the airborne mussels so that not one had time to fall back on the sand of the beach. At eight years old, I had not yet met My American Friend Martha and I had never heard her phrase 'strickly for the birds', but that day I had the feeling that in my grandmother's opinion the Miss Boyds, like Bella Beagle's left-over mussels, were 'strickly for the birds'.

After my grandmother's diatribe nobody had much to say and the remainder of the dinner passed in silence and everyone, except me, after the washing-up had been done and the fire stoked up, went off to have their Sunday sleep. I gave Fly her dinner, and after she had eaten up every piece of her bone from the beef she and I took ourselves a walk west from the house and soon came to the Strip of Herbage, which was the western boundary between the arable land and the moor. I had not, at eight years old, begun to think of it as the Strip of Herbage— that came later when I had read FitzGerald's poem—but as I now can think of it by none other than that name I have used it here.

Reachfar land was rich in valueless rock, the most of the arable land had been claimed from the rough, virgin moor within the memory of my grandfather. The field known as the 'West Parkie' had been 'taken in' in the childhood of my father and my uncle, and it was still yielding large lumps of rock to the plough. This meant that, every spring almost, the Strip of Herbage altered its character a little, as another boulder or two were rolled out into it, for it was a line of big stones that had been rolled there from year to year. In the contrary way of nature, however, although these rocks would not grow the crops my people fought for, the crevices between them grew all the things I loved—the violet, the sweet briar and the wild tansy rooted there and flourished; the lichens, like green pincushions full of golden pins, colonised the uptorn stones; the dog roses and the foxgloves came too and, as the rocks weathered to grey boulders, the wild thyme, which, like the Assyrian army, was all purple and gold, marched its cohorts across them in the summer sun. As when the coal boat came in, anything could happen at the Strip of Herbage. The proper way to behave at it was to get on to the big boulder at the south-west corner and make your way by hop, step and skip from boulder to boulder, treading on nothing but grey stone, to the big boulder at the north-west corner. This way, you saw from above every new plant that had taken root, every new flower that had come out. You could stop as often as you liked, and on a propitious day the Strip of Herbage could take you a whole afternoon to see it properly. Another desirable thing to have while hop, step and skipping was a song, and it was remarkable how, once you started off, the song would come to you, so I hopped, stepped and skipped today to a new song that came as I went along:

Bonnie Maddy—Lou—Lou, How do you do—do?
While the bells were ringing, your smiling voice was singing.
I'm glad I saw you there, there, with your curly hair, hair.
You are cute too, too, Bonnie Maddy Lou-Lou!'

I finished the Strip of Herbage fairly early that day, and when Fly and I went back to the house everything was still dead quiet, and when we had gone quietly into the kitchen the clock on the mantelpiece, with the flower-painted panel below the dial, said only quarter-past four. Sunday tea was not until five-thirty.

In a corner of the kitchen there was the 'little table' whose top held newspapers and a book or two, and which had two drawers, one of which held string and odds and ends and the other of which held my 'bitties'. These consisted of small things which I might leave lying about, such as a shell from the beach or a particularly handsome spruce cone or shiny chestnut from the Poyntdale trees, and there was always an end of pencil in there, too. My mother was very good about my 'bitties' drawer, and would always put into it any odd piece of clean paper that could be written on and sometimes, even, a few sheets of Proper Writing Paper from her own box which I was not allowed to touch. Today, there was a half-sheet of paper from her box, so I took it to the table and with great care I wrote down my Maddy-Lou-Lou song, which took me all the time until the clock on the mantelpiece began to strike five.

In that moment the house and farmyard came alive. There were movements upstairs, a rustling from my mother's room as my father laid aside his newspapers which he did not have time to read during the week, Fly began to stretch and scratch herself and, outside, the hens began to squawk for their evening meal. My aunt, who was the youngest person in the house except me, came into the kitchen and swung the kettle on its hook over the fire, where it began to sing. She smelled very nice, I noticed—she had been trying 'that stuff' on her face again—she was always at capers like trimming hats or doing her hair a new way at Sunday sleep.

'Nice smell,' I said, sniffing.

She looked at me. 'Lay the table for me!' she said and dashed out to the wash-house. By the time I had got the cups and saucers out of the dresser she was back and the kitchen was pervaded by a strong odour of carbolic soap.

'That's fine,' she said. 'You're a smart little craitur. Go out to the milk-house and bring me the little blue cream jug and I'll do the rest.'

My grandmother was the last to come into the kitchen, and she paused in the doorway and sniffed. 'What a stink of carbolic!' she said.

'It's me, Granny,' I said. 'I got some soot on me and used the carbolic soap.'

This was true. I had been at pains in the interval to do both.

'Then you had no business! The carbolic is very dear and not for you to waste, Janet. Go and wash that stink off your hands with the proper white soap!'

I did as I Was Told, but the kitchen still smelled nicely and concealingly-for-my-aunt of carbolic, and all eyes, except those of my unsuspecting parents and grandparents, were downcast and seeking the hidden corners of the room.

We had just taken our places round the table when there was an unusual noise outside, which became a gradually increasing crescendo of screeching, fluttering and giggling as it came nearer to the open door, and my silent grandfather became very upright at the end of the table, looked accusingly round at us all and said in a stern voice: 'And *what*, for goodness' sake, is *that?*'

Had I dared to speak, I could have told him, but I did not. In no time at all six Miss Boyds appeared in a covey of frills, feathers, gushes and giggles in the kitchen doorway, and out of the general babel of sound came the words of one of them: 'The door was open so we walked right in!' followed by another chorus of giggles.

Slow, majestic, silent and dark as a thundercloud rolling over Ben Wyvis, my grandmother rose in her place at the end of the table.

'So,' she said, 'I see.'

The giggles stopped. The silence was deadly. Not a hen squawked outside. She turned to my mother, who sat at her right hand.

'Come, Elizabeth,' she said, and to my aunt: 'Kate, tea for —' Her cold eye moved over the covey. '—eight of us, in the parlour, please.' And like one of the mighty warships in the Firth, with my mother in her wake, she clove a furrow through the massed Miss Boyds and led the way to the parlour.

'My Lord God Almighty!' said my aunt, which was an Awful Swear, and collapsed on to a chair.

Tom rose in the same moment, seized a plate of scones and a dish of jam and with a 'Come on, for God's sake, George, man! Bring our cups!' the two of them went out through the back way through the wash-house faster than I had ever seen them go anywhere in All My Born Days, carrying their tea with them. I ran to follow them, but my father thundered: 'Janet! Stay here and help your aunt!' so that was that.

'The second-best cups, Janet!' said my aunt, and while my father and my grandfather finished their tea in silence she and I plunged into the fray.

The Reachfar kitchen was a well-equipped place, both as to food and utensils, and my aunt, trained by my grandmother, was a swift worker, but that was the quickest meal ever prepared at Reachfar, so anxious were she and I to get through to the parlour to see what was happening. My Aunt Kate was— and is—one of the 'dark' Sandisons, which means that she is also one of the beautiful ones. Her dark waving hair had in it none of the Scandinavian reddishness to make it brownish like mine, and her dark eyes have none of the Scandinavian blue that lightens mine, and her skin in those days had a clear soft warmth brought to it by the inherited limpid rains of my grandmother's native West. In nature she was—and still is—as full of mischievous gaiety as a brown trout jumping on a summer evening. 'Are we ready?' she asked, the brown eyes dancing. 'I'll pour the tea, you carry the cups to them. Got your wee tray for the cream and sugar? That's right.'

Ceremonially, she and I carried the tea-tray, the trays of scones, cake and biscuits into the parlour, and I, with my 'wee tray' at the ready, took up my position beside her as my grandmother said to one of the oldest Miss Boyds: 'Strong or weak, Miss Boyd?'

'Oh, just as it comes, thanks,' said the Miss Boyd, while my aunt and I, at the side table, suppressed our uprising giggles.

It was a dreadful tea-party. When I think of it now, forty years later, my flesh crawls, and what my poor mother—I am said to resemble her very strongly in some ways—must have gone through as she sat at my grandmother's side I cannot bear to imagine. The Miss Boyds were cowed beyond all thought of a giggle and afraid to make the slightest fidget with their frills or gloves, and my redoubtable grandmother had reduced them to this pathetic state, I knew, without making a single gesture or speaking a single word that did not conform to the letter of social intercourse and to the law of Highland hospitality. She chatted about the weather, the crops, and listened to their attempts to be coherent about the beauties of Achcraggan, and, at the same time, by sheer force of pent-up disapproval, reduced them to a jellied mass of dithering subjection, so that, when tea was over, they did not even have the strength of mind to get up and go away. I am probably biased and my exaggerated view is probably erroneous, but I have always felt that if my grandmother had paid a visit to Kaiser Wilhelm of Germany during July 1914 the Great War of 1914–1918 would never have come to pass.

My aunt and I carried our trays out of the parlour and she said: 'We'll leave the dishes till later—come on back!' and the two of us went back to the other room.

'Janet,' said my grandmother, 'you can go off for your walk now.'

'Yes, Granny,' I said and left the room at once. My aunt was allowed to stay.

Usually George, Tom and I went for a Look Round on Sunday evenings, but I did not know where they had gone now, so I went to my 'bitties' drawer and got out the paper with my Maddy Lou song and took myself round to sit on the bench at the end of the house with Fly. I had not been there for five minutes when who should come walking towards me across the Long Park but Lady Lydia and Maddy Lou. This was indeed being a Memorable Sunday. I did not know what to do, for our parlour would hardly hold one more person with all these Miss Boyds in it, and my grandfather and my father had disappeared like Tom and George, so I had a moment of panic as I rose from the bench to make my curtsy. However, let it be said to the honour and glory of my family that never has it deserted me in an hour of need, and just as Lady Lydia came up Tom and George appeared round the north side of the house.

'Good evening, all,' said Lady Lydia, leaning on her ash-plant. 'How are you, George? I didn't get a chance to speak to you at church this morning.'

'Fine, thank you, your leddyship. And yourself?'

'Well, thank you. Mrs de Cambre, did you meet Mr Tom and Mr George at church this morning?'

'Ah wish Ah ha-ad! How a-ah you? An' Jah-net, too,' she smiled.

'The rest are in the house.' George hesitated and gave the back of his neck a rub with his left hand. 'But, to tell ye the truth, Leddy Lydia, all that Miss Boyds that's come to Achcraggan to stop is in there and Tom and me was just—well, we was just—'

Lady Lydia gave a pealing laugh and choked it off short with a glance at the house. 'Keeping out of the way, were you?'

'That's about it,' said George, looking relieved.

'My friend and I will just rest here a moment,' said Lady Lydia and sat down on the wooden bench along the gable.

I was still holding my paper and my pencil and Mrs de Cambre said: 'You been drawin', Jah-net, honey?'

'No, Mrs de Cambre.'

'She would be at the writing likely, madam,' said Tom. 'She'll often be at the writing for a whilie when she has the time. What is it the-day, Janet?'

'Nothing,' I said, that hopeless defence of a child as a reply.

'Oh, come, Janet!' said Lady Lydia.

I put the paper behind my back, but, of course, that was fatal. Even my 'clown' of an uncle would not let that pass.

'Give Leddy Lydia the paper, Janet,' he said gently, and I had to hand it over.

Lady Lydia began to read, then glanced at her friend and then began to read again with concentration.

'Well!' she said at last. 'Maddy Lou de Cambre, you had to cross the world to get a poem addressed to you! Listen to this!' and she read my song aloud. I could not look at any of them, but stood there, scarlet, blind, beyond all feeling or movement until suddenly Mrs de Cambre sprang up from the bench and caught me in a perfumed hug. When she came so close, I could see tears in her eyes, and, somehow, the tears made everything all right, but, in a second, she was laughing again and her smiling voice was saying: 'My, that's jus' the cutes' thi-ing Ah evah heard! May Ah have it to keep, Jah-net?'

'If you like,' I said.

'Ah mos' sut'nly *do* like! Why, that's jus' the nices' thing that evah happened tuh me!'

George and Tom were embarrassed now, too, at the contents of the paper, and serve them right, I thought. *Poop* to them for making me show it, anyway.

'Och,' said Tom, 'she'll often be at the writing when she is by her lone, madam. Chust any kind of capers and nonsense that will be coming into her head, like.'

George gave the back of his neck another rub and then: 'My mother—her granny—will not be knowing about her writing that way, of coorse. That kind of capers is chust for bairns and foolish ones like Tom and me.'

'A-and *me!*' said Mrs de Cambre, and winked in a very clever way with one long-lashed eyelid over one sparkling eye as she folded the paper and hid it away in the pocket of her tweed jacket. Lady Lydia smiled and then looked at Tom: 'Sir Torquil was telling me you have another fine new litter from the white sow, Tom?'

'Aye, your leddyship, a bonnie enough puckle piggies— would ye care to be seeing them?'

In his pride in the young pigs Tom had forgotten that to reach the sty we had to walk east past the front of the house, and, of course, when we reached the porch there was my grandmother, shooing the six Miss Boyds in front of her like a flock of frightened chickens. 'So it's yourself, Leddy Lydia! Good evening to you,' she said, and the Miss Boyds broke into a fluttering and giggling. 'The Miss Boyds was chust leaving,' she added in a voice of doom, and silence descended not only on them but on all of us, until it was broken by Lady Lydia.

'Oh yes, the Miss Boyds.' She gave them a collective smile and bow. 'I believe I saw you at church this morning, but I did not have an opportunity to meet you. You have come to stay permanently in your house in Achcraggan now? That is very nice. I am sure you will soon get used to it although it is so different from the Town. Good evening.'

She smiled again, and, sucking Mrs de Cambre, Tom, George and myself into her wake, she made her way through the silent ranks of the Miss Boyds into the Reachfar kitchen, she and my grandmother somehow giving the impression of 'speaking' each other in passing (though silently), as might the great liners *Queen Mary* and *Queen Elizabeth* do if they had to pass one another among the small craft on a summer day on Southampton Water.

Nothing more was said, in my hearing, about the Miss Boyds, but on Tuesday morning, when at breakfast I asked my grandmother to get their basket ready as early as she could because I wanted to get back early to go round the sheep with Tom, she said: 'The basket won't take you long, Janet. I arranged with the Miss Boyds on Sunday that you would leave it with Granny Fraser at Rosecroft and they can send there for it.'

'Oh? Why, Granny?'

'Why! Hark at her! And her forehead like a last year's tattie with wrinkles from asking questions! Because we have more to do than dress *you* to go trailing off to Achcraggan every Tuesday, that's why. ... Off you go and pick out the wee tatties for the hens' pot for me, like a clever bairn.'

'All right, Granny.'

The new arrangement suited me very well. I had no particular wish to 'go trailing off to Achcraggan' every Tuesday, for, by my standards, the Miss Boyds were less interesting than many of the things I could find to do at home; and although the hens' pot did not come into the interesting category, it did not take long and it kept my grandmother quiet.

*   *   *   *   *

In the course of the week I forgot all about the Miss Boyds, and, indeed, I did not remember them at all until the Friday, when they were mentioned again as the butter, eggs, honey and Red Cross items were being loaded into the trap.

'And the Miss Boyds, Tom,' said my grandmother. 'Chust

leave the basket with Miss Tulloch as I told you. ... George! Are you ready? If you are to get to the bank for Mr Macintosh this day it's time you were away. Tom and Janet are waiting for you!'

This was one of the Very Fine Market Days which came about once a month, when George had to go to Mr Foster, the banker, on behalf of his employer Mr Macintosh. Mr Macintosh was lame and did not go out much.

'Janet, have you got that pattern of thread for your mother? What are you to tell Mrs. Gilchrist?'

'The same as this or a little darker, and a little thicker rather than a little thinner, Granny.'

'That's right,' my mother nodded as George got into the trap.

'All right. Off you go,' said my grandmother, with a wave of the hand that the station-master at King's Cross might give as the royal train pulled out.

'Would I get coming into the bank with you, George?' I asked as I always did when Mr Foster was to be visited.

'No,' said George, which was how he always answered too, but no harm in trying.

In my own opinion I knew all about the bank already, but I always persisted in my efforts to enter it simply because every-one was always so putting-off about it, and I was wondering for perhaps the hundredth time why they were so secretive about Mr Foster's Bank as Dulcie picked her way down over the rough track on to the Poyntdale farm road and thence to the County Road on the shore. After all, we had a bank at Reachfar, the Bluebell Bank, which, in principle, was just the same as Mr Foster's Bank. The Bluebell Bank bred rabbits and Mr Foster's Bank bred pennies—that was the only difference. The Bluebell

Bank lay along the south side of the West Parkie, at right angles to the Strip of Herbage, and in summer it was covered and made blue all over by the nodding harebells that rang their rustling, faint chimes in the breeze. It was riddled through and through with rabbit burrows, and if you went there early in the morning you would see the families of young rabbits rolling in the dew on the grass at their doors like the slum children that you read about rolling in the dust.

Mr Foster's Bank did not have harebells, but it was a sort of rockery with a stone staircase going up through it to his house which sat on top, and I knew that in his house he had a lot of holes going into the rockery bank and that he put the pennies in these holes. My father had told me that if you gave pennies to Mr Foster to put in his bank 'they got more, the longer you left them with him', and I knew that one of the holes in his bank was mine, where the pennies I got when I sold my ducks at Christmas were breeding. I thought it only reasonable that I should be allowed into the bank to see the hole where my pennies were, and see how many farthing children they had at the moment. I could not see why everybody had to say that the bank was 'no place' for people who were not grown up. I had known for years where calves and kittens came from. What was so special and different about farthings?

'You're awful quiet, Janet!' George teased. 'Are you feeling sick?'

'Ach, you and your old bank!' I said. 'You can keep it.' I tried to think of something to say that would annoy *him* as he had annoyed me about Mr Foster's Bank and, the devil and I always having been firm friends, the words came to my tongue almost unbidden. 'I'll just go and wait for you and Tom at the Miss Boyds.'

The results of this were excellent. They were both far angrier than I had been about Mr Foster's Bank.

'You'll not go *near* the Miss Boyds!'

'You'll do dang a-all of the kind!' They both spoke at once.

'Why not?'

'You just *won't!*'

'I don't see why not—all that nice leddies—' I said.

'Hold your tongue, you wicked little clip!' said my uncle.

'George Sandison! I'll tell my granny on you—calling names like that! You should be ashamed!'

'Now, Janet—' he began in conciliatory tones.

'Don't you try your smooth tongue on *me!*' I told him in the voice of my grandmother. 'Being like that about the Miss Boyds, as if there was something *wrong* with them—'

'*I'll* tell you what's wrong with them!' Tom burst forth as the mare turned of her own accord on to the County Road. 'They're the dangdest, foolishest, hot-arsed-est lot o' ould bitches I ever saw in a-all my born days, and ye can tell your granny that if ye like, ye wee, cunning besom that ye are!'

'There, now!' said George. 'You've made Tom right wild angry at you!'

Things had Gone Too Far. This was really worrying.

'Tom, I'll *not* tell her!' I pleaded. 'And, Tom, I'll not go near the Miss Boyds, either!'

'That's right,' said Tom forgivingly. 'You'll just stop with Miss Tulloch as usual while George and me does our business at the bank and the Plough.'

'All right,' I promised.

I wanted to ask what that word 'hot-arsed-est' meant, for it was new to me, and I was always interested in words, but I decided to wait for a better opportunity.

When we reached Achcraggan, however, and I opened Miss Tulloch's shop door with its tinkling bell so that Tom and George could carry the baskets in, there were four Miss Boyds all giggling and nudging and fluttering in the middle of the floor, and they converged on Tom and George like wasps on a jam-pot. They invited us to tea. We did not have time. They would help us with our shopping. It wasn't so much the shopping, it was the business at the bank. Oh, surely we just had a wee while to spare? Well, you see, there was the horse. Oh, Mr Skinner would look after the horse.

'Mr Sk—? What? *Jock* Skinner? That twisted boogger? Beg your pardon, Miss Tulloch!' said Tom.

Miss Tulloch lifted up the flap of her counter. 'Chust come through, George—and you too, Tom. That thing you were going to look at for me is chust ben the back.' She dropped the flap again, separating the three of us from the Miss Boyds whom she now addressed in a business-like way: 'Then that will be a-all for you the-day, leddies? Oh, here's your basket from Reachfar! Good day to you a-all. Good day!' The bell tinkled and the Miss Boyds disappeared into the street, while Miss Tulloch ran through to the back shop to us, looked at Tom and George and gave herself up to helpless mirth.

'Well, I wasna born yesterday,' she said, 'but I never thought to see the day when the men o' Reachfar would be feared for their very lives! Aye, Geordie, maybe you better marry myself after a-all—you would be safe, then, maybe!'

Tom and George stood in the middle of the floor among the sacks of flour and barrels of herring, looking shamed to death, but she gave another squeal of laughter. 'Ach, it's a sin to be teasing you, that's what it is! But you're not yourselves in trouble. Every man in Achcraggan is running as if the devil was in it—even Bill the Post is sending Farquhar's wee laddie up to the house with their letters!'

'They canna be right in the head,' said Tom.

Miss Tulloch dried the laughter tears from her eyes with a corner of her white apron. 'Ach, you know what old maids are—the poor silly craiturs!' she said, and added soberly: 'It's a sin to laugh at them and them giving parties for Lady Lydia's soldiers and a-all. I fairly believe they would take some poor fellow with no legs if he was to make an offer. And not a thing to choose between the old ones and the young ones o' them —there's nothing in any of their heads but chust the one thing. Aye, you'll have to watch yourself, Geordie, boy! ... Are you for the bank? Here, chust go out the back way there and through to Mr Foster's garden. ... Mind the rat-trap there beside the drain!' She turned back to Tom and me. 'The place is chust fair rotten-infested with rats the-year. It's that Jock Skinner and a-all his old iron and dirty rags and trock that he'll be keeping in that old ruin o' a barn of his, the dirty, poaching rascal.'

Jock Skinner, being the Achcraggan dog with a bad name, was hanged every day and sometimes twice a day for all the village sins, regardless of whether he had committed them or not, so that even the very rats were laid at his door.

'Och, you should have let Janet know before now if you are plagued with rats, Miss Tulloch,' said Tom.

'Janet?'

'Aye, surely. She'll come down with Fly and Angus and sort them for you. She charges a penny a tail at home, but maybe, you being a friend, she will give you a special price.'

'I'll do Miss Tulloch's rats for nothing, so there!' I said.

To the horrified Miss Tulloch it was explained that Fly was my collie bitch and Angus my ferret, and Tom recommended us as the best rat-exterminating combination in the county.

'I'll tell you what we'll do, Miss Tulloch,' he ended. 'Next Friday Janet will come down in the morning with Fly and Angus and she can be going home in the evening with me as usual.' And this was agreed.

Shortly after that, Tom went away about his business and I went to Mrs Gilchrist's Drapery Warehouse, where the men's working shirts and cards of lace hung from the ceiling, and matched the thread for my mother.

'And Granny said to put it in the book, please.'

'Och, yes, surely, I'll be putting it in the book. ... And how many of you are down the-day?'

'Just George and Tom and me.'

'I hope your mother is well?'

'Oh yes, quite well, thank you, Mrs Gilchrist.'

Nobody ever asked if anyone else at Reachfar was well—they asked, always, only about my mother. It worried me a little, this.

'We are *all* well, thank you,' I added with emphasis.

'That's fine. And I hear the Miss Boyds was calling on you Sunday last?'

'Yes,' I said. 'They did call.'

'George would be showing them the place, I'm sure—or *one* o' them, whatever.'

My grandmother used to, and still does, come into my mind quite without my calling her into it sometimes, and I had once overheard her say that 'Teenie Gilchrist' was 'a good enough craitur in some ways but a wicked-tongued old limmer if you'd let her be', so I now recognised the presence of my grandmother in my mind and said the words that the presence inspired: 'Oh no, Mrs Gilchrist, not at all. My uncle had business with Lady

Lydia—she came up on Sunday too, with her visitor Mrs de Cambre. I am glad you had the thread my mother wants. Good day, Mrs Gilchrist.'

I left the shop, smiling and 'Good day-ing' my way through the crowd of female customers round the counter and went back to Miss Tulloch's.

I do not imagine that you are familiar with the word 'palter-ghost', which is a private word of my own, but I feel almost sure that you are familiar with the phenomenon which I use it to describe. A palter-ghost is a thing that comes to as follows, as My Friend Tom would say, when explaining something in a logical, scientific way. Imagine that one day you wake up with a pain in your knee, go to the doctor with it and he diagnoses housemaid's knee. When you emerge from his consulting-room, it is about a hundred to one that the following events —or something very similar to them—will happen.

(a) The woman cleaning the doctor's front steps will have a bandage on her leg that simply shrieks 'housemaid's knee'.

(b) The magazine that you buy to read on the bus on the way home will have a Home Doctor article on housemaid's knee.

(c) A woman with a shopping basket on the seat in front of you will be telling her companion a grim story of a second cousin twice-removed who had a complaint, diagnosed as housemaid's knee, but which was really gangrene and how, in the end, she died in agony.

(d) In the evening paper there will be banner headlines on the latest murder, and on reading the ghastly details you will discover that the unfortunate victim, far from deserving her gory end, had been a patient lifelong sufferer from housemaid's knee.

(e) Through the night, it goes without saying, you will dream that every joint in your body is afflicted with house-

maid's knee and that you are engaged in mortal combat with a murderer who is trying to bludgeon you to death on the steps of a bus with, for a weapon, a bandaged human leg which is afflicted with housemaid's knee.

That, that I have very baldly described, is housemaid's knee in the form of a palter-ghost, that phenomenon that palters in a mischievous, supernatural way with your daily life and your very reason. Anything, anything under the sun, given certain conditions which I am at a loss to tabulate, can suddenly take on the character of a palter-ghost and, although when I was eight years old I had not yet added this word to my vocabulary, 'old maids' became a palter-ghost to me. The expression recurred and recurred. No doubt it had always been used in family conversations, but it is a main characteristic of palter-ghosts that they always arise out of expressions which, hitherto, had no special significance, in precisely the way that poltergeists suddenly begin to haunt respectable suburban houses in Manchester or God-serving country rectories, instead of, as you might expect, some bloody-historied Norman keep or Madame Tussaud's Chamber of Horrors.

'No, no!' my grandmother would say, identifying some old acquaintance. 'Not *Lizzie* Mackay—the *older* sister, the one that died an old maid west Ullapool way.'

Or—'No, it was from the aunt that Robbie's money came —the one that was housekeeper to that man in Glasgow that left her the house and a-all and not a penny to his old-maid sister.'

Or—'Yes, Maggie was a bonnie lassie—it's funny she was an old maid.'

Or—'Och, she was always far too pernickety and parteeclar, poor Ina. She could never have made anything but an old maid, an old maid from the day she was born.'

Then, one evening, I remember, my father read aloud a letter to the editor of the county newspaper which was a diatribe against the schoolchildren of Dingwall for making a noise in the street on their way home in the afternoons. After reading this aloud, signature and all, my father said: 'Och, aye, poor old Annie. The bairns are ill-brought-up, she says. Well, well, they always did say that old maids' bairns are aye perfect.'

This statement was Too Much Altogether, and at the earliest possible moment I conducted an enquiry into the whole matter, with Tom, in the comfortable privacy of the straw barn.

'Tom, what *is* old maids?'

'Leddies that isn't married.'

'So Auntie Kate is an old maid?'

'Wheesht!' said Tom, with a frightened look in the direction of the kitchen. 'Hold your tongue! Saying a thing like that about your auntie!'

'But she's not married and *you* said—'

'I never said a word about your auntie!'

'But if she's not married and—'

'Your auntie is a young lassie that's not *married yet*—an old maid is quite a different thing.'

'Oh. Older? Like Miss Grant? Is *she* an old maid?'

'Hold your tongue, for God's sake!' said Tom. 'You'll have the both of the two of us in Bother!'

'But Miss Grant is older than *you* and she's not married and—'

'Miss Grant is an *unmarried leddy* and much respected,' said Tom, 'and if you'll be saying that things about her I'll tell your granny on you.'

'Ach, Tom! Is Granny Fraser an old maid?'

'Where could a woman that's a granny be an old maid?'

'You know fine that Teenie was a baby without a father—Granny Fraser isn't married although she had Teenie!'

'Well, she's not an old maid, anyway.'

'Because of Teenie?'

'Ach, be quiet with your ask-ask-asking!'

'I will *not!* ... Is it only people like the Miss Boyds that's proper old maids?'

'Yes.'

'Why?'

'It's myself that's half-deaved with you,' said Tom and then he sighed. 'There's some things that a person chust *canna* tell about right, but it's something this way. Weemen like the Miss Boyds gets known as old maids because they are for ever in among the men and making themselves cheap-like and none o' the men is wanting them. Your auntie isn't like that—you know fine yourself that plenty o' the lads will be coming about and taking her to the dances and things and she will chust be pleasing herself the ones she will be taking notice of.'

'And some man must have come about Granny Fraser before she had—'

'We will not be speaking gossip about Granny Fraser at a-all, the decent ould craitur, though misfortunate as a lassie.'

'All right. What about Miss Grant?'

'Nor Miss Grant, neither, forbye. Miss Grant was a very fine young leddy and it was a sad, sad thing when young Mester Colin o' Poyntdale was killed in India, away back before you was in it at a-all.'

'Mr Colin was going to marry her?'

'Aye.'

'So she's not an old maid?'

'No.'

'Will I be an old maid?'

'I hope not!' said Tom.

'It's a bad thing to be?'

'Well, not *bad,* ecksactly. It is chust better for a woman person to be married if she can and have a man to be looking after her.'

'Mick the Ditcher west at Dinchory doesn't look after Molly very much—he gave her a black eye again last Saturday.'

'God be here! It's try the patience of a saint you would do! Forbye, Mick's an Irishman.'

'Well, Jock Skinner and Bella aren't Irish and they are always getting drunk and fighting. If I was Bella I'd rather be an old maid.'

'Jock and Bella have no business to make a public exybeetion o' themselves.'

'You mean they should just not speak to each other at all like Mr and Mrs Macrae and sit one at each end of the house?'

'Well, maybe that would be more decent.'

'I would rather be an old maid than be Mrs Macrae.'

'I daresay,' said Tom. 'It would be a devil of a chob if you couldna be at the speaking. ... It's a whilie since you was last at the poetry-writing. That's far more inter*est*ing than a-all this speaking about old maids. The most o' them is very foolish craiturs with their everlasting cuppies o' tea and that one in Dingwall that was writing to the paper about the bairns is as daft as a ha'penny watch, sitting in yon roomie o' hers with yon old parrot and the cat with a red collar on it as if it was a good, sensible dog and feeding carrots out through the window to the coalman's horse. Yon is terrible foolishness and I canna be doing with it at a-all. ... No, you would be far better to be at the poetry-writing.'

'You can't be at the poetry when things is bothering you,' I told him.

'What things?'

'Things like old maids.'

'No. No, I can see that,' he agreed solemnly. 'There's nothing much o' poetry about old maids. The best thing to do, then, is to be forgetting about them. ... Is that the rain off? Because if it is we'd best take a puckle straw round to the old sow, the craitur.'

*   *   *   *   *

The following Friday, as arranged, I left Reachfar at a little after six in the morning with Fly and Angus. Fly was a dainty person, black, with a white 'shirtfront', tan paws, ear edges and eyebrows and the underlining plumes of her high borne tail were also tan. She was a small collie of the Shetland breed, a daughter of Old Fly, my grandfather's bitch, and related to Fan, Moss and Spark, who belonged to my father, Tom and my uncle respectively. Her father was Fionn, the chief dog of Mr Macgregor, the Dinchory shepherd, and Fly, as a pup, had been trained to follow me as a toddler who was beginning to roam about the moor a little. Fly had pulled out the tail feathers of the turkey-cock who tried to attack me, she had hauled me back from the rim of the well by my dress, and she and I had had many morning sleeps in each other's arms in the 'caves' she could dig in the bottoms of the haystacks on the sunny side. Fly was delighted to be 'going a place' with me now, this fine summer morning.

Angus was a little different. Everybody liked Fly, but poor Angus nobody liked except me and then Tom. Angus had been given to me by the Poyntdale gamekeeper for no better reason than that he, Robbie, had never before seen a little girl who was not afraid of a ferret, and Angus lived in a box with a wire-netting top, in the cartshed, and had a bowl of bread and milk daily. Everybody, while sitting in the kitchen, far from the cart-shed, would tell you that 'Angus is the most useful craitur about the place', but it used to give me a pain in my heart that, even so, they did not like him. Of course, Angus was *not* bonnie. He was exactly like a white weasel with pink eyes, but, somehow, I felt that *everybody* could not be bonnie—I was not bonnie like Jean Macintosh myself—and I loved him. And Angus loved me, which was nice of him, so, of course, as soon as I was out of sight of the house, I took him out of his bag which he hated and put him round my neck—which he liked—and wore him, head on one shoulder, tail on the other, as ladies often wore the skin of a dead squirrel which they had never known alive and which did not even have a name. If other ladies wore dead squirrels, why couldn't I carry Angus round my neck instead of in a bag? And my grandmother could not see me now, anyway.

Thus the three of us progressed, by all the field paths on my school route, until we came out at the 'Smiddy' above Achcraggan, where big John-the-Smith was smoking his pipe in the doorway and awaiting his first customers.

'Aye, good morning, Janet! And what are the three o' ye going to be at the-day?'

I took Angus from my neck and dropped him into his bag. 'Good morning, Mr John-the-Smith. We're going to be catching Miss Tulloch's rats.'

'There, now. Come on in and get a sweetie.'

I went into the smithy and had a hard 'mint imperial' that carried a faint, pleasant flavour of tobacco out of the tin box.

'Och, aye, and another one for the road,' said the smith in

his big, musical precentor's voice, so I took another and put it in the pocket of my kim-*oh*-no. 'You'll take a message back to your granda for me?'

'Surely, Mr John-the-Smith.'

'You tell him to bring his horses in for shoe-ing this very next week. Tell him all the mules from the Army Dee-pott is coming the week after and I'll be short o' time.'

'All right, Mr. John-the-Smith.'

He went to his cupboard on the wall in the darkest corner of his dark smithy and took out his flat black bottle and the cracked cup and had himself a dram, smacked his lips and put the bottle and cup back into the cupboard. John-the-Smith was 'inclined to be fond of a droppie', and sometimes people like Mrs Gilchrist would be critical of him, but, as Tom said: 'It's all very fine for *them* in their wee shoppies and housies selling a bittie lace or sweeping the floor, but the smiddy is hard, hot work that makes a man dry.'

In a way, John-the-Smith was like the smith in the poem that started 'Under a spreading chestnut tree...' except that there was no chestnut tree at his smiddy but a very bonnie row of rowans. John was a 'mighty man was he' and he had 'large and sinewy hands', but he did not *feel* the same as the smith in the poem. The one in the poem had what Tom would call a 'goody-goody' feeling about him, and there was nothing of that about John-the-Smith. No. John-the-Smith, although mighty, large and sinewy on the outside, might easily go stealing the Poyntdale apples or some laddies' caper like that, and very often, when he was not busy, he would stand outside his black cavern, throwing a horseshoe into the air and catching it while the whole hillside rang with his voice singing 'Annie Laurie' or some song like that, in just the way that I would bounce my ball to one of my own songs. You could not help liking John-the-Smith, and also I had heard Sir Torquil say that he was 'one of the finest craftsmen in the North'.

As I turned to go on my way, sucking my 'mint imperial', he said: 'Aye, Janet, so you are off then? Tell your Uncle Geordie a message for me, will you?'

'Yes, Mr John-the-Smith. What?'

'Tell him I am chust saying to him to keep his eye on them Miss Boyds.'

'Why?' I asked.

'He'll know fine why. Chust you tell him that's what I was saying.'

And he stood in his black, flame-lit doorway, holding on to the sides of his leather apron and you could have heard him laughing west at Ullapool.

'Keep your eye on them Miss Boyds,' I said to myself, memorising the message. It was a caper, of course, but John-the-Smith always had capers that worked out well, and I would certainly give George the message, and as publicly as possible—at the supper-table would be a fine time, I thought.

Miss Tulloch was surprised to see us so early, but pleased none the less, and Fly got a drink of milk, and I had lemonade out of a bottle with a glass ball in its neck and a plate of biscuits.

'And now I'll let you see Angus,' I said, and added sternly: 'And you are not to be frightened of him.'

But when I took Angus out of his bag Miss Tulloch was just like all the rest. She tried not to, but she just could not help drawing away from him and drawing her breath in at the same time.

'He is a nice little craitur,' I told her. 'Aren't you, Angus boy?'

'They—they're awful clever beasties, I'm told,' she said, which was good of her, and she did not skirl and run away like a lot of people.

She showed us how the rats came in and went down through a drain in the yard and seemed to come up somehow in her back shop and, sure enough, they had dug plenty of holes between the wall and the floor, the brutes, so I told her she had better go into the shop and shut the door before we started, and that, if Davie the Plasterer was at home, she should get him to come and stop the holes. She said she would send for Davie and went away, closing the door. I had my rat stick with me and Fly, who knew now why she had come to Achcraggan and had got a big bowl of milk, went about listening and sniffing while I blocked off certain holes at her direction with tight balls of sacking. Then we put Angus down the drain in the yard, and I quickly rolled a stone over it and dashed inside again, for Angus, too, knew why he was there and was off down that drain like a shot from a gun. We got three big rats at the first drive, Fly with her lip peeled back snapping their backs and tossing them over her shoulder in one black-and-tan flash of movement. Then she listened a little, sat down and all we had to do was wait for Angus to come out, stop that hole and start all over again.

By dinner-time Davie was there too, giving us a hand, and we had fifteen rats laid out on top of an old box in the back yard, for we had bolted a nest of four half-grown ones which always gives a rat bag a good lift, and most of the holes in the back shop were now neatly filled with plaster by Davie. Miss Tulloch gave us a good dinner—with meat that came out of a tin can, a thing I had never seen before, which looked red and raw, but it not being manners not to eat what people offered you, I took the first mouthful a little fearfully, then found it very good and ended by having a second helping before my stewed plums and custard. Fly was offered the custard that was left over, but would not eat it and Miss Tulloch looked hurt.

'Would you keep it for her, please?' I asked. 'You see, she is telling us there are more rats in it yet.'

'Is she?' Davie asked, looking at Fly's back as she sat in the doorway that led through to the shop.

'Yes,' I said, and Fly cocked her head over the other way. 'See her listening at them?'

'There canna be many more, Janet,' Miss Tulloch said, but I was sure they were there.

Miss Tulloch went back to the shop and Fly and I, with Davie to help, went out to the yard.

'It's that danged drain,' said Davie. 'What it needs is a grating across it to stop them getting in at all. It's up the drain from the shore they're coming.'

But the rats had a second way, Fly was certain of that. She was no longer interested in the drain, but more than interested in a corner of the walled yard in which stood Miss Tulloch's big stack of empty boxes.

'There's something in that corner, Davie,' I said.

'Well, we'll soon see!' said Davie and began to move the boxes. It took a long time, moving them all and stacking them tidily in another place, but when we moved the last one we found three holes that came out of Miss Tulloch's building and one that came through the yard wall.

'The danged brutes!' said Davie indignantly.

Fly was dancing about with her plumed tail high and murder in her golden eyes as she went from one hole to the other. Then she sat down and cocked her head at me. I took Angus from my neck and put him on the ground. He weaved his pointed head about along the row of holes, then flattened himself and disappeared down one that led into the shop. Fly, noiselessly, stepped along by the outside of the shop wall with her head cocked and then was off, in through the back shop, through the passage, into the front shop, which was full of Friday people, over the top of one counter, over the top of the other, while Davie and I with our sticks ran round behind. Chaos reigned. Fortunately, George and Tom were in the shop and I heard my uncle say: 'It's all right, leddies! It's only Janet and Fly at the rats.' But all of us had reckoned without the Miss Boyds. I do not know how many of them were there, but from the yells they set up at the word 'rats' I felt they must have multiplied since last Sunday into fifty Miss Boyds. The din was unbelievable, while Davie and I thrashed about in the dimness in the limited space behind the counter at the enormous rat, which, in Miss Tulloch's heavily stocked shop, had far too many places to hide. But at last Fly got it, on the broad shelf among the biscuit tins at the end of the counter, gave it her one killing shake and tossed it over her shoulder plumb into the midst of the screaming Miss Boyds.

To this day I can see George, Tom and Bill the Post—the only men in the shop—festooned with skirling Miss Boyds who were hanging round their necks and climbing up their arms; the dead rat in the middle of the floor, and all the Achcraggan women, Miss Tulloch and Davie lying at all angles against counters, barrels, boxes, helpless with laughter. And then, as the noise was just dying down and the three men freeing themselves from the encumbering Miss Boyds, like the last kick from the wings that the old music-hall stars used to give at the conclusion of their 'turn', Angus came out through the narrow space between the end of the counter and the wall, in that toothpaste-out-of-a-tube way that ferrets have. Before I could climb over the counter to pick him up, the first woman had seen him as he ambled across the floor with his back-arching lope, and with an eldritch screech she dropped her shopping-basket and made for the door.

George, Tom and Bill the Post, still draped with Miss Boyds shrieking harder than ever, were overborne in the panic rush and the entire crowd debouched wheeling and reeling into the street, where practically the whole population of Achcraggan had now gathered. I picked Angus up, put him on my shoulder and went to the door to see George and Tom shaking themselves and brushing Miss Boyds like flies from their arms and shoulders. Tom looked at me with dreadful bitterness: 'Gawd *dang* ye and that bliddy ferret!' he bellowed.

The women were now all in a covey, their eyes fixed on Angus and round with horror, but that meant nothing to me. Imagine My Friend Tom saying THESE WORDS TO *ME!* I snatched Angus from my shoulder and glared at the Miss Boyds who were the cause of all the trouble.

'It's throw Angus in among you that I'll do!' I shouted.

'Janet Sandison!' my uncle bawled. 'Get inside there this minute and put that beast in its bag!'

I did as I Was Told, but the Miss Boyds, with their skirts gathered round their bony knees, were running for home as if Angus was right behind them.

Our journey back to Reachfar was a silent one. Even their business at the Plough had not made George and Tom chatty and cheerful as it usually did and, to make matters worse, the news of the afternoon's ratting in Achcraggan was home at Reachfar before us. As soon as we reached the door of the house, my father, his eyes glittering with mischief, came out and said: 'What's this I'm hearing, Tom, about you and George kissing the Miss Boyds in Miss Tulloch's shop?'

And for weeks afterwards, indeed, Tom and George could not set foot in the village without being asked questions like: 'Have ye put up the banns yet, Tom?' or 'Now, which one o' them *is* it that ye fancy, Geordie?' while Bill the Post got to the stage of threatening to give up his job of postman altogether.

As a child of eight, my understanding of the impact of the Miss Boyds on the life of our community was very limited, but not all grown-up people were as discreet as the members of my family in my hearing, and I gradually gathered that the Miss Boyds, from the oldest to the youngest, were reckoned to be 'man-mad' and that this was a very undesirable thing for women to be. My pretty Aunt Kate was one of the most popular young women at the Red Cross Dances, Church Picnics and the like, and had a host of admirers, but my grandmother had very strict views about fitting behaviour and a scathing tongue when laying down these views, so that, one Sunday, on the way to church, she said: 'And Kate, don't let me see you and Sandy Farquharson ogling one another at the sermon today. If you want to behave like the Miss Boyds, go and live with them!' which turned my pretty aunt's face a blazing, shamed scarlet.

As a child of eight, still less did I understand the mentality of the Miss Boyds, of course, but, forty years later, I feel that when they sold their town house and took up permanent residence in Achcraggan they did a thing that was, at the least, foolhardy. They did not understand this remote community, and it did not understand them, for, apart from being used to town life, the Miss Boyds were Lowlanders by birth, and if ever there were two different races within the political boundary of a single country, there are two races in Scotland, or *were* in those days. Of the two, the Lowlander is by far the more honest, forthright person. He is shrewd and clever and he knows it, but he makes the great mistake of thinking that the slower-speaking, slower-moving Highlander is less shrewd and clever than himself, and, being a forthright person, he says aloud and honestly that he thinks so. The Highlander does not argue with him, for the Highlander is extremely polite by nature and would never contradict anyone about a point like that. He does not laugh with scorn in the Lowlander's face either, for that also would not be polite, but, in a quiet way, on his own home pitch especially, he can make rings of shrewdness and cleverness round the Lowlander, and what is smarter still, contrive to maintain undamaged the Lowlander's illusion that *he* is the shrewder, cleverer man of the two.

The Miss Boyds, who came to Achcraggan with some idea, apparently, of being big frogs in a small pond, who were going to show the natives some style in the way of tea-parties, some high fashion in the way of dress and some bright ideas of all kinds, were destined from the start to be lambs to the slaughter. Their unfortunate hunger for male society, coupled with their total lack of any claim to physical good looks, was bound to complete their downfall in a district where beauty and distinction in the women was a commonplace rather than a rarity. At this distance of time I have some understanding of, and consequently pity for, the Miss Boyds, as well as some estimate of the cruel herd instinct of a small community, but as a child of eight I laughed with the rest. Even at that, I did not laugh as much or as often as many did, for my life was really remote from that of the village, and when, in the autumn, I went back to school, any rude, crude, schoolchild references to the Miss Boyds which I brought home were received by all my family with frozen faces and the admonition from my gentle mother: 'Janet, don't be vulgar,' or, from my father: 'No gossip, Janet. This is Reachfar—not a village shop door. Get on with your supper.'

In spite of this suppressive attitude on the part of my family, however, I knew that they were as maliciously interested in the Miss Boyds as was the rest of the district, and I was aware that when I was not present their latest peccadilloes were discussed with enjoyment in the Reachfar kitchen. I had been aware, many times in the past, that certain subjects were discussed by my family out of my hearing—things like the pennies in the bank, for instance, and whether the red cow should be 'put to' the Black Angus bull or the Shorthorn at Poyntdale this time. But in a superior way I inwardly said 'Poop!' to my family about these things, for I already knew all I wanted to know for the present about pennies in the bank and the mating of cows and was willing to allow my family its silly, secretive discussions about them.

The Miss Boyds were a different matter. I did *not* understand as much as I wanted to about the Miss Boyds, and they were an ever-present, nagging problem to which I could find no satisfactory solution. The crux of this problem was that they were old maids who were despised for being old maids, but were despised still more for hanging round the menfolk and trying to alter their status. It did not make sense. I felt that people could not have it both ways. If to be an old maid was laughable and undesirable, was it not praiseworthy in the Miss Boyds to try to get married? Also, if men did not want to marry them, why did they not keep away from them as Tom, George and Bill the Post did? Why did a lot of the village men like Mrs Gilchrist's Hughie and Lewie the Joiner's Donald go to parties at the Miss Boyds' and be seen giggling with them outside the post office and things like that? I questioned Tom on this last point.

'Ach, be quiet with your ask-ask-asking about them danged Miss Boyds!'

'I will *not!* I'll tell Granny about you and George laughing about what Alex the Slater told you Miss Iris said to him on Saturday—that's what I'll do!'

'Och, now, Janet, ye wouldna do a thing like that.'

'Well, *why* do Alex and Hughie and Donald and them all go about the Miss Boyds if they don't want to marry them?'

'Och, it's chust taking a rise out o' the silly craiturs that the young fellows will be!' he said. 'It's only for a choke.'

'What kind of joke?'

'Och, it's chust kind of comical and amusing the capers they will be at with their face powder and their scent and a-all. And all that love stories they will be reading and for ever talking about.'

'Auntie Kate would put powder on her face if Granny would let her, and she's got *dozens* of love stories up in her room.'

'Ach, Auntie Kate is only a lassie—no' a foolish old maid!'

There it was again, the complete vicious circle.

*   *   *   *   *

Late in September, on a bright harvest Sunday, when the new-cut stubble was golden in the sun, the Firth blue as my aunt's dance dress and the Ben purple as the pansies in my grand-mother's Sunday hat, my family retired for its Sunday Sleep and Fly and I decided to go and have a Look Round at the old quarry. The old quarry was at the south-easternmost corner of Reachfar, where our march fence on the east divided us from the upper moorland of Seamuir, and where, on the south, it divided us from the lower moorland of Greycairn. The quarry had been disused for about seventy years and had never been a big working, but had yielded enough freestone for the church, the manse, the school, schoolhouse and one or two walls in Achcraggan. Old Murdo the Mason was the only man in the district who could remember stone coming out of it and Murdo did not know when he himself was born. At that time it had been the property of Seamuir, but when the farms had been properly fenced at the turn of the century Captain Robertson's father had told the fencers to take a straight line north and south, which left the disused, useless quarry on the west, and Reachfar, side of the march.

The quarry was a little like Angus and the Strip of Herbage —it was popular with no one at Reachfar except myself—but for me it had many attractions, not the least of which was that it was Absolutely Forbidden Ground. It would have been a circular green basin lying on the sloping hillside except that its more elevated side, instead of being a continuation of the curve, was a straight line where the old quarry face had been. The stone of this face, being soft and friable, had a deep fissure running diagonally across it, in which three rowan trees and two wild cherries or 'geans' had taken root, and, in lesser fissures, ferns, pale foxgloves and strange trailing mosses had made themselves at home. It was a dank sort of place. The basin-like hollow that was the quarry floor was carpeted with mossy green grass, out of which grew clumps of whin and broom, wild raspberries and brambles, and in the centre of the hollow a spring seeped up, forming a small, weedy pool which was inhabited by a fascinating family of newts.

When I had been a small child, free to roam, attended by

Fly, the two forbidden places had been the well on the moor above the house and the old quarry. The well, I was told, was inhabited by a fierce old man called Sandy, who had red whiskers and was always on the lookout for children to steal, and the quarry was even worse, for it was the home of a fearsome character called Rory, with black whiskers, who lay in wait for children to come along and then caused lumps of freestone to break away from the quarry face and kill them. The psychology of this, as applied to me, was bad, for my family had overlooked the fact that my grandfather and many of my best friends had whiskers and that I was therefore convinced of the essential benevolence of all men with whiskers. For this reason, Fly had had to drag me back from the rim of the deep well by my dress, because I had crawled through the fence to visit Sandy who lived there, and as soon as I was old enough to walk the four miles to the quarry I naturally went there too, to pay a call on the black-whiskered Rory.

By the time I was six years old, of course, I knew that it was all a Pack of Lies about Sandy in the well and made Tom and George admit it, but the quarry was a different proposition. My grandmother and my father and mother were the ones who gave the orders about where I could and could not go, as a rule, but about the quarry Tom and George were the most virulent forbidders, so that I did not dare discuss Rory with them at all, much as I wanted to. You see, it was *true* about the quarry. Some mysterious person *did* live there, in the cave with the narrow mouth at the foot of the rock face, although I had never happened to find him at home and he had never hurled any lumps of rock down on me. Instead of a door, his home had a big boulder about twice the size of myself in front of the cave opening, but I had several times peered round the side of it into his darksome place. Inside he had a few odds and ends of buckets and bottles, and some bags that looked as if they held oats which were protected from his dripping roof by some rusty corrugated sheeting. Away back, in the dimmest part of all, was his fireplace where he did his cooking, and on this there was a funny round pot with a long spout from its top that seemed to go up his chimney and became invisible in the black, dripping darkness above. It was a frightening place, although it was very interesting, because it was so very, very secret. I could not go there very often because of the risk of being caught by Tom or George, who were smarter at catching you at things than the rest of my family, but when I had an overwhelming need for a shiver of Tremendous, Thrilling Secret, I would go there and take a look inside.

Rory, I decided, must be a hermit, who did not want to see anybody, ever, for he could not be away from home *every* time I went there and called Good Day to him, or perhaps he always went out on Sunday afternoons, which, of course, were the only times I could go to the quarry with real safety.

On this Sunday Fly and I left home immediately after dinner and 'went straight' to the quarry, for I hoped that if the hermit went to tea with some other hermit friend on Sundays I might be in time to see him leave, even if he would not speak to us, but when we arrived at the quarry, there it was, green and damp and quiet as usual, the boulder in front of the cave and not a movement to be seen. Oh, well. We had a dabble in the newt pool, got some newts out on to a stone, had a look at them, put them back, had a look into the big dark pipe that carried the water out of the pool and through the green basin wall of the quarry to trickle away to join the Seamuir Burn, and we floated a few pieces of stick into the pipe and ran round to see them come out on the other side. We were just setting a really large piece of bark on its way through the pipe when Fly cocked her head, listened and looked towards the little path through the broom that led into the quarry basin. It could only be my father, Tom or George. They had followed me. Like a flash, Fly and I were into the middle of a thick clump of broom together, and in another flash I had the belt of my kim-*oh*-no wound round Fly's muzzle, but my heart was sick, for I knew that at the first whistle from any of them Fly would succeed in barking, bound muzzle or not. But it was not any member of my family that came over the green rim of the basin. Fear and guilt streamed out like hot water from the tips of my fingers and toes and my hand dropped away from the belt on Fly's face. It was that Miss Iris Boyd and that son of the cattleman at Whitemills that was home on leave from the Army, and he had his arm round her waist and she had her head on his shoulder and was giggling in a way so silly that I was red hot all over and rooted to the ground with shame for her. Before Fly and I could feel calm enough to move, they suddenly sat down right beside the clump of broom that held us, and he began to pull at the front of her blouse and she was saying: 'Now don't, Jamie!' and giggling, and then again: 'Jamie, you mustn't !' and not really meaning it at all, and his face was looking sly and his eyes were bright and his mouth was open and the lips wet and slobbery. And, always, from Miss Iris there would come that silly, ineffectual, guilty, furtive giggle and the 'Now, don't, Jamie! You mustn't take advantage!' After what seemed a very long time of this, she suddenly sprang to her feet and ran, clumsily like a crab but giggling all the time, across the grass by the pool, but I saw Jamie catch up with her and they threw themselves down by another clump of broom where I could see only their feet and his hand, now, pushing the skirts up from her skinny legs with the black stockings and the pink garters below the knees. Fly and I crawled out, silent and unseen, on to the path, then took to our heels and left Miss Iris and Jamie wrestling in the quarry. ...

It was all Dreadful, dreadful in a way that I could not describe, for my brain would not think about it without having red sparks of shame, and my stomach felt sick. And I was afraid to go home, not because the broom bushes had torn my hair ribbons off and had made a big rent in my kim-*oh*-no, although these things were bad enough, but because I felt that some of the hideous, sly guilt of Jamie's slobbery mouth was somewhere on *me* and that my family would see it. I felt that, for the first time in my life, I had been in contact with Real, Awful Sin— the kind of sin that shamed and degraded—and that it was My Own Wicked Fault for going to the quarry where My Friend Tom and My Friend George had told me I must not go. If I had not gone there I would never have seen Jamie's horrid face as he tried—tried—what were her words?—as he tried to Take Advantage. He had been trying to couple with her as the stallion at Poyntdale did with the mares, but this had not been clean and natural as the animals were. Jamie and Miss Iris *knew* it was not. *She* called it 'Taking Advantage', and his eyes and mouth had shown his guilty knowledge of shame and ugliness.

When I came within sight of the house, which stood darkly outlined between me and the sunset light above the Ben, I sat down behind a tree and began to cry. I would be late for tea. I would get a scolding. I did not care. If only—if *only* my family could scold me enough to take away all that appalling ugliness, I would never, *never* go near the quarry again.

I do not remember how I passed that evening, nor do I remember much of the week that followed—I remember nothing except my Burden of Sin which went everywhere with me and was behind my shoulder as I fed Fly and Chickabird, and on the next Sunday I remember how I wanted to cry when, after dinner, both Tom and George announced that they did not want a Sunday Sleep and that the three of us would go out and have a Right Good Look Round for the whole afternoon. If they knew, I thought, about my Burden of Sin, they would never invite me to go for a Look Round with them again.

When we had passed through the moor gate we took the south-easterly path that led to the Home Spring about half a mile away, from which the water flowed down a little trench through the heather to feed the well where the whiskered Sandy was reputed to have lived. Tom and George showed little inclination for conversation, for which I was grateful, because my Burden of Sin made me that I could neither think nor talk with any pleasure. When we reached the Juniper Place where the spring was they sat down on the green turf among the juniper bushes which had the grotesque shapes of pillars, pincushions, deformed dwarfs and queer animals, took out their pipes and looked around them at the quiet fir trees that ringed the small clearing among the heather.

'Aye, a grand day,' said George, and reached into his pocket for his tobacco, but, instead, he took out two of my hair ribbons and a kim-*oh*-no belt. 'So you were having a bit Look Round at the old quarry last Sunday, Janet?'

This was it. Sin had Found Me Out. I began to cry.

'Ach, wheesht, now!' said Tom. 'There's nothing to be crying about and worrying the way you have been doing a-all the week past. ... Wheesht, now.'

'Was you seeing anything going on up there?' George asked.

'I saw everything!' I sobbed. 'I saw it all! I know all about it! It is dreadful and awful!'

'Ach away with you!' he said. 'There's nothing dreadful and awful about it at a-all! Where is the harm in a wee bit caper like that?'

'It *isn't* a caper! It's a dreadful, awful, wicked *sin* and people shouldn't be *doing* things like that! God will put a *curse* on people that's doing things like that—'

'Where would God put a curse on George and me for making a droppie good—' Tom burst out.

'Hold your tongue, man!' George broke in sharply, but he was too late. My raw, flayed perceptions had caught the 'George and me'.

'George and you?' I stared at Tom while the tears tickled my cheeks as they ran down. 'Making a droppie? A droppie *what*?'

'What are ye speaking about?' George enquired blandly. 'What would we be making? You didna hear right—what Tom said was—'

'You're making *drams!*' I shouted. ' *Drams!* In that pot in the Hermit's cave!'

'Be *quiet*, for God's sake!' snapped George with a haunted look round him at the silent bushes and trees, and then he stared at Tom's stricken face and said with terrible, long-drawn-out vehemence: 'Da-a-amn ye to hell with your long, foolish tongue!'

I stared wildly from one of them to the other. Never, never had I heard George be angry at Tom, and never, never had I heard George Swear an Awful Swear like that one he had sworn at Tom. It was all my fault for going to the old quarry; my Burden of Sin was growing bigger and bigger. It overwhelmed me. I cast myself face downwards on the short rough grass and sobbed until I thought my heart must burst.

'Wheesht, pettie!' said Tom, his big hand rubbing my shoulders. 'Come now. It's all right. George and me has done away with the bliddy thing—come now, pettie, don't you be worrying. It's not such a terrible big sin to make a dram now. Wheesht, pettie—'

'I don't—I don't care if you'll be making a—making a *loch* of whisky,' I sobbed. 'Dad said when the Excisemen caught the man at Ullapool that people would be at far bigger sins than that and so they are! So they *are!* Terrible, *awful* sins!'

'Here, come now,' said George in an authoritative voice, much more like the voice of my father than that of my clown of an uncle. 'Sit up now and tell Tom and me about this. *What* people? *What* sins?'

'That Miss Boyd and that man—'

'When?'

'Last Sunday at the quarry—'

'What the bliddy hell was one o' that danged bitches doing on Reachfar ground?' Tom bawled. '*What* man?'

I told them. I told them everything—black stockings, pink garters, 'Don't take advantage' and all. They listened in rigid silence to my recital, and when I had finished I looked from one of them to the other.

'For myself,' said George, 'I am hard put till it not to be laughing!' and suddenly he rolled over on the grass towards Tom, caught him round the neck and said: 'Come on, Tom, dearie, give me a nice kiss, now!'

'Now, now, Geordie!' said Tom with squeaky refinement. 'Don't be taking advantage!'

They began to roll about on the grass together until I could hardly believe that they had not been with me the Sunday before and seen the whole episode for themselves. The longer it went on, the funnier it became, and by the time Tom sprang up and began to run, giggling, away, with his toes turned out, his hands holding up his trouser legs as Miss Iris had held her skirt, I was holding my aching sides as I laughed, and the dogs were barking their delight and jumping round in circles.

'Was that the way it was, at all?' George asked, after they had sat down again and caught their breath.

'Yes—but not funny like that,' I told him.

'No. That was because they weren't doing it for pure foolishness, like Tom and me. But it was chust foolishness that was in them, a-all the same, although that Miss Boyd is too foolish to know when she's being foolish, like.'

'That's chust the way of it,' said Tom. 'And her that ugly, with the pink garters on her, and a-all.'

'Yes,' I agreed.

'Iphm. ... But, George, man, we'll have to sort it so that they will not be at their foolishness on Reachfar ground—in the old quarry, in parteeclar.'

'Aye,' George agreed, and to me: 'They wouldn't be going near the cave, do you think?'

'No,' I said. 'It's dirty and wet near the cave.'

'And the leddy might be getting mud on her pink garters,' said Tom, with which they both began to laugh as though they would burst. Somehow, my Burden of Sin had now disappeared and my relieved mind went off on a new tack.

'A fine to-do,' I told them severely, in the voice of my grandmother, when they had stopped laughing. 'You two telling me a Pack of Lies about Rory with the black whiskers and you making drams in that cave all the time!'

'We will not be speaking about that at a-all,' said Tom with dignity.

'Not to nobody,' added George firmly.

'It's tell Granda on the two of you I should do!'

'Telling yarns like that is no use to nobody,' said George in a superior way. 'You have to have proof of the like o' that.'

'There's plenty of proof!' I said. 'The bags and yon big pot and everything!'

'All right. Away ye go and *tell* Granda and take him to see the pot, and ye better send a tellygram west for the policeman when you're at it, ye wee limmer!'

'Aye, and get the Exciseman over at the same time, ye wee besom!' added Tom.

I stared from one blank face to the other. 'You've shifted it!' I said.

'What?'

'The pot and things.'

'*What* pot is it she keeps speaking about, George?'

'I wouldna be knowing. I never heard of a pot being in it at a-all myself,' said George and lay back and puffed smoke at the sky.

'That's a Pack of Lies!' I shouted at them, but they merely lay back and stared at me, half smiling and impervious. 'If that pot is on Reachfar, I'll *find* it!' I threatened.

They still made no reply. That day, or any other day, they made no reply. That day and many another day, I spent many hours hunting over Reachfar for that pot, but it was like the Rainbow's End. I knew it was there, but I did not ever find it.

Thirty years later I questioned them about it, for I am extremely persistent about a thing that interests me.

'Why you were never caught, I don't know,' I told them.

'Och,' said George modestly, 'Tom and me were never the ambeetious kind to go in for anything in a big commercial way, to be making money at it, like. Any jobbies that him and me ever went in for—like taking a bit fish out of the river at night or the like o' that—we aye did it chust for pleasure, in a quiet way, among ourselves and our cronies. Tom and me was never clever enough to get ambeetious. It's when people will get ambeetious to be making money at a thing that the bother comes in—that's what I always think, whatever.'

'Yes, and me too, besides,' Tom concurred.

Following my experience in the old quarry, however, Tom, George and I had a number of discussions about the basic 'fool-ishness' of the Miss Boyds and the general ugliness and undesirability of behaviour such as theirs which, as Tom said, 'made nothing but a speakylation and a laughability of a person', and we also decided that 'we would not be speaking of Miss Iris in the old quarry in the house or to the family at a-all'. Apart from these decisions, we added the Miss Boyds in general to our repertory of people to be imitating, such as the Reverend Roderick and Lewie the Joiner, and we agreed among ourselves that Tom's flair for 'doing' a Miss Boyd speaking to a gentleman was utterly surprising as well as completely brilliant.

'It's always been myself that acted the leddies before,' said George, after a particularly successful tour de force by Tom as Miss Daisy receiving the letters from Bill the Post.

'The thing about it, George, man,' said Tom, reapplying himself to his job of forking straw, 'the Miss Boyds is *not* proper leddies.'

At all events, by one means and another, George and Tom contrived to blot out all the ugliness, shock and outrage of what I had seen in the old quarry with a clear wash of laughter. They convinced me that what I had seen was 'chust not worth a real person's time to be bothering about', and, in return, I made no 'bother' for them about the things I had seen in the cave but which had since been removed. We 'chust did not speak of these things, in the house, or to the family, or to anybody at a-all.'

∗   ∗   ∗   ∗   ∗

By the beginning of October the Miss Boyds' name was enjoying a rest from people's tongues at school, in the village and on the hills around, for we now all had something else to think about, which was the Poyntdale Harvest Home, which I was to be allowed to attend for the first time in my life. I was delighted and, at the same time, amazed to think that I was to be allowed to penetrate this annual mystery.

'But I thought it was a Big People's Thing, Mother.'

'So it is, but every time you have a birthday you grow to be a bigger person,' my mother said, 'and you are big enough now to go to the young people's part of it. But you can't stay all night, like Auntie Kate and Tom and George, of course. You and I will come home after supper.'

This seemed to me 'only reasonable', and I went away with Fly to the Thinking Place to give consideration to this idea of growing to be a Bigger Person every year which made you able to go to more and more Things. By the time I was as old as my grandmother, I concluded, there would not be a Thing in the Whole Wide World that I had not been to or did not know about, and the world was a very wonderful place indeed.

The Harvest Home was to be on Friday, and on the Saturday of the week before Danny Maclean came to Reachfar with his fiddle. I loved Danny. He was a strange, mysterious person, who lived all alone at the bee croft away west on the Dinchory moors, with his dog called Rory and his millions of bees. He had black, lank hair, and queer, brownish, leathery skin on his face and hands, and a big smiling mouth full of big white teeth, and bees loved him. They would settle all over him when he had caught a queen and never think of stinging him, and when he was not working with his bees he would be playing his fiddle. He very seldom left his bee croft. He came down to Dinchory once a week to pick up his groceries, tobacco and copy of the local newspaper which were left with the Dinchory shepherd, and occasionally he would come to Reachfar to see us when the heel of the sock he was knitting for himself would not come right, and then he would bring us some sections of his honey and have his fiddle with him. Since I learned to knit several years ago, I knitted a pair of socks for Danny now and again, and in return he taught me to dance the Highland Fling and the Sword Dance, only, not having a sword, we used the poker and tongs from the kitchen fireplace instead. Danny said I had a 'grand sense o' time and could put a fine lift in it', and when I had learned all the steps he would stand against the dresser, long and lean and that brownish colour of his, and say: 'One-two-three-four!' and off we would go. It was easy to 'put lift into it' to Danny's fiddle. As Tom said: 'Danny could play to make a cat dance', and Tom had a very low opinion of cats.

On this evening, when Danny arrived, my mother took me to her room, brought a cardboard shoe box out of her wardrobe and took out of it a pair of proper dancing pumps that were just my size. Until now I had always danced bare-footed.

'When you go to the Harvest Home on Friday,' she said, 'Lady Lydia wants you to dance for the people.'

'Oh, Mother, no!' I wanted to run away to the moor and hide. The dancing was just for Danny and me and my family and I could imagine with terror those *hundreds* of people at the Harvest Home all *looking*. 'Mother, *no!*'

She laid the beautiful fine leather pumps down on her bed.

'When you go to a thing like the Harvest Home, Janet, you don't go just to eat the good supper and take everything you can get for nothing, like Jock Skinner's bairns coming to school on Christmas Eve just to get their apples and oranges. If there is something you can do that people may enjoy you have to do it. And Lady Lydia thinks that her visitors may like to see you and Danny at your fiddling and dancing.'

'Danny will be there?'

'Of course! It wouldn't be a Harvest Home at all without Danny with his fiddle and Bill the Post with his melodeon and your father with his pipes.'

'Dad plays the pipes for them?'

'Every year. Everybody does something—those that *can,* anyway.'

'What do *you* do, Mother?'

'Lady Lydia usually puts me to sit with her visitors from the South so that I can explain our local ways and customs to them and answer their questions. Wouldn't you like to try your dancing with the pumps on?'

'Yes—but, Mother—what if people laugh at me?'

'Well, what of it? If they'll be laughing, they'll be happy, and the Harvest Home is a happy thing. You wait till you hear them laughing at Tom and George doing their reel to the pipes!'

I began to laugh myself, then, at the very thought, for George and Tom at their reel were enough to make a cat laugh, but I had never known that they did it anywhere except in the privacy of the Reachfar barn. I put on the lovely shoes with the leather tassels on the ends of the long laces that tied up round my ankles and went through to the kitchen where the big table had been pushed back against the wall and Danny stood against the dresser with his fiddle.

'My,' he said, 'but that's a right fine pair o' shoes! I better see that this ould fiddle o' mine is in good tune for that shoes.' And he put the fiddle under his chin, snuggled it the way Fly did when she had pups and then went 'Tap, tap, tap, tap...' round the four sections of it with the end of his bow and played the little tune called 'The Old Four-poster Bed', which ended again with the four taps from the butt end of the bow on the wood to make the four posts.

'Aye. She'll do,' said Danny. 'We better take the Sword Dance first, Duncan, while we have plenty o' wind. That's a devil of a thing you have there.'

From the little table my father picked up an enormous sword with a big, cairngorm-set, basket hilt and drew it from the long silver-mounted scabbard.

'The Clansmen cried Claymore! Claymore!' bawled Tom and George in lusty chorus. 'I will rise and follow on! Rise and fight for Charlie!'

'Hold your noise, you two!' said my grandmother.

The claymore belonged, I knew, on a rack above the fireplace in Sir Torquil's study and I had never seen it at close quarters before. Lying on the floor, crossed over its scabbard, it looked enormous, the basket hilt over which I had to dance seemed to be about a foot high, and the area around blade and scabbard seemed to cover about half an acre. The poker and tongs had been easy compared to this. And if Sir Torquil had sent the claymore to Reachfar this was serious. He really *required* that I should dance at his Harvest Home. I was on the brink of wishing that I was not Big Enough Yet to go at all.

'The great thing is,' said Danny, 'to try and get the size o' the bliddy thing in your mind and then not be looking at it at a-all. Chust as if it was the poker and tongs that was in it. I will be seeing some o' the exheebeetion dancers looking down at their swords with their shoulders humped like dogs looking into jeely jars. Now, when the clansmen in the old days shouted "Claymore, Claymore!" like Tom said, they used to doon wi' the sword on the heather and wallop into it—and not looking at the sword, for if they was looking down at the ground like that, how would they be seeing the Englishmen coming?' He gave a pluck or two at the strings of his fiddle. 'Right, Janet—chust you mind to be chumping a little higher and a little further than usual and be looking *up* at the fiddle. *One* and *two* and *three* and *four!*'

'Hwee-ow-ow-oooch!' yelled Tom and George, and Danny proceeded to raise the ghosts of the clansmen through the floor of the Reachfar kitchen into the toes of my new dancing pumps.

When we came into the 'quicktime' at the first practice I forgot to 'chump a little higher and further', caught my flying toe in the basket hilt and ended in a heap on the hearthrug, but after about four turns through the whole thing Danny decided that we would 'do', and while we had a rest Tom and George had a go, clowning their way round to their own 'deedling' for music in their big working boots until my father picked up the claymore in case they would damage the hilt. 'And you'll have to take her yourself for the Fling with your pipes, Duncan,' Danny said.

'Och, no, man!' said my father.

'Och but *so!* The fiddle is fine for the hoose here, but the Fling is better to the pipes, and the Poyntdale barn has plenty of room for them. And you can make as good a chob of the

Marquis o' Huntly as ever I heard.' He turned to my grand-mother. ' You'll have to put up with the pipes in your kitchen for a wee whilie the-night, mistress.'

'Och, well, well, Danny,' she said assentingly.

The great night came along and all of us except Aunt Kate set off for Poyntdale—Auntie Kate would go down to the dance when my father brought my mother and me home; and the dance and the midnight second supper being the parts she liked best, everybody was happy. Driving down in the trap, with the claymore wrapped in an old pillowslip at my feet, and dressed in my white Sunday skirt and blouse with a big sash of my mother's tartan tied in a big bow at the back, I was wishing that it was not Harvest Home, but just any other ordinary evening of doing my knitting or doing a little reading and writing with George and Tom, but when we reached Poyntdale Square I forgot all that, and even forgot about the claymore and the dancing. This was better than the coal boat. I had always told myself that Everybody came to the coal boat, but now I saw that that was not true, for there were people here that one never saw anywhere except at their homes, like old Granny Fraser and Johnnie Greycairn's wife and just Everybody. And, of course, six Miss Boyds, dressed to kill, giggling in a covey in a corner by themselves. People continued to come in from all angles, and my father, Tom and George disappeared to attend to the disposal of the many horses, traps and carts. Sir Torquil took my grandparents, my mother and me away in our trap to the Big House, to the big drawing-room where Lady Lydia, Mrs de Cambre and some other ladies and gentlemen were and said: 'The Reachfar party, my dear. I'll come for you all when we are ready to start.'

In my opinion everything had 'started' long ago and,

breathless with excitement, I wondered what was to happen next, but for the moment I could concentrate only on the beautiful dresses of the ladies and the funny black-beetle sort of coats that the gentlemen who were not wearing the kilt had on.

'Janet,' said Lady Lydia, after I had made my curtsy, 'there is something here you will like.' She turned to one of the gentlemen and said: 'Would you lift down the old music box, Drake?'

He lifted a long wooden box with a glass top, through which you could see a lot of machinery, down from a table and put it on the carpet and he and I sat down beside it. When he had wound it up with a little handle, shaped like the thing for turning our sharpening stone at Reachfar, it began to play music, tinkling music like the sound the dry bell heather made in autumn, but much, much better to listen to. I did not want to leave it when my mother said we had to go now, but of course I had to, and another thing I realised I had to do was get into a governess cart with two of the ladies and two of the gentlemen and none of my family there at all, and drive with them to the barn. I saw that this was all right, for my mother too was separated into a different trap from my grandmother. Mrs de Cambre was in my governess cart, wearing a long pink satin dress with sparkling things on it, with its pink train all bunched up on the floor at our feet, and she had a pink feathery thing fixed in her dark hair with a jewelled brooch. She was very, very beautiful, I thought. My aunt had told me that the dresses the Poyntdale House ladies wore for the Harvest Home were always the talk of the countryside until the next year, and that seeing them was the biggest treat of all, for you could hardly believe that such beautiful clothes could exist. I realised now that this was true. Here were the trains, the long gloves, the feather fans, just like the picture in our parlour of Lady Lydia going to see the King at Buckingham Palace before the war, only in the picture the dress looked plain white and not pink or green or blue as were the dresses tonight.

'A'ah you gonna write a pome about all this, Janet?' Mrs de Cambre asked, and said to the others: 'This sweetie is a poet, you-ou know.'

'And her grandmother is a witch!' said the gentleman called Drake, who was Lady Lydia's brother. 'Isn't she, Janet?'

'Wha-at?' Mrs de Cambre's eyes were round.

'Sometimes people will be saying so,' I said, for this was true.

'But witches a'ah scary people! Miz Sandison ain't like tha-at!'

'But Granny isn't a scary witch,' I said, adopting this new and descriptive word. 'Granny is the clever, kind sort of witch, except when people are thinking about doing badness, and then she can see it in them. As long as you don't think of doing any badness, she is very nice.'

'Yuh hear?' said Mrs de Cambre to the other lady and gentleman. 'Don' you-all get to thinkin' 'bout any badness!'

And then we all laughed and we were at the barn door. The ladies and gentlemen all went to sit up in a corner beside the big threshing mill which was covered tonight with a green tarpaulin and decorated all over with sheaves of oats and barley and big bunches of flowers and vegetables from the Poyntdale garden. Lanterns hung in rows from the rafters, and all round the walls were the sheaves again. In one corner there was a low platform, hemmed in by freshly painted ploughs, with shining shares as if they were split new, and on this platform was My Friend Danny

with his fiddle and Bill the Post with his melodeon and a lot
of ploughmen and gamekeepers whom I knew, but had never
known they could play the instruments they were holding.
John-the-Smith was there too, already singing a little to himself
in his big tuneful voice. My mother was right, as she always
was—at Harvest Home everybody contributed *some*thing. I
was quite pleased now that the big claymore was lying at the
back of the platform in its pillowslip.

I found My Friend Alasdair, who was also having his first
turn at the Harvest Home, and we went round the end of the
big mill and had a peek into the big straw barn next door, and
in there you never saw the like. Mrs Fergus, the fierce, black-
dressed housekeeper of the Big House, with the bunch of keys
hanging from the belt around her waist, was in there, with all
the servants and the ploughmen's wives, all with aprons on
over their best dresses, and tables and tables covered with white
cloths and more dishes than I had ever seen in my life, and
there was a grand smell of roast beef coming from somewhere.
Alasdair and I were going to follow the smell, but, of course,
Mrs Fergus turned us back. Tom said that Mrs Fergus was
enough to frighten the devil himself, and I told Alasdair so, but
when we were out of her hearing Alasdair said: 'Ach, I'm not
heeding her. There isn't a *Mr* Fergus, and she's only an old maid
that's in it after all!' but I knew that this was just boastingness,
for he *had* heeded her and how could she be Mrs Fergus if there
was no Mr Fergus? Alasdair told some real lies now and again.

Then Sir Torquil made a little speech and said how glad he
was to see us all, and the soldiers and sailors who had come,
and his visitors from the South and from America who had
never been to a party like this before, and then he asked John-
the-Smith to be ready. Then the Reverend Roderick said a short

prayer about thank you for the Harvest and then John-the-Smith sang the Hundredth Psalm, but it was far bonnier than in church, for all the fiddles and melodeons played it too, and I wanted to cry but before the tears quite got the better of me it was over, and after a moment the fiddles began to dance and John began to sing his comical song about 'The Wee Cooper Who Lived in Fife'.

For me, after that, the evening was full of sheer wonder. The proceedings had started about five in the afternoon, and although the lanterns were burning in the rafters the evening sun was still streaming through the open doors of the big barn, and now through these doors came eighteen sailors in *white* jerseys and *white* bell-bottomed trousers, six of them carrying brass instruments like horns such as I had never seen before. These six went up on to the musicians' platform and the other twelve formed two lines in the middle of the floor, folded their arms high across their chests and with their right feet forward began to tap out the rhythm of the gay tune that came from the platform. Then, with incredible precision and fantastic lightness of foot, they all began to dance the Sailor's Hornpipe.

This was over much too soon for me, but then I was swept away by Tom and George coming up with stern faces to the Soldiers' Matron who was standing beside us in her pretty white veil, and Tom said: 'Matron, we've come to get you for the boys to be doing an operation on you!'

Matron, who was red-haired and Irish, yelled: 'Begorra an' ye'll not now!' and ran away round the barn, and now the soldiers were coming in with a white table on wheels and the stable barrow and they all had big knives, and one had a carpenter's saw and another had a big axe, and George and Tom were chasing Matron round and round the barn until John-the-Smith suddenly out with his big fore-hammer from the platform and hit her on the head and her eyes looked across one another and she fell down and Tom caught her and lifted her on to the table. I got very frightened, but my mother said it was all just pretending and to wait and I would see that Matron was all right. So I watched and the soldiers started on her with their knives and they pulled strings and strings of sausages and black puddings and two or three horseshoes out of her and threw them into the barrow; they sawed, and threw a leg in a long black stocking into the barrow and one way and another you would not believe what they did to poor Matron on that table, until suddenly she sat up, hit *Tom* on the head with the hammer so that he fell into the barrow and then she wheeled him out through the door.

I was still holding on to Alasdair and laughing about Tom in the barrow, when Tom and George pushed the big sack platform for the mill into the middle of the floor and Sir Torquil said: 'And we have a new performer this evening, ladies and gentlemen. Janet Reachfar is going to dance for us. Come, Janet.'

All I saw clearly in the big ring of faces was My Friend Danny, smiling over his fiddle at the front of the platform, and then my father, George and Tom sitting on the edge of the platform at his feet. Sir Torquil picked me up, stood me on the sack platform, then drew the claymore from its scabbard and crossed one over the other at my feet. I stared at it for a moment, the slanting sun struck a golden ray from the big cairngorm in the hilt and: '*Poop* to you!' I thought, gave myself a shake, put my hands on my hips and looked up at Danny. He smiled at me, snuggled his fiddle with his chin, 'Hee-eee-ow-ooch!' shouted my father, Tom and George in the time of the opening four beats and we were off. It was the easiest thing in the world. The big claymore might not have been there at all—it might have been the poker and tongs at home, the way my feet came over and back dead on Danny's beat, for after that first shout *all* the people began to shout on the turns and all the fiddles and melodeons began to play, so that it felt as if all the people in the barn were dancing through my feet. When it was over, and they were all shouting and clapping their hands, I bowed all round as my mother had said and then bowed to Danny. Danny, laughing all over his leathery face, bowed back to me over his fiddle, and then I jumped off the platform and ran to my mother. Danny had been pleased, I knew, and I was very happy.

After that the Dinchory shepherd's wife who was from Skye sang one of her beautiful Gaelic songs to Danny's fiddle, and then the minister rose and went into the middle of the floor.

'I have been asked to announce a special new item, ladies and gentlemen. The youngest chentleman among us is now going to play a waltz, to be danced by six people whom we a-all know to be some of the best waltzers in the county.' And as he finished speaking, who should come slow-marching through the door with his little boy's pipes on his shoulder but My Friend Alasdair, with the last sun shining on his carroty head! But more amazing to me still was what followed. First my father came and bowed to Lady Lydia, who looped her train over her wrist and they began to waltz round and round Alasdair; then Doctor Mackay came and got my mother and *they* started to dance, and then Sir Torquil bowed to Mrs Mackay and the three couples were revolving round the boy with the pipes that were playing 'Over the Sea to Skye' in perfect waltz time. I watched Lady Lydia's blue satin, Mrs Mackay's golden-yellow silk and my mother's black velvet with the cream lace swirl past in a happy dream of sheer astonishment. I had never known before that my father and my mother could dance. What things you discovered when you were Big Enough to Go Out!

Since that time I have seen many performances of one kind and another, but I have never seen anything more satisfying to the heart than those three couples revolving round the small boy with the pipes while all around them the happy people sang the song and swayed to and fro in time to the music.

When it was over, Sir Torquil came back to the corner and said: 'Well, supper now, I think,' but the minister came up and whispered something to him and eventually he nodded and said: 'Oh, all right, all right!' He then announced: 'Our friends, the Misses Boyd, who are now among us, will now entertain us with a song.'

Fluttering and giggling, the six Miss Boyds rushed into the middle of the floor, separated, giggled, coalesced into a covey again, giggled some more, rushed over to whisper to Danny and the other musicians, rushed back, separated again and at last faced each other in two rows of three. By this time an uneasy titter was running round the big barn, George was rubbing the back of his neck with his left hand, and my mother's long nervous fingers had taken a grip on the back of my white blouse that was almost stopping my breathing.

The Miss Boyds, accompanied by the fiddles and melodeons, got started. Their choice was a ballad, called, I think, 'Huntingtower', which was usually sung as a duet between a man and a woman, but in this case three Miss Boyds were the man and three the woman.

When ye gang awa', Jamie,
Far across the sea-ee, laddie!
When ye gang tae Germanee,
What will ye bring tae me-ee, laddie?

carolled the female section, not quite in tune and not quite together.

I'll bring ye a braw new goon, Jeanie ...

the male section promised in an off-key contralto.

It was agonising in every way. Six Miss Boyds, all over-dressed and badly dressed; six pairs of steel-rimmed spectacles flashing in the slanting last light; three Miss Boyds simperingly coy and another three dashingly swashbuckling. My mother's hand took a strangle grip on the bunched-up back of my blouse; Mrs de Cambre's knuckles pulled her gloves to splitting point as her hands gripped the stem of her ostrich feather fan; Lady Lydia and my grandmother, side by side like twin queens enthroned, stared straight ahead and kept at bay, by sheer personal force, the rising tide of tittering and giggling from the young farm-hands and the pink-cheeked servant girls.

At long last it was over. There was an immediate burst of applause from Sir Torquil, the dominie, the doctor, and the men of my family, which was quickly taken up by the rest of us, and then Sir Torquil announced supper.

Alasdair and I went away to join some of our school compan-ions, and ate an enormous supper of roast beef, raisin dumpling and apples, but just as we were starting on our fourth apple my grandmother's voice, from the table where she was sitting, said: 'Janet, Alasdair, come here.' We looked at each other. 'You heard me,' said the voice. It was not loud at all. I had wondered if I had imagined it, but Alasdair, from his face, had heard it too.

'Yes, Granny?' I said.

'Just sit there, the two of you. That's all.' She indicated two chairs in a corner beside her and turned away to her table com-panion again, so that we could do nothing but sit down. There were no more apples or anything within reach. Mrs de Cambre looked at us, gave us her one-eyed wink and said to Sir Torquil: 'They tell me that Miz Sandison is a wi-itch. Is that true?'

'Quite true,' said Sir Torquil solemnly. 'Like your fortune told, Maddy Lou?'

'Ah surely wou-ould!'

'Tell her fortune by the yaavins, Mrs Reachfar?'

'Surely,' said my grandmother with her queer, secret eye-smile.

'What's that, for goodness' sakes?'

Sir Torquil reached up to one of the barley sheaves on the wall and pulled off an ear with all the yaavins or whiskers on it. 'You do like this,' he said, and rubbed the ear between his two cupped hands until they were full of grains and broken yaavins when he held them out. 'Then let the grains run off like this.' He tipped his hands forward and the grains fell to the floor, but some of the broken yaavins clung to the skin of his hands. 'Then hold your hands out to the spae-wife.'

'Spae-wife?'

'Fortune-teller. In this case, Mrs Reachfar.'

'Let the leddy choose her own ear o' barley,' my grand-mother said, and Mrs de Cambre went to a sheaf and chose an ear. 'Now, be careful not to get yaavins on your dress. They'll stick for ever and you'll be finding yourself with one itching you next time you wear it. All right—rub it out.'

Mrs de Cambre rubbed carefully with her pretty small hands, after taking off altogether the long gloves that had been dangling from her wrists, let the grains run to the floor and then held out the two hands across the table.

'The hands of a leddy,' said my grandmother, putting her own strong but shapely hands under the small fingers. 'There is nothing sudden or startling in any way in your fortune, madam, but a bonnie, happy fortune for all that. A *woman's* fortune. Your life will be a long and a very happy one. You have a son, madam?'

'Yes, Miz Sandison.'

'And a big boy, and you so young.'

'He is eighteen, Miz Sandison.'

'Well, I have told you you will have a long and happy life with all your own people around you. And there is a big happiness connected with a son of yours—it is the one boy you have?'

'Yes.'

'It is through him that the happiness will come. I cannot tell you what it is, but something that you and your husband have wished for. It takes the form here of a three within a three —will you mind on that?'

'A three within a three, Miz Sandison?'

'Aye. That's right.'

'Ah'll remember.' She looked down at the broken yaavins on her hands. 'A three within a three.'

'Aye, madam,' said my father's voice, 'is the ould spae-wife at her capers?'

'Please tell mine, Mrs Sandison,' someone else was saying.

'Surely. Pick out your own ear o' barley, lassie.'

The rest of us went out to the threshing barn again for the rest of the concert, but my grandmother stayed in a corner of the straw barn telling fortunes. Truly, people brought the strangest gifts to the Harvest Home.

All too soon Tom and George—the latter dressed in a skirt, blouse and bonnet of my grandmother's—had danced their reel, I had danced my Highland Fling to my father's pipes and it was time for my mother and me to go home, but I was tired too, never having been out of bed so late, and my mother said that I would not enjoy the crowded grown-up dancing.

'Before you go, Elizabeth,' Sir Torquil said to my mother, 'come and see the stackyard—there is a fine moon.'

Lady Lydia and a lot of the others came out to see the stackyard too. We went to the end of the Square, along the gable of the barn, where, facing us, were the nine front stacks. These would be the last of the big stackyard to be threshed, and they were all securely thatched against the winter, but woven into the thatch of each stack in dark-green broom, which showed black in the moonlight, was a letter, so that the front row of stacks spelled 'Poyntdale'.

'My, but that's pretty!' said the voice of Mrs de Cambre. 'I nevah saw a thi-ing like that befoah!'

'And you probably won't again, Maddy Lou, anywhere in your travels. Stacks like that are a dying art.'

'Who did it?' some man's voice asked.

'Duncan Reachfar, the grieve. He and his brother and Tom, their man, are the only men left about here that I know who can do it now. Old Reachfar taught them. But the very art of good stacking is dying out. That's only the finishing touch to a high-class job, but it's bonnie.'

I thought that Sir Torquil's voice was unduly sad when he said that only the men of my family, in our district, could thatch and mark his stacks like that, for what was he worrying about? Even if my father got sick (a thing I had never known to happen) at harvest-time, Tom or George would come down and thatch his stacks for him, for it was impossible that they could all be sick at once. 'Dying out,' he had said. Dying. Did he mean that when my father, George and Tom died there would be nobody left who could—? But that was not possible! These men were *not* mortal! They had always been there, they were never sick, people like a person's father and a person's friends did not die! Only old, old people died—people like old Granny Macintosh, maybe. ... But everybody was getting older all the time. Even I was Big Enough now to come to the Harvest Home! And if I was a year older, my father was a year older, *everybody* was a year older than last year—a year more like old Granny Macintosh. ...

Suddenly, from the dark shadows among the stacks, came the voice of my father, in no way weak and enfeebled with age but raised in anger and yet hoarse with fury: 'In God's name! Are ye *mad,* smoking in there? And them danged cigarettes at that! Come out o' that, ye senseless booggers!'

'Great God!' bawled Sir Torquil and sprang over the gate. 'Where are they, Duncan? Who is it?'

'I think, Elizabeth,' said Lady Lydia, 'we had better go.'

But before we could move, my father, very silent now, was opening the gate in the stackyard wall and ushering through it three sailors and the three youngest Miss Boyds.

'It's all right,' my father was saying. 'Just mind, though, lads, that a stackyard can go up as fast as your ship's powder magazine.'

The Miss Boyds, giggling, ran along in the shadow of the barn wall, followed by the sheepish-looking sailors, while my mother's nervous grip on my hand was squeezing my fingers in a vice, before she expelled a long breath and said: 'Janet, we must get home and let Auntie Kate come down to the dance. Say goodnight to everyone.'

I made my curtsy and thanked Lady Lydia and Sir Torquil. For me the Harvest Home was over.

For George, Tom and me, however, a thing that we had enjoyed was never really over and we talked about the Harvest Home for days, until my grandmother said she was 'fair deaved' with us, although she would still laugh, almost against her will, at the recapitulation of one or another incident by Tom or George.

The day after the Harvest Home, which was a Saturday, Tom and George, not having been to bed at all but having just arrived home in time for breakfast, decided that it would be a fine day to thatch the Reachfar stacks while my grandfather was 'sleeping himself clear o' the night before and would not be bothering them'. Being further up the hill, and on less fertile land than Poyntdale, the Reachfar harvest was always a week or two later. Tom and George were in fine form, with 'skirts' of sacking tied round them to protect the knees of their trousers from the sharp ends of the sheaves on the stack sides, reliving the events of the night before while they worked and Fly and I helped them. At one point, while Tom was up the ladder, George nudged me to keep quiet, cut off a short piece of hairy rope and applied a match to the end of it, holding it between his fingers like a cigarette.

'What was your father saying last night?' he whispered.

Seeing what was required, I started to shout: 'In God's name! Are ye *mad*, smoking in there? And them danged—'

I could go no further. George, in his sacking skirt, went cackling and giggling and running through between the stacks in classic imitation of the Miss Boyds, while Tom clung, helpless with laughter, to the slope of his stack at the top of his ladder. Having started on the Miss Boyds, there was no stopping them, and Tom descended from the ladder to take the female part in a rendering of 'Huntingtower' and was unbelievably coy in his sacking skirt.

'Man, George, yon was terrible,' he said soberly when they had finished.

'It was something like Miss Iris at the old quarry, but not so bad,' I put in.

'Well, it was bad enough,' George said. 'It was like as if you and me had set ourselves up to sing the Psalm like John-the-Smith, Tom. It is an awful thing when folk has no idea what's expected o' them.'

'How does folk know, George?' I asked.

'Ach, if a person has any sense they can see for theirselves what they should do and what they leave alone. You wouldna be dancing your Sword Dance if Sir Torquil wasna asking your father. And Tom and me wouldna be at that capers o' the reel if folk wasna *at* us to be doing it. It is chust common *sense.*'

'Av coorse,' said Tom, 'anybody that's kind o' *good* at a thing gets asked to do it—like wee Alasdair with his pipes. He is a grand piper for a wee fellow. But when Sir Torquil has all that fancy visitors there, he's not needing people to be making fools of theirselves, except the like o' George and me. People knows we canna dance or sing good, and they know we are being foolish at it on purpose. There's a-all the difference in the world between being foolish on purpose and being foolish because you are too foolish to *know* you are being foolish, like.'

'Would you two be going to thatch the rest o' the stacks the-year or chust leave them till next back-end?' my grandmother enquired with heavy sarcasm from the top of the garden.

'Aye, aye, Mistress,' said Tom. 'We was chust sorting a puckle straw.'

'I never heard o' men that sorted straw with their tongues before,' she said and went back into the house, carrying the big cabbage for the dinner.

'I hope she'll be boiling a bittie suet with the cabbage the-day,' George said. 'A bittie suet with it makes a-all the difference. What more is for the dinner, Janet?'

'That hen the red cow kicked and broke its leg.'

'That dirty ould Leghorn brute? That hen's near as ould as maself!—Och, well, Tom, we might as well tie another rope or two.'

Having got on to the subject of food, we ate again in memory the supper of the night before, which started Tom and George off again.

'Have a little more of the dumpling, Miss Boyd,' said Tom.

'Oh, well—well, chust a sensation!' said George coyly. 'Gawd be here! Who ever heard o' a sensation o' dumpling?'

* * * * *

With all the talk about the Harvest Home, I quite forgot that we were into October now and that there was no mention of the coal boat, and I do not know how long I would have forgotten about it if my father had not come home and announced one evening that Sir Torquil was not certain that the coal boat would come at all this year.

'Tom,' he said then, 'you'll have to take a walk through the moor and mark a good puckle trees for cutting.'

'Ach!' said Tom disgustedly. 'Hack, hack, hacking away at the trees! The Home Moor is the only bit of high shelter in three parishes an' with all your hacking away you'll have it fair useless.'

'It's not my will to cut the trees, Tom, man! But if the coal boat canna come, it's not chust ourselves—there's all Achcraggan looking for fire for the winter!'

'Achcraggan?' Tom was outraged. 'Where in the world have

126

we got trees for the whole place?'

'We are not being asked to serve the whole place, Tom,' said my quiet grandfather. 'Sir Torquil and Mr Macintosh and Captain Robertson will do their best, like always, but Reachfar has a little wood too. You will mark the trees, Tom.'

'The railway?' Tom asked. 'Surely the railway can be bringing in a puckle coal?'

'You know the railway can hardly carry the sailors coming north, far less coal, Tom,' said George. 'I'll stop home on Saturday and mark the trees with you. There's no need to take young ones or straight ones. The wood will be better clear o' them old twisted ones.'

'We-ell, maybe,' said Tom. Tom loved trees, young, old, twisted or straight, and still loves them. 'Dang this war!'

'Aye, dang it, right enough!' said my grandfather, although nobody was allowed to say 'Dang' in the house and it was a word he seldom used anyhow, and I was not allowed to use it at all.

'Yes, indeed. *Dang* it!' I said.

'Janet!' said my mother. 'That is enough.'

The great thing about the discipline at Reachfar was that, no matter what the crisis, as far as I was concerned my family never let up on it for a moment.

It was a queer feeling to know for the first time in your life that you could not be certain of having the coal boat to look forward to. It left the year looking very naked of things for looking forward to. There would be the 'tattie holidays' in October as usual, which the village children liked but which I hated. It was all very well for them, but I would have preferred to be at school. If they handled as many potatoes as I did in the course of a year, what with hens' pots and pigs' pots and people's pots, *they* would not be so anxious to gather them in a field either, even if they did get pennies for doing it. It was the 'tattie holidays', I think, which were originally responsible for my still-firmly-held belief that *some* money is not worth its weight in potatoes.

So, the next Saturday, which had to be cold and showery, just for spite, George, Tom and I spent a long dreary morning on the moor, 'marking trees'. Usually, if George, Tom and I went to the moor—to count sheep or cut a few old dead trees for the Reachfar fires, or plant a young tree or two, or mend a fence or a dyke or anything—we had a riotously happy time, out of hearing of my grandmother, with George and Tom clowning about and telling yarns about old Sandy Bawn who had gone to America in the long ago, had come back and told fearful stories of the size of the trees there.

'And he would tell them as solemn as if it was the God's truth he was telling you, man!' Tom would say.

'Aye, yon one about the redwood tree—was that the name of it? That he said was as big around as the steeple o' Achcraggan Church!' George would add. 'What a danged liar the man was, Tom, when you think on it.'

'Och, something terrible, man. And him swearing on his Bible oath it was the truth. Av coorse, there was always a soft bittie in Sandy Bawn, George—he was for ever thinking he was far cleverer than others, and a man has to be gey soft to be thinking like that.'

This day, though, as we plodded through the wet heather, there were no stories and no clowning, and we did not mark many trees, either, from the can of red paint we had with us. After all, there were three of us, all capable of thinking up excuses as to why this tree and that one should *not* be marked.

In the afternoon, when we came out after dinner to have a go at the west end of the moor, we were holding a debate about the very first tree when the dogs put up a fine young hare from his lie under some juniper bushes, and, one way and another, in the excitement of heading the hare off and eventually catching it I fell over the can of paint and it all sank into the wet moss of the moor, so then George gave the can a kick with his big boot which stove in its bottom, and Tom said: 'To hell with the danged pent whateffer! If Sir Torquil wants *us* to mark trees for his sawyers, he'll chust have to be giving us another puckle pent.' He gathered all four feet of the hare together and tied them with a string from his pocket. 'Janet, you'll have to be taking this brute down to Leddy Lydia—she'll eat them everlasting. Chugged hare, the cook calls it, although why people will be putting a hare in a chug is something I've never understood right.'

'What will we tell Granda about the paint?' I asked, for, after all, I was the one who had spilled it.

'Ach, we'll chust not be mentioning it at a-all,' said George.

'A-also, forbye and besides,' said Tom, 'what a person doesna know canna hurt them.'

After that we spent a pleasant, wet afternoon on the moor and caught another hare and three rabbits, but as we neared the house in the dullness of the evening my conscience began to rear its ugly head on several distinct counts. We had marked no trees, we had spilled the paint, destroyed the can and we had, in general, been guilty of the sin of wasted time. I slipped round to the rear of George and Tom, being wise to their caper of wheeling smartly into the barn and leaving me to take the first shock of my grandmother's attack, but today, by a special providence, this manoeuvre was unnecessary, for the Poyntdale trap was standing in the yard and the pony was in the loosebox. My two companions in crime stopped dead at the moor gate.

'Will Sir Torquil be here, think ye?' said Tom.

'I wouldna be sure.' George looked over his shoulder at the serried ranks of fir trees with no red paint on them. 'Janet, just run down to the house like a clever lass—'

'I will *not,* George Sandison! Besides, it's the governess cart that's in it and Sir Torquil says he wouldn't trust his backside in that bloody washtub for all the whisky on Speyside.'

'Janet Sandison! What kind of words is that to be using?'

'It was Sir Torquil that used them.'

'When?'

'Down at Poyntdale one day.'

'It's hard,' said Tom, 'for a man to believe the ears that bairns have and the memories that's in them. Well, we better be going down to our tea.'

'You have no business,' said my uncle virtuously, 'to be imitating Sir Torquil's way o' speaking.'

'And you've got no business kicking his paint can!'

'Hold your tongue, you blethering little limmer!' said George.

We took off our wet coats and boots in the passage and put on our slippers, and when we went into the kitchen Lady Lydia and Mrs de Cambre were just finishing tea with my grandmother, my grandfather, my mother and my aunt. My father was not yet home from Poyntdale.

'There you are!' said Lady Lydia, rising. 'We really came to see Janet for a moment and we want to get home before dark.'

'How do you do-do, Janet! Ah brought you-ou a li'l somethin'.' And she put a big cardboard box into my arms. 'Open it!'

'Thank you,' I said and laid the box on Lady Lydia's chair.

Now, you may not believe this, and I had never seen such a thing in my life before, but when I opened that box there was a *baby* inside it—a baby, sound asleep, in a long white gown, a white woollen jacket and a white woollen bonnet.

'It's yours, Janet,' said Lady Lydia when I drew back from it in admiration. 'Pick it up.'

I could not believe it. Babies came like calves, and mothers who got them *never* gave them to other people, never, never, and the cows cried for days when you took their calves away.

'No,' I said.

'But it *is* yours.'

'From Mrs de Cambre,' said my mother.

It must be all right. If my mother said that Maddy Lou was giving this baby of hers away to me, then I could have it. I picked it up carefully, with a hand behind its woolly bonnet, for you always had to be careful of the heads of young things like calves or babies, and then I put my face against its cheek. It was cold. Its face was ice cold. It was DEAD.

'It's dead!' I shouted. 'It's a *dead* baby!' and the dresser tilted sideways before my giddy eyes, the bones of my arms melted with terror and the dead baby fell to the floor. ...

The lifesize doll's head struck the steel fender and broke into a thousand pink-and-white splinters of china, while the eye mechanism rolled into the ashpan.

I do not remember any more of what happened that evening, but Lady Lydia and Mrs de Cambre came to see us all the next day. My mother had explained to me in the morning about little girls sometimes having imitation babies that they called dolls to play with, and how Mrs de Cambre had been kind enough to think that I might like one, and she showed me the little clothes and the little bootees that the doll had worn. But I knew it was not a doll. I had seen dolls in the village, and they were made of cloth, stuffed with sawdust. I felt haunted.

'Where is it?' I asked, shuddering.

'Dad buried it.'

'That's right,' I said.

'Mrs de Cambre says that you can have another doll now that you understand. Would you like that?'

'No, Mother.'

'Then, when she comes to see us today, just tell her No, thank you, and ask for something else instead. She wants to give you a present and it is very, very kind of her.'

'All right, Mother.'

When Lady Lydia and Mrs de Cambre arrived I felt shamed and dreadful and guilty at first for not wanting the doll that they thought I ought to like, but Mrs de Cambre was so smiling and kind that I soon felt better and she said: 'It's only silly kids that play dolls anyways. When Ah go to Invahne-ess nex' week, yuh kno-ow what Ah'm gonna do?'

'What, please?'

'Ah'm gonna buy the bigges' book for readin' an' the bigges' book for writin' that they got in that town. Would you-ou like that?'

'Yes, please.'

I felt fine now. Who would not prefer real reading and writing books to an imitation, unreal baby? The next week I received a complete set of the works of Louisa M Alcott and two big books full of white paper, and along one side of each page was a row of holes so that you could tear the sheet out neatly and send it to someone if you wanted to. In the parcel there was also a pencil with a little hat to protect its point, a big rubber, a bottle of ink and a queer black pen which, after my father had read the paper in its box, could be filled with ink and write for weeks without having to dip it.

'That,' said Tom, 'is a most wonderful invention. Fountain-pen, is it, they call it? A very remarkable contrivance, that's what it is.'

I had to write a proper letter of thanks for this magnificent present, which I did on the first tear-out sheet of my first new book, beginning 'Dear Mrs de Cambre' and ending 'Yours sincerely, Janet E Sandison', but my mother allowed me to add at the very bottom: 'PS Bonnie Maddy Lou Lou, I thank you-you.' And the other thing that I remember about all this is that with 'pennies' earned by myself—and the first I had ever spent—I was allowed to buy a King's picture, called a stamp, at the Post Office, put it on the letter, carefully watched by Tom to see that 'His Machesty was sitting square with his head the right way up', and post it in the red slot in the wall.

The dismal 'tattie holidays' came along, and the school-children spread over the farms for a fortnight to help gather the crop, but we did not have extra children at Reachfar, for my grandfather, Tom, my aunt and I could manage by ourselves, and we had some of my aunt's admirers, in the form of four sergeants from the Army Depot, to give us a hand, which, of course, resulted in my grandmother's decree that 'with all that men in the field, you'll have to send Kate into the house to help with the cooking'. It was enough to drive a person out of her head, this sort of thing, I thought, as I hurled potatoes into the wire basket. My grandmother would end up by making an old maid out of my aunt, the way she would hardly ever let her even speak to any nice young men.

Towards the end of the potato-lifting, which all of us at

Reachfar were agreed was the worst crop of the year and the only one we actively disliked, we were all cheered, far and wide, by the news that the coal boat was coming after all. She was late, but she was coming, and all we had to hope now was that there would not be a gale at the time of her visit. We school-children were cock-a-hoop, because we had already had the 'tat-tie holidays' and there would be another clear break for the coal boat.

The day of her arrival dawned frosty and clear, with a light breeze and no more coming north-easterly from the sea, but cold enough to make you prefer walking to riding behind the horses in their spotless carts. We set off with the Reachfar string before it was light, and Dick was inclined to caper on the way down to Poyntdale. He danced on the stony road until the sparks flew from his shoes, arched his neck and tossed his head in the dawn breeze and would hardly wait for us to open the field gates. I was coming second, holding Betsy's bridle, and at the bottom of the Long Field Tom pulled Dick aside and said: 'Go you first with Betsy, Janet, and I'll put this ould boogger's head in her cart and see will he behave himself.'

My grandfather, coming behind with Dulcie, agreed, and I took Betsy round into the lead. Betsy, if anything, was worse than Dick had been now that she had the open road in front of her. She danced, she side-stepped, she threw her head up into the wind with me swinging on the bridle rein, and at the march dyke between Reachfar and Poyntdale my grandfather called a halt.

'What the devil's in them the-day, Tom? The wee mare back here is at it too. ... Is there weather in it?'

They both looked away across the Firth, then west to the Ben, then back to the horses.

'I'm not smelling weather, Reachfar. Are you?'

'No-o. But I don't like this capers for the County Road. Neither you nor me is fit to hold that brute Dick, Tom, if he takes badness in his head.'

I could see the whole great day in jeopardy. 'Wait a minute!' I said, and climbed out on the tram of the cart and on to Betsy's shoulders before they could protest. 'Let's try now—up, Betsy!'

She walked sedately now, with no side-stepping or dancing, but she was still tossing her head and sniffing the breeze, and I could feel that she was restrained from dancing only by the long training of 'going canny when the bairn was up'. Every muscle, every drop of blood, every hair of her hide was pulsing with the desire to run wild.

'I'll speak to Duncan at Poyntdale,' said my grandfather. 'Maybe he can lend us a man.'

The last part of the road down into the Poyntdale Farm Square was very steep and the horses behaved more quietly as they picked their way down, but perked up again on the smooth Poyntdale road, and as we rounded the corner by the cattle courts into the Square, and Dick saw the Poyntdale string of horses lined up, he decided to show these soft plainsmen what the hill folk were made of. He pulled out sharply from behind Betsy and me and went off at full gallop across the cobbles of the Square, the sparks flying from his shoes, his harness glittering in the morning sun, Tom standing in the cart, his feet braced and all his considerable weight pulling back on the reins. Dick was not bolting, he was simply having fun, and when he reached the other end of the Square he stopped, blew out a cloud of steam and looked back along his side at Tom.

'Ye bliddy ould limb o' Satan!' Tom bawled, and lashed the rein ends down on his shiny rump.

Dick merely shook his head as if a fly had brushed him, poised one forefoot on the point of its shoe like a ballet dancer and stared at the Poyntdale string in an insolent way. The Poyntdale horses, spirited people all, did not care for this at all, and began a little nonsense of their own so that the men at their heads had difficulty in holding them. My father, a calm-tempered man as a rule, was looking unusually flustered, and when my grandfather asked if he had a horseman to spare he barked: 'Coming in here with that capering brute! As if *this* bliddy lot wasna bother enough the-day!'

'It must be the weather,' Sir Torquil said. 'What was the Ben like from the hill, Reachfar?'

'I wouldna say there was weather in it—' my grandfather began, and, at that moment, round the corner came the Dinchory string with my uncle at the head of the first horse, a big black with white feet, whose nostrils were wide and whose big eyes rolled over the Poyntdale string with a glare of insolent disdain.

'God be here!' said my harassed father. 'Look at that brute Jet!'

He sprang into Dick's cart. 'Tom, get in with Janet and give Dick to me—I'll go first.' He was driving out of the Square before he had finished speaking.

'Reachfar and I will go next,' said Sir Torquil, jumping into Dulcie's cart. 'You come in line next, Janet.'

The other carts fell in, and from Betsy's shoulders I could see, back along the line, my powerful uncle having a fine old tussle with big Jet from Dinchory, while my equally powerful father out in front had all he could do to hold the cavorting Dick. But everyone was at least reasonably safe now, for Jet and Dick, the ringleaders, were in control, my grandfather had Sir Torquil, one of the best horsemen in the county, to help him, and Tom had me, with my blackmailing long relationship with Betsy. Still, it must have been a nerve-racking drive for my father and George, knowing all the horses in the strings as they did, and knowing also the weaknesses among their men, most of whom were a little too old or a little too young—the best-aged men being at the war—to hold a horse that had the devil in him. Every animal was a highly-trained, intelligent individual, but as we made our way along by the Firth, where the ships were lying in the deep channel, their hulls pale grey in the morning sun, there was a queer feeling of uneasiness in the air. Dick was still capering out in front, I could feel the strange excitement emanating from Betsy into my legs and buttocks, and, as Dulcie was behaving better than most, Sir Torquil spent his time in the main on foot, going up and down the long string.

'We won't take them on the pier, Duncan,' he called up to my father out in front.

'Not this devil, anyway, for a while,' my father called back, not moving his eyes from Dick's tossing head.

'What's in them, Tom?' he asked next as we passed him.

'God knows, Sir Torquil.—Ach, it's that big devil of ours. He chust upset the whole lot with his capers.'

The boat was there, just drawing in to the pier as we came round the bay into Achcraggan. The tide was still filling and we should have a good day, I thought, and have all the clean cargo off before dinner-time, if only the horses would settle down and behave themselves. I was very fond of Betsy, but I could think of many more amusing things to do at the coal boat than sit on her shoulders in the biting wind that was striking my bare knees like a whiplash and blowing the short, pleated, tweed skirt up round my face, exposing my matching tweed knickers to all and sundry, who would not know that I had clean white ones on underneath.

Everybody, as usual, was at the coal boat, including the policeman from 'west the country', the outpost of whose district was Achcraggan, and who came there about once a month on his bicycle. He always chose an occasion when there might be a drink going to pay his visit, for which he could not be blamed, when you consider that Achcraggan pier was about fifteen miles from his village station.

'Morning, Campbell,' Sir Torquil said to him.

'Good morning, sir.'

'I'm glad you're here. I don't want any women or children on the pier this morning—the horses are a little fresh.'

Betsy, Tom and I were already on the pier, for my father had taken Dick into the field beside the Plough and was galloping him round and round, cart and all, while my grandfather had stopped at the pierhead for a moment to talk to Captain Robertson.

'What apout that craitur, sir?' the policeman asked, pointing at me.

'Janet Reachfar? Don't be a fool, Campbell! She's in charge of a horse. Children *playing*, I mean.'

Poop to Sir Torquil, and Constable Campbell, too, I thought, for now I did not dare to climb down from my perch on Betsy's back.

'And wha-at, sir,' said the policeman, 'apout the leddies what iss on the poat?'

'Ladies on the boat? What the devil d'ye mean, Campbell?'

'I haf to report, sir, that there iss quite a fair puckle leddies on poard the poat,' said Campbell officially.

'Great God!' Sir Torquil looked wildly round him and saw the captain climb over the rail and jump on to the pier. 'Ah, there you are, Captain Greig! Very pleased to see you here again. … But, what's this I hear about you having women on board?'

'Hoo ur ye, Surr Torkull, surr?' said Captain Greig from Glasgow. 'Weemen? Weel, Ah've seen wecmen an' weemen in ma time. Ah'm a sea-gaun man.' He took his pipe out of his mouth and spat sadly into the lapping water. 'If they yins ye see forrit therr is weemen, maybe Ah'm a mermaid masel'. Aye.' He spat again. 'Therr's fower o' them.'

'Four?' said Sir Torquil and looked at the boat. 'Holy suffering cats!'

Up in the bows of the boat were four Miss Boyds, giggling and cackling and nudging each other while two of the deck hands worked self-consciously with a rope.

'Cats is richt,' said Captain Greig, looking into the dark and noisome bowl of his pipe. 'An' gey skinny auld tabbies at that. Ah'm awa' up tae the Ploo'.'

'No, you don't!' said Sir Torquil. 'Get these—er—ladies off that boat! And you, Campbell——'

'Yessir!'

'*You* get them off the pier!' and with a step that said 'I am not the local magnate to do my own dirty work' Sir Torquil slipped under Betsy's nose and was lost in grave discourse with Tom, with the horse and cart between him and the route that the evicted Miss Boyds would have to take.

How the Miss Boyds had got *on* to the boat I do not know —there was no gangway, as the cargo was swung over the side and the crew simply straddled the rail and then jumped—but a large number of men were involved in getting them off. They screamed and cackled and shrieked and giggled, while Betsy fidgeted, and Tom cursed under his breath, and Sir Torquil, cursing quite audibly, went to the head of the next horse behind us.

'I can't! I can't! I'm going to fall in!' shrieked the fourth Miss Boyd, with a leg on each side of the top rail and a foot on the second and a foot on the third, and clinging to the hand of Dominie Stevenson on the pier. At that moment there came the proverbial seventh wave of the incoming tide which is said to be more powerful than the preceding six, the boat swayed on its swell, the water lapped the pier and—Dominie Stevenson was a very wicked, mischievous, old man. The fourth Miss Boyd did indeed fall in, remarkably clear (when I think of it now) of both boat and pier, and was gallantly fished out, dripping, cold and covered with seaweed, by Dominie Stevenson, the doctor and Bella Beagle's young cousin. After that all four Miss Boyds went home, while the three rescuers betook themselves to the Plough to 'warm' themselves after their gallant act.

The day was now made. Something *always* happened when the coal boat came in and we had got away to a good start and, too, the horses were now a little less lively, for Dick had had a 'lesson' in the field beside the Plough while Jet, from my uncle, had been having an equivalent lesson up and down the sand of the shore. The other horses, now that the ringleaders were slightly subdued, decided to behave themselves, but every string that came in, the man in charge of it said that he had had unusual trouble with his horses that morning. At about nine o'clock, Tom remarked to me that it was funny that Johnnie Greycairn and Diamond had not got down yet, for by this time he and I had delivered a two-cart haul to Mrs Gilchrist's Drapery Warehouse, and were back at the pier, but even as he spoke, across the crescent of the bay, on the road on the far side, was seen a remarkable sight. Johnnie Greycairn, like some devil-inspired Ben Hur, bolt upright in his little cart, with a long fir branch in his hand, was lashing old hairy Diamond along the road like a man demented. Even the sailors on the boat stood at gaze when Johnnie allowed the foam-flecked Diamond to stop at the pierhead.

'For God's sake, Johnnie!' said my father. '*What* have you been doing to your horsie?'

'Horsie, you say!' squealed Johnnie, waving his fir branch like a claymore. 'It iss a stallion he thinks he iss! It's defy me that the boogger would do the-day—dancing and capering and running and chumping as if the very devil himself wass in him! And so it's *learned* him that I did, with this bittie stick. He'll maybe *think* a little before he'll be trying to chump a gate again and him yoked to the cartie and a-all!'

Poor Diamond, panting and flecked with foam, looked as if he would never 'think' again, and Achcraggan heaved a regretful sigh, for, obviously, he was not going to liven the proceedings by diving off the pier today.

Sitting on Betsy's shoulders, her reins in my left hand, my right hand holding the stick of toffee that Mrs Gilchrist had given me, while Tom and the men loaded the carts, I was in a fine point of vantage for seeing what was going on. The sun was fully up now, it was warmer and the hoarfrost was melting and running in streaks down the slate roof of the Plough. The Miss Boyds, Miss Violet none the worse for her early dip in the sea, were back and sitting like a row of birds on the low wall, opposite the inn, between the road and the sea, but they were less conspicuous now, for a number of the village and fisher women were about too, down to have a look at the boat. The policeman had relaxed his discipline, and some of the older boys were around the pier, now that the horses had quietened a little. It was probably the first frost of the year that had got into them all, Tom said, and he was probably right. I licked at my toffee, pressed my knees into Betsy's comfortable hide and looked out over the Firth, thinking.

The Reachfar horses were always fresh and inclined to caper, for, as my father said, they did not have enough to do. It was because they were not crofters' horses, like Johnnie's little hairy Diamond, but big, heavy Clydesdales, as well bred as the Poyntdale and Dinchory horses. This was because, all his life, my grandfather had been accustomed to the well-bred animals of Poyntdale, and would have had 'no pleasure' in handling 'a puckle hairy Shelties' about his own little place. It had taken a lot of care with the Reachfar 'pennies' to get into the good class of horses and cattle, but now that we *were* in, it was paying us well at the markets. The 'unctioneers' were always 'very civil' now about Reachfar stock, as civil as if we were a big place like Poyntdale.

Up at the pierhead, Dick, even now, was still blowing off steam, tossing his head and stamping his big, hairy feet, although he had hauled several heavy loads into the village, and, behind me, while they were loading him again, I could hear my father telling the boys to keep well clear of him and threatening to take him down to Poyntdale, one of these days, and 'sweat the hide off him' at the turnips. Poor Dick! When he was taken down to Poyntdale to do a heavy week's work, he was always so glad to get back home that he used his remaining energy to jump every gate in the place and annoyed everybody all over again. Dick, I thought, was a little like myself—he could get into Bother no matter how hard he tried to keep out of it.

It must be getting on for dinner-time, I thought, as I licked at my toffee. What a lot of ships there were in the Firth today too. There was a big cruiser away far up at the big pier near the naval base, and a line of big dreadnoughts down the deep-water channel, and all around them were destroyers and smaller craft, while just a short way west of Achcraggan I could see three of the submarines that could sail under the water like herrings. It was hard to believe that, but my father said that they could, so it must be true. And two aeroplanes came flying over, right across above Reachfar. Now *that* was a thing that Dick did not like when he was ploughing or anything. If an aeroplane came over, Dick would forget what a careful, skilled worker he was and begin to dance and trample his big feet over tatties, turnips or anything. Poor Dick, he just could *not* keep out of Both—

Suddenly, round the Point, east by the Fisher Town, a destroyer came dashing into the narrows of the Firth, and as she came past the village she began to blow a deep-pitched, booming horn. I had time to see her big, white bow-wave, her string of bunting from stem to stern, and the froth of her long wake, and then my toffee was in my pocket, both my hands on the reins that went past my sides and my knees holding on to Betsy's neck for dear life.

'Hang on! Hang *on*, pettie!' Tom yelled as Betsy went up on her hind legs and he ran to her head. 'Hang *on*, bairnie, for *Christ's* sake!'

It was not difficult to hang on. Betsy's big saddle was behind me, and the loaded cart was behind Betsy, and I had strong legs and strong arms. Tom got her down, but there was another outburst of noise and up she went again.

'I'm fine, Tom!' I yelled, catching the excitement as I went up in the air for the second time and saw all the 'eyes' of the

143

ships winking at one another which made me think in a flash of Maddy Lou's one-eyed wink. Down Betsy came with a clatter on the stone of the pier, and 'Hang on!' came Tom's voice as up we went again. The noise was something infernal. All the ships were now blowing sirens, whistles, horns and ringing bells, and the sound was going out to the surrounding hills to reverberate back redoubled, and the pier, the road at the pierhead and the yard of the Plough were full of plunging horses and shouting, struggling men.

I do not know how long it all lasted, or how many times I went up and came down with Betsy, but I suddenly realised that we were at the pierhead, with Tom on one side of her head and Sir Torquil at the other, and that as Sir Torquil lifted me down My Friend Alasdair dashed past, waving a big yellow lion rampant flag and yelling: 'The war's over! The war's over!'

'You all right, Janet?' Sir Torquil asked.

I gave my bottom a rub, I had got quite a bump when I went back against the saddle the first time up. 'Yes, thank you,' I said, and reached for my toffee.

A few yards away, my father, the doctor and Dominie Stevenson were standing round Dick's head, and a further few yards away my uncle and two other men were round big Dinchory Jet.

'Gawd be here, Janet!' called my 'clown' of an uncle. 'It's myself that thought the end o' the world was in it! You all right?'

'I'm fine, George!' I called back, and he did his big laugh.

Gradually the last echo of noise died away up the Glen to the west at the foot of the Ben, and there was a strange silence, broken only by the now calming breathing of the horses. Then there was the clop-clopping of hooves and the Reverend

Roderick came round the corner from the village in his trap.

'You heard the news?' he asked into the silence. Nobody spoke. He took off his black hat and his noble head and bearded face took on majesty as he looked up at the bright sky. All the men took their hats and caps off and I put my toffee back in my pocket.

'Thank God!' said the Reverend Roderick, and after a moment he looked out over the sunlit water. 'My,' he said, 'but it iss a *peautiful* day!'

He replaced his hat, gave his reins to one of the boys and climbed down from the trap. 'Well, and the coal boat is in, I see. That's fine, now, that's fine! ... Alasdair Mackay! Come down off that roof—you'll break your neck, boy!'

'Yes, sir!' called Alasdair, but the lion rampant was now flying from the chimney of the Plough, and everybody began to talk about the war being over.

Shortly after that I was sent along to Miss Tulloch's to have my dinner—the rest of the Reachfar people had theirs with all the other men at the Plough, or the manse, or the doctor's or the schoolhouse or anywhere, but Miss Tulloch always had only me, because she was far too busy with her shop, my grandmother said, to be feeding a lot of big hungry men.

'It's yourself that's in it, Janet!' she said, when I went into the shop, and I smiled and said: 'Good day, Miss Tulloch.' This greeting given by my people had always amused me, and I used to wonder what they would think if, one day, I said: 'No, I am somebody else today, Miss Tulloch.' Today, indeed, I *felt* as if I were somebody else, what with all the excitement and Betsy rearing and it no longer being dinner-time now but nearly 'half-yoking', which was the middle of the afternoon.

'I'm sure you are hungry, but there is a whole can of that

beef you like and plenty o' tatties and just you dig in. … I've had mine, and I'll be back and fore to the shop all the time, for the people is just fair daft with the war being over and, indeed, I am feeling a little foolish myself.'

I 'dug in' to the block of tinned beef and the potatoes grown on Reachfar and was glad to know that Miss Tulloch, too, was feeling a little 'foolish'. While she ran to and fro at the tinkle of the shop bell, and I sat eating at the table in her room, we conducted a broken conversation.

'And they tell me one o' that daft Miss Boyds fell in the sea o' the morning?' she asked.

'Yes.' I nodded, with my mouth full of beef. 'Miss Violet. She fell right in with a big splash and the dominie and the doctor and Willie Beagle had to pull her out.'

'Lord be about us a-all! What will they do next, think you? They held a Hallowe'en party the other day, the foolish craiturs, and had some soldiers and sailors at it an' Jock Skinner, if ye please, and them all with turnip lanterns and eating treacle scones off a string from the roof like bairns, they tell me. And they left one o' their foolish lanterns oot in the back sheddie where they keep their paraffin and put fire till the sheddie and a-all their firewood and the week's washing that was in there. They're as daft as ha'penny watches, the whole lot o' them. … Eat up that beef, lassie, for it will only be wasted—I don't care for it, myself. … Och, aye, a right night of it we had at Hallowe'en with them. The party was over before the fire got going, and after the noise they was making—it's a wonder you didn't hear them up at Reachfar—after the noise was over, the village went to their beds, and the next thing I heard was Doctor Mackay galloping his pony down the street an' bawling oot o' himself something fearful. It seems he was called out at three o' the morning for the baby at the Seamuir shepherd's an' wee Willie, the shepherd's laddie, that had been put down to get the doctor was roarin': "The Miss Boyds iss on fire! The Miss Boyds iss on fire!" You never saw such a night in Achcraggan, with the weemen skirling an' the men runnin' doon the street tying the troosers on them as they went, an' this one wi' a pail, an' the minister's man wi' yon fancy waterin' can wi' the wee spoot on it!' Miss Tulloch went off into a gale of laughter and began to mop her eyes with the corner of her white apron. 'But it's a-all very fine to laugh,' she added soberly, 'but there's something not *dacent* aboot them when ye think on it.'

'But what about the fire?' I asked. 'Did they put it out?'

'Och, lord sake, aye. Mind you, the ootside sheddie is burnt till the ground. ... And then the Miss Boyds was for the men to come intil the hoose to get a droppie tea for their work and apparently old Katie Beagle up and said: "Johnnie Beagle! If you set foot in that hoose o' sin, ye'll never come back to *my* bed!" You know the loud way the fishers will be speaking—everybody heard her. Lord bless me, there *never* was such a night in Achcraggan!'

Miss Tulloch, who had been swept away in the drama of her narrative, suddenly realised that she was talking to *me* and not to one of her contemporary village cronies, wiped her eyes, rose and said: 'Ach, the poor craiturs. It's wickedness in us to laugh at them. To be right, it's sorry for them we should be. ... Well, if you canna eat any more you'll have to be going back, for Tom will be needing you.'

When I went back to the pier, however, Tom was not, apparently, 'needing me'. The horses were all unharnessed and nosing about among the bundles of hay in several of the Seamuir fields, the carts were all standing about up-ended, their trams pointing to the sky, and not a man was around the pier. A few groups of women were chatting here and there, the school-children were playing with balls—the boys kicking them, the girls bouncing them—in the yard by the Plough, and the four Miss Boyds were sitting, as before, on the sea wall. Several trim naval launches were tied to the pier on the side opposite to the shabby coal boat, and the seagulls were planing in long swoops and screaming as the turned tide began to recede from the shingly beach. From the Plough came the sound of countless male voices raised in raucous song.

I went into the Plough yard and joined in one of the ball games, but we had not been playing long when another naval launch was seen making in to the pier, so we all went over to see her made fast. The sailors in her were all of the peaked-cap kind, called 'petty officers', who did not wear the jerseys and wide trousers that I liked, and they took a lot of wooden boxes out of their launch and carried them into the Plough. Alasdair said that the boxes had gunpowder in them that was left over from the war, but I did not think so, for they made a sort of chinking noise like the basket did when I carried jars of jam to Granny Fraser, and what would they want with gunpowder in the Plough, anyway? Alasdair said they were maybe going to blow it up like Guy Fawkes with the Houses of Parliament, so we all sneaked round to the back of the Plough and climbed up and had a look in through the windows. I think every single man I knew was in there with a glass in his hand, and the petty officers were putting the boxes in behind the counter in a fur-tive sort of way, so I thought maybe Alasdair was right after all, and that these English-tongued petty officers were nothing but a pack of Guy Fawkes's after all. And there were all the men of my family and Sir Torquil and the dominie and everybody, just standing there, waiting to be blown to smithereens. I pushed my head in through the window and yelled: 'Dad, Tom, George, Granda! Come *out!* Come out before they blow you up!'

All the faces inside turned upwards. 'Ye wee limmer!' Tom shouted. 'Get down out o' that!'

But my father did more than that. He put his glass down on the counter and made for the door with a purposeful look in his eye, and, without words, I, Alasdair and all the lot of us sprang down from our perch and took to our heels, up the Seamuir field that was just behind the Plough's back garden. We soon discovered, though, that we were not being pursued and stopped running and turned back to look. *All* the men were now pouring in a black stream from the door of the Plough into the road and over on to the pier.

'It's going to asplode, sure enough!' said Alasdair, jumping with excitement.

But the Plough did not 'asplode'. What had happened was that the tide had gone away and left the coal boat high on the beach, her rusty bottom well settled into the sandy shingle. When we children had gathered the courage to go down, the men were giving up the effort to refloat her, and Captain Greig, swaying a little, was standing at her stern with a glass in one hand and a black bottle in the other. He emptied the last drop out of the bottle into his glass, drank it off and broke the empty bottle with a crash over the stern of the boat. 'Ah hereby christen ye the *Cutty Sark,* ye ould bitch!' he said. 'And ye sittin' flat on yer arse at Achcraggan Pier!'

All the men cheered like anything, and, led by Captain Greig, went back into the Plough.

Before they went, though, I got hold of Tom and asked him about the boxes the sailors had brought and he said: 'Ach, no, nor gunpowder. It is chust a droppie beer to drink to the war being done.' So, after that, Alasdair and I had a few friendly slaps at one another and we went back and played some more ball games. The games were enlivened and varied periodically by a drunk sailor staggering out of the Plough, going down the pier and getting himself safely, by instinct only, into one of the launches which had now been moored down at the end of the long stone-flagged slope, but it must have been about tea-time when Jock Skinner's wife arrived and went into the Plough (a thing no woman, not even the queer Miss Boyds, did) and the singing stopped and a lot of shouting started. We children, of course, gathered round the door, for, in spite of what Tom had said, Alasdair was still spreading propaganda about Gunpowder Plots. Again the Plough did not 'asplode', but out came my father with Jock Skinner held by the scruff of the neck, and out came my uncle with the screaming Bella held by both arms from behind, and my father said: 'Now, be off, the two of you, and do your fighting at home!' and he and my uncle went back inside and shut the door. Then the fun began. Jock was reeling drunk, as he frequently was, and Bella was very angry, as she frequently was, and she picked up an empty bottle, swung it like a club and began to chase Jock round the pierhead, shout-ing: 'Home wi' ye, home wi' ye, ye drunken devil!' Jock tried to do as he was told and make for home, but she caught up with him, hit him over the head with the bottle and he collapsed in a heap by the sea wall, a little past where the Miss Boyds were sit-ting. Nobody moved or spoke except Bella, who, contrite now, hurled herself at Jock and cried: 'Jockie, boy! Ah didna mean it! Are ye all right, Jockie, boy?' Jock gave a grunt and settled himself for sleep, and she rose to her feet. 'Ye drunken boogger! she said. 'Chust you *stop* there an' be sleepin' yerself sober!' and, swinging her bottle-club defiantly, she strode away down the village street.

The children went back to their ball games, but I did not go back this time. The sun had gone in and the afternoon was dull and grey, and I wanted to go home, so I went to the gate which Betsy was looking over—she wanted to go home too—and climbed from the gate on to her back. She gave a little whinny of pleasure at seeing me, and I sat there patting her neck and looking around at the darkening water of the Firth.

The village women were calling their children now and drifting away back to their warm firesides; and then I saw the Miss Boyds help Jock Skinner to his feet and walk away, helping him, along the road. It was kind of them. His head must be sore. The children were laughing and shouting still as they went to their homes. I wanted to cry.

But, with their way of never failing me, just then the men of my family came out of the Plough and I was happy again.

'Bring Betsy over, Janet!' my father called.

I got down, opened the gate, climbed up on it and up on Betsy again, and she went of her own accord and stood by her own cart. My father put her harness on, backed her into position and brought the trams down, talking to the village and farm men all the time.

'No, Hughie, it's very good o' ye, man, but not the-night. Aye, Alex, we'll have a dram tomorrow, maybe. No thank ye, Rory, I have to get home with my father and the bairn. I'll see ye another day.'

George and Tom, yoking Dick and Dulcie, were arguing in the same way, while my grandfather was talking to Sir Torquil.

'It has been a great day, Reachfar,' Sir Torquil said. 'When that destroyer came up with her bunting on, dammit, I couldn't believe me own eyes!'

'I knew,' my grandfather said quietly, 'that there was something in the wind the-day. I knew it on the horses o' the morning.'

Sir Torquil did not argue the matter. Nobody did. How could they? What *had* the horses felt in the air that morning?

It took a long time to marshal the Poyntdale and Dinchory strings and get the horsemen out of the Plough, but at last we were under way, the horses plodding steadily and quietly now towards their stables, and just as well, for in several cases the horse was in charge of his drunk driver asleep in the cart. The last thing I remember was the sound of the song that the sailors were singing in the Plough as we drew away into the twilight.

There were three something-something
Hanging on the wall,
Three something-something, hanging on the wall.
If one something-something should accidentally fall,
There'll be two something-something hanging on the wall.

The same 'plan' of a song as Ten Little Nigger Boys, I thought, and a fine tune. What could the something-somethings be? A pity I had not heard it properly. I fell asleep in Tom's lap in the gently swaying cart.

We had four days of coal-boat holidays that year, because we had an extra two days because of the war being over, and just as well, because through celebrating the end of the war we had got ourselves, as Tom said, 'all through-other with our work and the boat stuck on the beach and a-all'. The next day, though, Tom, Granda and I left Reachfar at dawn again, went to Poyntdale and loaded with wood from Sir Torquil's sawmill and then on to the boat, stacked the wood on the pier, carted the minister's coal, then loaded with our own coal and came home. It went on like that for two more days and became very dull. I had a feeling that the whole business of the coal boat had reached its climax at that moment when the destroyer had dashed up the Firth and that it would never be the same again. The greyness had come down, gradually, after that, and had ended in the dreary, sordid fight between Jock Skinner and his wife and the sad ugliness of Jock reeling down the road in a covey of Miss Boyds. I did not know it at the time, but that greyness was the grim dawn of a new era, the Post-War Period. All I knew was that the greyness and Jock Skinner and Bella and the Miss Boyds among them had sullied the bright joy of the coal boat and that the mark would be there for ever and ever. I remember thinking about it all deep inside the Thinking Place among the tall, close-ranked fir trees above the Reachfar well, and I must have done this thinking on a Saturday or a Sunday, for it was forenoon, and after I had settled it all with myself, and accepted the darkening of the bright coal-boat memory, Fly and I went round the moor and scraped the red paint marks off the trees with my knife. The war was over, the coal boat had been in and we would not have to cut the trees now. The trees were salvage from the wreck.

Part II

hat winter of 1918 into 1919 was long and bleak and wet. The moor and field paths were so sodden with rain that they were almost impassable, and I had to go round the full three and three-quarter miles by road to school, morning after morning, plodding along in the driving rain, meeting no one between Reachfar and the County Road except perhaps the Poyntdale shepherd, who was always a little wetter than myself and a little more morose too. The rain continued on right through March and then, in a spiteful way, froze itself up and descended on us in blinding, driving snow, in a bitter 'peewits' storm' as March turned into April. Throughout the long dreary wet winter my grandparents had been predicting a 'peevies' storm' as they called it, and, as usual, about the weather and most other things, they were right.

An old man of the Scottish Border, the opposite end of Scotland from my own, has told me that in the Borders they used to refer to these days when March turns into April as the 'Borrowing Days' and that they had this rhyme about them:

March borrowed from Apryle the first three days and they were vile.

The first o' them was wild and weet, the second o' them was snaw and sleet,

The third o' them was sic a freeze, it froze the birds' nebs tae the trees.

At Reachfar, during these March-end days, after a snowless winter, we expected the peewits' storm, which was so-called because the lapwings, having laid their eggs in the hollows of the bare ploughland, would call and call with their eerie cry as they flew low among the 'wild and weet and snaw and sleet'.

But after the peewits' storm was over spring broke in beauty over the countryside like a fresh young girl who had, after circumventing angry parents, arrived a little late but flushed with triumph at her first ball, her eyes sparkling, her cheeks glowing, her breath coming fast with expectation, and I, affected by the spring in my own fashion, began to inspect the rabbit families in the Bluebell Bank and dance down the Strip of Herbage again. I was dancing to a new tune this year—

Six something-somethings hanging on the wall …

I had discovered that, starting with six and working down to 'one something-something', jumping on to certain stones the while, I could go from one end of the Strip to the other without having either any stones or any song left over. The only unsatisfactory thing, now, was, what could the something-somethings be? I thought of six Betsy's collars, and six Granny's bonnets, but these things never fell, either accidentally or any other way, and then the white light of the poet's inspiration was vouchsafed to me:

Six Miss Boy-idds sitting on the wall!
Six Miss Boy-idds sitting on the wall!
If one Miss Boy-idd should accidentally fall,
There'd be five Miss Boy-idds sitting on the wall!

I was pleased with this as children (and poets) are with their own songs, and I danced the Strip of Herbage to it, collected the eggs to it and did all my small jobs to it for several weeks, until one day my gentle mother called me into a quiet corner and said: 'Janet, the song is not about the Miss Boyds. It should be six *green bottles hanging* on the wall.'

'But, Mother, I like it with Miss Boyds in it.'

'*I* don't. And, Janet, please don't sing it that way.'

'But, Mother! Why not?'

'Never mind why, this time. Just don't sing it that way, to please *me*.'

'All right, Mother.'

My mother had never before given me such a reason for doing or not doing anything. One of the nice things about my mother was that never did she say like my grandmother: 'Do it because I tell you.' My mother would say: 'You have to curtsy to Lady Lydia because she is a fine and good lady and a little girl like you has to have some way of showing her respect.' The great thing about my mother was that she was full of Real Sense.

So I gave some thought to her spoiling my song about the Miss Boyds which, I felt, was not a very harmful or rude song compared with some of the things the schoolboys shouted after the Miss Boyds in the village street, but I would probably have given up thinking about it, in my usual fickle way, except that, the very next week, on the Tuesday morning, when I was ready to leave for school, my grandmother said: 'Janet, take this basket, and at your dinner-time go round to the Miss Boyds and hand it in.'

'What's in it, Granny?'

'A bittie butter and some jam, and carry it canny.'

'Are the Miss Boyds buying *jam* next?' I enquired. It was a *disgrace* to buy jam from the shop or anywhere else. People had to make their own, unless they were too old, like Granny Fraser.

'Janet!' said my mother. 'That will do. Take the basket to the Miss Boyds and tell them that Granny sent it and come away and don't stay chattering. Do you understand?'

'Yes, Mother.'

I set off in silence for school, my satchel on my back, the basket in my hand. This was Awful. My mother had even been Cross. *Poop* to these Miss Boyds! They meant nothing but Bother. In fact, *dirt* on these Miss Boyds!

The dominie kept the basket by his desk until dinner-time, and then I had my sandwiches and milk in the playshed with my friends and set off. It was skipping-rope time, and I wanted to play, but I had to go on this (danged-into-myself) errand.

'Where are you off to?' Jean Stewart asked.

I did not like Jean Stewart much. She was a fisher girl, with a tongue as sharp as an east wind, as Tom would say, and always teasing the 'wee ones' in the baby class at playtimes. I was already bad-tempered enough about this errand and it was none of her business anyhow, but Reachfar people were supposed to be 'civil'.

'To the Miss Boyds,' I said.

'What for?' she pursued.

This was Too Much. This was Pure Nosiness. 'Nothing to do with you!' I snapped and walked towards the school gate with my basket.

In a second Jean's sycophantic clique of friends seemed to spring from the ground around her and took up the cry that she gave them. 'Jock Skinner's weemen! Jock Skinner's weemen! Bairns wi' nae faithers! Jock Skinner's weemen!'

I stopped in the wide gateway. 'Shut your mouth, Jean Stewart!' I said.

They began to dance round me like gadflies, their ragged

black hair flying, their sallow, spindly legs kicking, Jean's mouth emitting shrill word after shrill insulting word. 'You're anither! You're anither! Jock Skinner's weemen!—'

The words, in the shrill fisher accent, were extraordinarily obscene to me. Raw, red rage swelled in my brain and chest and my gentle mother's voice saying: 'Decent people don't fight— especially ladies. Decent people don't fight—' was becoming fainter and fainter. Suddenly my mind could no longer hear that voice. I hung the basket on the gatepost in icy calm, and then, whirling round, I had Jean Stewart by the wiry black hair and down on the ground while her mouth was still forming its latest insult. She was a year older than I was, and wiry, but the small fisher breed was no match for the brawn I had inherited from Reachfar. Before the doctor came along, going on his after- noon round, pulled up his pony and jumped down, I had Jean senseless, with blood flowing freely from her nose and from her head where it had struck a stone when I pulled her down. Her sycophants were all bellowing as if *they* were being murdered. One of the boys got the doctor's bag from his trap and opened it and the doctor held a bottle under Jean's nose and gave her a good shake. She opened her eyes, saw me, cringed and started to bellow.

'Janet Sandison!' said the thunder of the dominie's voice. 'Did you do that to Jean?'

'Yes, sir.'

'You should be ashamed of yourself!'

'Hold on, Dominie!' said the doctor and called sternly to his own son. 'Alasdair, you and the boys were here. What hap- pened?'

'Jean was calling names at Janet and Janet hit her.'

'*What* names?'

Alasdair kicked a stone about with the toe of his boot.

'Speak up, boy! *What* names?'

'Names that you told me I wasn't to say about Jock Skinner's weemen, Dad.'

The doctor gave Jean another shake. 'Stop that bawling, you little besom, or it's a dose of castor oil you'll get! Go into the cloakroom and I'll come and wash that cut. ... Come here, Janet!' He took some cottonwool from his bag, put stuff from a bottle on it and wiped the three big claw marks on my check. 'You'll do fine,' he said and gave me a friendly slap on the bottom.

'And any more name-calling among you girls, or fighting—' said the dominie, 'and I'll take the boys' cane to you! Disgraceful, on the public road. ... Whose basket is this?'

'Mine, sir.'

'Well, here you are. Get back into the playground.'

'Please, sir, Granny said to take the basket to the Miss Boyds.'

'Oh. Oh, I see. All right, be off then! ... John Watson, what are you doing with that catapult? No catapults in the playground—hand it over. ... Good day, Doctor. Thank you. Good day.' Grumbling to himself, the dominie went back to his interrupted dinner and I went off to the Miss Boyds.

I could not tell you how it was, but the Miss Boyds' house and the Miss Boyds' garden and the Miss Boyds themselves looked different. Only the two old ones and Miss Annie were there, and the two old ones did not speak at all. There was no fluttering or nudging or giggling now, but they were not like ordinary people either. They seemed very anxious that I should come in, so I did, but then they did not seem to have anything to say. Miss Annie took the basket, unpacked it in a wondering, startled sort of way, as if she had never seen a basket before, and then said: 'But why did your granny send *us* some of her butter and jam, Janet?'

They *were* funny people. They did not know any of the ordinary things that everybody knew.

'Oh, it's just a compliment,' I explained. 'My granny sends people compliments all the time.'

I knew, for I had to carry these compliments most of the time, or Tom and Betsy and I had to carry them when it was the minister's firewood or the dominie's light oats for his hens.

'A compliment?' Miss Annie asked, still not seeming to understand.

'Yes. And all you have to do is give me back the basket and tell me to thank my granny for the kind compliment or something like that.' I knew all about this business of compli ments. Very slowly, Miss Annie folded the napkin, put it into the empty basket and handed it to me. 'There, then, Janet,' she said. 'And tell your granny that we are all thanking her for her kind—kind—*kindness*' she got out at last.

Dominie Stevenson would not think much of her as a scholar, I thought, when she could not remember two words like 'kind compliment' from one minute to the next. She would not make much of a job of reciting 'I to the hills—' at Scripture Lesson, I thought. And then I noticed that her face had gone all twisted and funny the way Lady Lydia's did when she came to tell my grandmother about her young brother being killed at a place called Mons, and I was sent out of the kitchen.

'I have to go now,' I said, and went to the door. 'But when you'll be having a little time you should come up and see my granny. Good day, Miss Boyds.'

I could not think of anything better to do or say, so I closed their door and then their garden gate and went back to school. That was the best thing they could do, I thought. People who were in trouble so that their faces got twisted and funny like that could not do a better thing than come and see my granny. My grandmother who made you behave, and Mrs Sandison who was much Respected in the District, and Mrs Reachfar who was a grand vet, a devil for a bargain and a Bit of a Witch besides, were all quite different people from my granny, although they all lived inside the same person. You did not see my granny very often, but she was very, very good for people who had trouble.

I was far too interested in afternoon school to think any more about the Miss Boyds, and too busy paddling up the Reachfar Burn, with my shoes and socks in the basket, on the way home, to remember about my fight with Jean Stewart, so that when I walked into the house at about half-past five the whole of my family was there, and so was the news of my fight. My mother fired the first, and telling, salvo. 'Janet Sandison! Look at your face, scratched like some tinkerwoman! How dare you behave like Bella Skinner in Achcraggan Street?'

I had not been aware of being unhappy all day, but I now felt very unhappy indeed. I sat down on the fender stool and burst into tears. I seldom cried as a child, for I seldom had anything to cry about. Indeed, the only people who, until now, could make me cry at all were my mother and my father, but this crying was different from any crying I had done before. I was not crying only because I had done something wrong that had made my mother angry. I was crying with a wretchedness that had in it some of the greyness of the first day of the coal boat, some of the sordidness of Bella hitting Jock on the head with the bottle and some of the dreadful numbness that had pervaded the Miss Boyds' kitchen that day. I did not really know what I was crying about, but I could not stop. My faithful friends and allies, George and Tom, plunged headlong to my aid.

'Ach, the poor bairn!' said Tom. 'As I was hearing the story from the shepherd that got it from the doctor himself, there was good provvycation—'

'Hold your tongue, Tom!' blazed my mother. 'Provocation or not, I will *not have* my daughter fighting like a hooligan! You hear me? I—'

'Hey, Elizabeth, lass,' said George, making a good try, 'you have to mind that there's some o' this coorse Reachfar blood in her too!'

'Stop! Stop, *stop*, George!' I sobbed. 'Stop! Stop!'

Tom bent down, scooped me off the fender stool and made for the door.

'Dang the lot o' ye for being *at the* bairn!' he bawled. 'Ye thrawn black-haired booggers that ye are! I'll not *let* ye be at the craitur and her sobbing herself seeck with ye bawling at her about a bairns' row at the schoo! Did none o' ye ever—'

'Come back here, Tom,' said my father suddenly. 'Give her to me.'

He took me on his knee. 'Come now, Janet; your mother was angry about you fighting and rolling in the dirt, but that's all past now and you won't do it again. Come now.'

'It's the Miss Boyds!' I sobbed. 'It's the Miss Boyds!'

'*That* poor craiturs?' my granny asked in my granny's voice. 'What about them? Were they not nice to you when you took the basket?'

'Yes, they were nice, Granny. They were very nice. But—it's the Miss *Boyds!*' I bellowed and began to sob all over again.

Everybody began to argue with everybody else and I did not, even then, blame them. I could not tell them what I meant, and none of the meanings they suggested were true, and, all the time, Tom was keeping up a running fire of 'Dang ye all for being *at* the poor bairn!' and 'Stop crying, pettie, stop crying for Tom', until in a final scream of near-hysteria I yelled: 'Granny, you'll have to go and see the MISS BOYDS!'

'Kate,' said my uncle, 'warm a droppie milk. Tom, go ben to the parlour and bring the whisky. I'll calm that bairn down if it's the last thing I do.'

On my mother's lap, now, and very ashamed of myself and afraid of my own outburst which I did not in the least understand, and shocked, too, at the upset I had caused in my family, I sobbed and hiccuped my way through my cup of warm milk with the teaspoonful of whisky in it. When I think of it now, many child psychologists could have taken lessons from My Friend Tom, for he sat there with his dram of whisky, beside my mother and me, and said: 'A lot of people will be saying bad things about the Miss Boyds. Now, I think myself that they are very nice craiturs when a body gets to know them.'

'And *not* hot-arsed-est!' I said between sobs. I did not know what it meant, but it had a derogatory sound. There was a pregnant sort of silence, but Tom took the matter in hand with what I now recognise as considerable courage.

'Not at all,' he said. 'No, not hot-arsed-est in the least, although a person might have said so before knowing them right. No. I believe they are a very nice lot o' leddies. Don't you think that yourself, George?'

'Well, now,' said the other natural master of psychology, 'it's a good whilie since I saw them. What did you think o' them the-day, Janet?'

'They were sad,' I said. 'Very sad, and all alone, and just the three of them—'

George and Tom (and probably the whisky) had me talking now, and I poured out all I knew and felt and could find words for about the Miss Boyds, including the greyness when I sat on Betsy outside the Plough and watched them walk away supporting Jock Skinner. I even told of how I had 'pooped' them and said 'dirt on them' to myself and everything. I told them about Jean Stewart's name-calling and, in the end, came back to their sadness and their loneliness and how I had told them to come and see Granny and how I did not think that they would come, because they seemed to be afraid of everybody now, even of me.

'The poor craiturs,' my granny said when I had finished. 'But don't you worry any more, Janet, for tomorrow Tom will yoke Dulcie and *I* will go and see *them*.' She turned to my family. 'I haven't been to Achcraggan on a weekday this twelvemonth. Aye.' She straightened her back and her face became very stern. 'Iphm. We will leave after dinner, Tom, and fetch Janet from the school on the way back. Dulcie will do fine on that back green at the Miss Boyds.'

This meant that Tom was to take a nosebag for Dulcie. It also meant that Achcraggan was to have time to see that Mrs Reachfar was spending the afternoon at the Miss Boyds.

'What do ye think, Granda?' she asked, appealing to the only law that she ever recognised.

'Chust you do that, Mistress,' he said quietly. 'We mustna leave the craiturs alone in their trouble.'

We all had supper after this decision had been taken, and after my grandfather had said the grace my 'clown' of an uncle, leaning back in his chair, spoke behind me to Tom. 'Tom, I have a special grace of my own to be saying for us three the-night.'

'What's that, George, man?'

'You have to shut your eyes, Tom. And you, Janet.'

'George!' my grandmother said in a warning voice.

'God bless the Miss Boyds,' said George, 'for getting Tom and Janet and me a dram out of the parlour bottle and us not even sick. Amen.'

When we opened our eyes, my grandmother, my grandfather, my mother and my father were all looking hard at my 'clown' of an uncle, but they did not say anything. How could they? It had been a very nice special grace and had been spoken with all due reverence. I felt a lot better, ate a big supper and went off to bed as usual afterwards.

When I came out of school the next afternoon my grandmother, Tom and Dulcie were waiting in the trap at the gate.

'Did you see them, Granny?' I asked as I climbed up over the wheel into the trap.

'Yes, Janet, and I had a cup of tea with them and it was very nice.'

'Were they sad?'

'A little quiet, maybe.'

'Why are they like that, Granny?'

'We won't be gossiping, Janet. ... Tom, stop at Miss Tulloch's. Maybe she will have some of these fancy buns from the baker west the country and we'll take a few home for the tea.'

When my grandmother went abroad, which was seldom, there was always a special 'eating' treat. My fickle mind left the Miss Boyds and concentrated on the choosing of the buns—a whole two dozen of them, three for each member of my family—and there were three kinds: square gingerbread ones, round ones with big lumps of white sugar on their shiny brown tops, and queer ones like long snakes coiled up with currants inserted in the coils. While my grandmother talked to Miss Tulloch I put eight of each in the big white paper bag and then came over to where they were talking, holding the bag open.

'Look, Miss Tulloch—eight of each kind and three eights is twenty-four and that's two dozen.'

'Yes, Janet.'

'And you'll mind to write them in the book?'

'Yes, Janet. Now take two more, one for you and one for Tom to eat on the way home; Granny doesn't want one. And give these sugar lumps to Dulcie for me.' I went back to the tray of buns and Miss Tulloch turned again to my grandmother. 'Aye, I see what ye mean, Mrs Sandison. Och, yes. The poor craiturs. Och, aye, it's true enough, I will be thinking. Lizzie Fraser saw her in Inverness that time she was up when her sister was sick and Lizzie said there was no mistake. Five months she would have said it was, she said, and Lizzie should know. She has nine of her own.'

My grandmother said something which I could not hear and Miss Tulloch spoke again. 'Och, the bairn is busy with the buns, Mrs Sandison, although I'll give you that she's a lively little clip.' They were talking about *me,* and I thought how foolish grown-up people were, for now that my granny had been to see the Miss Boyds I was not interested in them, or *would* not have been if they had not talked about *me* in between. But, now that they had brought me into it, where, before, I had been hearing without attending, I now began to listen hard to their low-pitched conversation.

'The trouble is there right enough,' Miss Tulloch said.

'Are they saying who?' my grandmother asked.

'Aye.' Miss Tulloch smoothed her apron and brushed a little flour off the counter.

'Iphm?' said my grandmother, very much as the Inquisition might have asked a question.

'Jock Skinner—the night o' the Ar*mis*tice, they say.'

'Mercy on us!' My grandmother rose from her chair and spoke in a louder voice. 'Well, it's myself that would take it kindly, Miss Tulloch, if ye was to be calling on the Miss Boyds when you'll be having the time, just to pass the time o' day. Aye. You, and Mrs Gilchrist and the post-mistress and a few o' the local leddies. It's lonely for them, and Reachfar is a fair way and I'm getting a little old for a lot of jaunting.'

'Yes, Mrs Sandison,' said Miss Tulloch.

'And if there should be any bother or any remarks passed that you don't care for, chust let me know. I'm getting old, but I'm not fair done yet. … Come, Janet. Thank Miss Tulloch for the buns. We have to go home now. Good day, Miss Tulloch.'

I gave Dulcie her sugar lumps—she always got the ones that had fallen on the shop floor or something like that and were a little dirty—and then we drove home. I gave a little thought to the Miss Boyds and their 'trouble' but not a great deal, for it was a fairly common occurrence that people would be having babies without getting a father for them first, which was the proper way to have them. People were different from horse persons like Betsy. Betsy could have a foal fathered by the Poyntdale stallion, and we at Reachfar would help her to look after it and feed it, but people were different. People, partly because of what it said in the Bible, and partly because human children needed more pennies to bring them up properly, ought to have both a mother and a father there all the time—the mother to wash the baby and look after it, and the father to go out and work to earn the pennies to buy things like clothes and sugar (that did not grow on the place) for it, and some extra pennies to put in the bank in case the baby might grow up to be clever and able to take the Higher Eddication, at a university, maybe. I had known all about this ever since I could remember, and thought it all very simple and 'only reasonable'.

Of course, the Miss Boyds would manage very well for pennies for their baby, I thought, even without a father being with them, for they had a 'puckle money among them'. It was the Bible side of it that would be the trouble in their case. What the Bible said made it a Disgrace to have a baby in the house with no father for it. That was what the village people said, although my grandmother thought differently in that queer way of her own of thinking differently about all sorts of things that offended against the village laws. I remembered, about a year back, when Mary Junor that worked in the canteen at the soldiers' camp had a baby with no father, one of the village women said it was because she was a bad girl, and my grandmother said in her sternest voice: 'You hold your *Bad Tongue,* Kirsty Graham. Bad girls don't *have* bairns.' And she looked at Kirsty as if she could see a Bad Girl right there in front of her. Kirsty held her tongue after that and my mother made clothes on our sewing-machine for the baby and I sewed the little buttons on. Mary's baby had been, somehow, Because of the War. The war was such an upset that it caused people to have babies without fathers for them, even, but the war was finished now and probably the Miss Boyds' baby would be the last one of its kind that we would have in the district, I thought.

When we were home, and my grandmother had gone into the house, and Tom and I were unharnessing Dulcie, I said: 'Tom, which one of the Miss Boyds is it that's having the baby?'

'God be here!' said Tom. 'Don't let your granny be hearing you!'

'If I'd wanted her to be hearing me, foolish, I'd have asked herself!'

He looked down at me over Dulcie's neck. 'Why are you needing to be knowing?'

'Just to be knowing.'

'You're far too danged knowing already!'

'Tom Reachfar, that's a Bad Thing to say! My father says that people can't *ever* be knowing too much. Not even the minister can't still be learning, he says!'

'There is good knowing and bad knowing, though.'

'Babies is *not* bad ! My grandmother says that *no* baby can be bad!'

'Ach, to the devil with it!' said Tom. 'You would argue the leg off Johnnie Greycairn's Diamond. They tell me it's the young one, the one they'll be calling Vi'let.' He put Dulcie's small trap harness collar on its peg. 'Away and open the gate of the Wee Fieldie and put her in for me.'

I opened the gate of the Wee Fieldie, Dulcie ran through and I closed it behind her. 'Tom, will you swap me your sugary bun for my ginger one?'

'Aye—if you'll be holding your danged tongue about things,' he said.

*   *   *   *   *

The sun swung round on its high summer course. My Red-Crossing apron, which I had outgrown and which I did not need now because there was no war and never going to be another war, was turned into a cloth for polishing the spoons, and my mother unpicked the Red Cross from Tom's Saturday bonnet. The soldiers' camp was all broken up and the heather began to grow again where the huts had been, west on the Dinchory moor. At Poyntdale House the big ward had all the beds taken away and the billiard-table was brought back in from the coach-house and set in place. It seemed to me that the only person whose life was not changed in some way was Janet Sandison. I had no Red-Crossing to do now, but the Miss Boyds were practically a Red Cross in themselves, the number of baskets and things I was always having to carry for them. However, they were not sad now, although they still did not giggle and nudge as they used to do, and their house was always quite cheery when you went there, with Miss Tulloch or somebody in having a yarn with them. And the schoolchildren—even Jean Stewart—seemed to have tired of the sport of calling after them in the street.

June came along, and with it its big event of school 'coming out' for the summer holidays and Prize Day. Prize Day at Achcraggan School was something like the coal boat, for Everybody was there. Lady Lydia presented the prizes, Sir Torquil and the minister made speeches, and Dominie Stevenson called out the name of the child and what the prize was for and handed it to Lady Lydia. But the great thing about Achcraggan School was that, by the time they had finished, *every* child had a prize and some had several. There were first and second for each subject in every class, and then all sorts of 'specials'. The minister gave a Bible as the Special for Scripture, Miss Tulloch gave a Special for Fancy Sewing, Lewie the Joiner gave a Special for Woodwork, my grandmother gave a Special for the Best Bouquet of Wild Flowers (as chosen by Lady Lydia, who got it to take home as her presentation bouquet), and I was not allowed to enter for this. My grandfather gave a boys' Special for the Best Tray of Vegetables grown in the school garden, as selected by himself, and he presented *it* to the minister. And then Lady

Lydia gave a Special (always a small but good brooch) for the Girl Dux of the school, and Sir Torquil gave a silver watch for the Boy Dux. Among some fifty children nobody came away from it all empty-handed.

On Prize Day I did not have to be at school until eleven, but Tom, George and I set off together at nine, for Tom and George, of course, had a little business to do with their cronies at the back door of the Plough before coming to the school, while I had to go to Miss Tulloch's and sit still and not move in order to keep my white Sunday clothes clean until it was time to go up to the school with her. The school playground today was full of traps, and the minister's glebe field was full of horses, and among them was the Reachfar trap which had brought the rest of my family except my aunt. She had been left to look after the place, but she was always allowed to go to the Prize Day Dance in the Church Hall in the evening.

All we children had to form up from the gates to the school door to welcome the Poyntdale wagonette, and then, while the minister welcomed Lady Lydia and Sir Torquil, we all had to go inside and the dominie called the roll right through the whole school. Today, at the appointed time, instead of the smart trot of the wagonette greys down the road, there came a noise far more frightening than the sirens of the ships at the Armistice; all the horses in the glebe field rushed away up to the far corner and plunged about wild-eyed, and round the corner came Sir Torquil and Lady Lydia, sitting in a Thing, with a man in front holding a handle, and there were no horses near it at all. This dreadful Thing came at the school gates, where I was standing, in a cloud of dust and an inferno of noise, and I was so frightened that I would have run away up the hill to the horses if the bones of my legs had not melted. I could not move; I could not even look away from the dreadful Thing, for even my eyes would not move. 'It's a motor car! It's a motor car!' shouted My Friend Alasdair who was beside me. 'Hurray! Sir Torquil's got a motor car!' All the other children were far quicker-witted than I was and they all took up the cry, even the wee ones in the baby class, so, of course, I who was in the top class in the Dominie's Room could not show my terror. But I could not cheer either. I held grimly on to the bar of the school gate, while the Awful Thing thundered past me, up the playground to the school door, and the words of the Frightening Hymn that we had sometimes in church echoed through my mind:

His chariots of wrath the deep thunder-clouds form,
And dark is His path on the wings of the storm.

The Thing let Sir Torquil and Lady Lydia climb down out of it, down some steps it had, and then it took the man with the handle down to the playshed and suddenly stopped its noise, although it was still filling the air with its awful smell, and the children and the people, regardless of the smell and the danger that it might decide to move again, crowded round it. But not all, after all, I saw with relief. My grandfather, Tom, Johnnie Greycairn and several other of the grandfathers stayed in a tight group under the big tree, and I knew they did not like the Thing either, so I went over to join them.

'Tom,' I whispered, 'I don't like it.'

'Nor me neither, the stinkin' thing!' said Tom.

'Are you frightened of it, Tom?'

'Och, no! Where would a person be frightened of a thing like that that canna move unless a mannie with a funny bonnet on him will be turning a handle?'

'It wouldn't *come* at a person, Tom?'

'Where could it come at a person and it with no brains in it?

No, no. Now, *Dick* would come at a person he didna like, but not that contrivance. It *canna.*'

'Well,' my grandfather was saying to old Mr Ramsay, 'the Laird has to move with the times, but I don't think it is as bonnie as the horses myself.'

'No, indeed, Reachfar, nor as wise either,' said Mr Ramsay.

Then the dominie rang the bell for the children and we all had to go in for roll call, and the people all had to come in too, but I noticed that the man that the Thing had with it did not come in. He had to stay beside it as if it would not let him go. I was not at all sure that he was not afraid of it, and that, in spite of what Tom had said, it would not come at him if he tried to leave it, like a spoilt child that would kick and scream at its mother and not go out to play by itself when she had visitors.

When the dominie began to call the roll from the oldest child in the school down to the youngest the next thing went wrong. The first three pupils answered 'Present, sir' all right, but when he called out 'Margaret Skinner' there was no answer. He tried again, sternly, with the more familiar name 'Maggie Skinner?' There was still no answer. The dominie clicked his tongue and went on down the roll, then: 'Thomas Skinner.' No answer. 'Tom Skinner?' Still no answer. By the time he reached the end, all five Skinners who should have been there were missing. This was very queer. The Skinners might have to be 'whipped in' every other day of the school year, but they were usually there for their apple and orange at Christmas and 'to see what they could pick up for nothing' on Prize Day. However, after a colloquy and some nodding between the dominie, the minister and Sir Torquil on the platform, the proceedings went forward as usual. The speech was made, the prayer was said and the Baby Class was given its prizes first because it was difficult for the wee ones to sit still for too long and the lady teacher had them all near the door so that she could take them out to play if they became restive. At last, I went up and made my curtsey for First Girl in my class and as usual, too, Alasdair went up and made his bow for First Boy, and then they got started on the mass of Specials. I usually got the Special presented by Doctor Mackay for General Intelligence and Alasdair usually got the Special for Nature Knowledge presented by Captain Robertson of Seamuir, but here the schedule went wrong again and these prizes went to other people. Ever since the Armistice, it seemed to me, you could not depend on anything being as usual any more. I sighed and watched the bees in the honeysuckle at the window while the dominie droned his way through all the Specials.

'And now,' he said, 'pay attention, everybody, for I have a situation here that has to be explained and I want everybody, young and old, to understand it. As you know, Mr Murray at the Academy sets the paper for the Top Class for the examination for the Dux prizes presented by Lady Lydia and Sir Torquil, and I send the written papers back to Mr Murray to be marked. Some of the older people may remember that some years ago Sir Torquil's prize went to Hector Gunn, who was five years younger than some of the others who wrote papers. Hector Beagle, as we all know him, is now doing very well at the Marine Engineering in Glasgow, so we can all have confidence in the marking of Mr Murray and his Committee at the Academy. This year, the Dux prizes *both* go to a girl and a boy who will have to stay here for another year with me before going to the Academy, as they are both only nine years old. These two are Janet Sandison of Reachfar and Alasdair Mackay, the son of our good doctor.'

Alasdair and I went up to Lady Lydia and I got the brooch, which is a little circle of river pearls, and Alasdair got the watch. It was indeed a very, very queer Prize Day and my mother seemed to have got a cold in her head or something the way she was blowing her nose, and Tom and George were smiling the foolish way they smiled sometimes if their business at the Plough took a little too long.

When the Prize-giving was over, with a short prayer from the minister, we children usually lined up again to see Sir Torquil and Lady Lydia drive away, but not me this year. They could all say what they liked, but I did not trust that Thing, so I gave my book and the blue velvet box with my brooch to my mother and went away into the school garden and had myself a swing. I heard the noise of the Thing going away, and then I came back into the playground where my grandmother was standing talking to the three oldest Miss Boyds and Tom was yoking Dulcie to the trap.

'I am very pleased you came out to the Prize Day,' my grand-mother was saying. 'It is a nice outing and the bairns are always amusing with their sewing and woodwork and all.'

I thought she would never stop gabbing so that we could get along to Miss Tulloch's for the tea and cake that she always provided to tide us Reachfar people over on Prize Day, and all the other women kept going over to join them and my grand-mother kept calling this one and that one over and they would all chat for a little longer. In the end we were the very last peo-ple to leave the playground, my mother and the three Miss Boyds, if you please, riding in the trap with George at Dulcie's head, then my grandmother and Miss Tulloch walking behind, then my grandfather and my father, then Tom and me. And where do you think we went? Not to Miss Tulloch's at all. We went to the Miss Boyds', and had a proper dinner, in the room they called the dining-room, round a big table, Miss Tulloch and all. It was a first-class feed, of soup, then fried haddock and potatoes, and then a cold pink pudding, and then tea and fancy biscuits and all carried in by Bella Beagle's Martha, who was very handy about the house, and had been in the kitchen at Poyntdale before her mother brought her home to be handy about their own house in the Fisher Town. On the way home Tom and I agreed that we had never been to such a Prize Day in all Our Born Days.

'My, but I am chust terrible full,' Tom said. 'I think it was that third droppie of the pudding that did it. … We must tell Auntie Kate about that pudding—maybe she would make it for us of a Sunday, sometimes.'

'Bella Beagle's Martha could teach her,' I suggested.

'We-ell.' Tom was doubtful. 'I wouldna say anything o' that the-now. No. We'll chust tell her that it was a by-ordinar' good pudding and it that bonnie pink colour and a-all.'

'All right,' I agreed. 'Anyway, it was very good of the Miss Boyds, Tom.'

'Yes, indeed. Aye. They're a puckle very nice leddies, the Miss Boyds. … Would you be giving me a wee bit turn of your brooch to wear in my bonnet when I'll be going to the market next?'

'Ach, stop your foolishness!' I told him.

When we reached home I was taken out of my white clothes and put into my kim-*oh*-no and the holidays had started, so Fly and I after tea went off to have a Look Round the moor. Now that I did not have to go to school for a while, and it was summer, I was allowed to stay up till nearly nine o'clock if I was clever—half-past eight if I was not—instead of having to go to bed right after supper-time. We went by the Picnic Pond and inspected the double buttercups, and then went up by the edge of the swamp that fed the pond and where the ragged robins grew, and Fly started a rabbit or two here and there, but merely in a playful way, for they were young ones that were not worth catching. Then we went on again until Fly flushed up a cunning old hare who had been there for years, and of course it got away again with only two of us there, but we accidentally got into the swamp in the excitement, so I took my shoes off, hung them on a tree to dry and went on barefooted through the soft, gurgly moss of the swamp, which flowed up in a pleasant way between the toes. The swamp went all the way up to the march dyke between Reachfar and Greycairn, but the trees stopped at the dyke, and the Greycairn moor on the other side was stony, with heather and tussocky grass, and the swamp became less interesting from there up to the Greycairn Spring, with no ragged robins or marigolds or double buttercups, only a few bog cottons blowing their tattered white banner-heads in the hill breeze. Fly and I decided not to cross the dyke, but to have a sit-down on its loose, warm, brown stones and then have another paddle down the Reachfar swamp.

We had not been sitting long, 'gawping about us' as my grandmother called it, when I saw something glittering in a tussock of grass in the Greycairn moor. Down near the shore, and nearer the village, you often saw pieces of glass glittering in the sun near the roadside or on the beach, but you seldom saw anything like that up here, for the people in the farm lands had more 'more sense' than to leave a broken bottle lying in the sun among dry grass, heather or fir trees. That was how fires started, like the one in Dinchory Spruce Plantation, that cost a lot of very valuable trees before it was put out, not to mention Tom's scarf which I had knitted for him, which he had hung, with his jacket, out of range, as he thought, and which had been overtaken by the raging fire. Fly and I went over to the glittering thing to take it away, but it was not glass, it was a bright metal teaspoon. This was indeed an odd find, but we could not think of an explanation, so I put it in my kim-*oh*-no pocket, and, being now on Greycairn ground anyway, we went on to have a look at the water bubbling up through the heather by the big grey boulder where the spring was. I sat on the boulder while Fly had a drink and gave her muddy feet a wash, and 'gawped about me' again, and then I noticed the cart tracks that went east to west through the swampy ground that ran south to north below the spring. That too was funny. What would a cart be doing in here on the rough slope, when there was a road going east to west, that bridged the swamp too, just a few yards to the north, on the Reachfar side of the march dyke? Hamish the Tinker, likely, the foolish old craitur, I thought. You never knew where Hamish and Cripple Maggie and their old cart would turn up next. But no. The hoof-prints were those of a shod horse and Hamish's little hairy Sheltie had never worn a shoe in its life. Johnnie Greycairn and Diamond? No. The wheel-marks were too close set for Diamond's cart. No. It must be some new travelling tinker in the district—that would account for them travelling on the moor instead of on the road by the dyke. If they had come in through Greycairn from the south side, they would not even know that the road was there at all, if they were strangers.

Fly and I made a big round of the moor before we went home, and saw sundry other things of interest on the way, and then marched back side by side in time for supper to a new song that I had been making:

On the Greycairn Moor
I found a silver spoon.
It must have lain there many nights,
Underneath the moon.
I found it in the sunshine,
Lying in the heather.
I'll put it in a parcel for
A Present for my Mother.

At the end of this stanza we would halt smartly like the soldiers, Fly would do three barks: 'Ow! Wow! Wow!' and then
we would set off marching and do it all over again. Fly was very
good at learning to do her bit of any song we happened to have,
and we worked the last repeat of the stanza so that it took us
right to the door of the house and Fly did her three barks inside
the porch.

'The fiend's in that dog of yours today, Janet Sandison,' said
my aunt, who was coming down the stairs in her pretty blue
dance dress with the big bow at the back. 'She barked the whole
morning, nearly.'

'Is Tom putting you down to Poyntdale with Dulcie?' I
asked. 'Can I get coming?'

'Ask your mother,' she said and gave one of my pigtails a
tweak. But she smiled, so I knew I would be allowed to go,
because she would help me with the asking. So, as an end to a
great day, Tom and I drove to Poyntdale with my aunt in her
pretty dress and her big white shawl and handed her over to
Bobbie Mitchell from Drumtosh to go in *his* trap to the dance
and then Tom and I drove up the hill home in the dusk, long
after bedtime, singing 'Over the Sea to Skye'.

The next morning, at breakfast, the table was agog with the
news that my aunt had brought home from the dance. Jock

Skinner and Bella and all their children had upped and run away and the policeman was looking for Jock because he had been 'dealing' with the Army people when the camp was broken up and he had run away without paying them the money for the things he had 'bought'.

'What a scandal!' said my grandmother. 'What a Disgrace and a Scandal! As if he hadn't done enough harm already without bringing the *police* about the place!'

Dirt on Jock Skinner, I thought. I had my silver spoon in a parcel in my pocket for my mother, but it would go practically unnoticed if I gave it to her in the midst of this how-d'ye-do about Jock Skinner. *Poop* to Jock Skinner! So, after breakfast, I put the spoon parcel back in my room in my hidey-hole and went out with Fly and Angus to look for a few rats to sell to my grandfather, and did not give the spoon parcel to my mother until supper-time in the end, for I wanted my whole family to be there for the presentation, but even then it was spoiled, for before my mother could open the parcel Fly and Moss and Fan and Spark started barking and going a fearful length until, as Tom said, 'you would think it was the Chermans that was in it'.

And it was nearly as bad as an invasion of the Germans at that, for it was Constable Campbell and another policeman, and none of us at Reachfar caring over-much for policemen, things became so serious that Tom and I had to lock all the dogs in the barn, while Dick came to the moor gate and stamped his big hairy feet at the strange men as they wheeled their bicycles along the yard to the door. My grandmother gave them tea and scones and boiled eggs, and then they started asking a lot of questions and asking the names of everybody we had seen yesterday.

'God bless me, Campbell!' my father said. 'We were all at the Prize-giving—the whole district was there.'

'Dang it!' said Constable Campbell. 'So nobody was on Reachfar at all?'

'Oh, Kate was here. We always leave somebody on the place.'

They started to question my aunt, but what with my grandmother hissing about scandal and the dogs howling in the barn, you could hardly hear a word.

'Nobody at all, all the time!' my aunt almost shouted.

'And you *heard* nothing?'

'No.' Then she thought for a moment. 'But Fly—the bairn's bitchie, you know—barked for about two hours solid.'

'When was that?' my father asked.

'Shortly after you all left, she started. I went out to the end of the house to see who was coming, but there was nobody.'

'Would you be knowing the time, Miss Sandison?'

'I'm not sure. I had just fed the young pigs. Wait a minute—the mail train was just at the end of the Firth, turning north, you know.'

'That's fine. And the dog barked for a long time?'

'Yes.'

'Dad,' I said, 'Fly would be looking at where she was hearing.'

'Which way was she looking, Kate?'

'Up to the moor. She was at it until after the clock struck twelve. I was half deaved with her.'

They went on and on with their questions until I was half deaved with *them* and thoroughly tired of the whole thing and their foolishness. Where would Jock Skinner run to Reachfar when he knew he was *never* allowed to set foot on our ground?

'Mother, open the present, Mother!' I said.

So, with a Look at me, she opened it, but not in a nice way—only in a way to keep me quiet—so that I wished I had not given it to her until the next day or else had held my tongue.

'Janet, where did you get this?' she asked, without saying Thank you first, which was very unlike her.

'I found it on the moor last evening.' I was frightened now, because her face was so serious, and backed myself in between Tom and George, even although I did not see how there could be a Bother if you told the Whole Truth. My mother handed the spoon to my father.

'Whereabout on the moor, Janet? All right, nobody is angry.'

'Not our moor. The Greycairn moor, Dad.'

'Could you be showing me the very ecksact spot if I was to be walking up there with you and the policemen?' Tom asked.

'Yes, surely.'

'See the crown on the back of it?' the questioning policeman asked Constable Campbell. 'Can the lassie show us the place, Mrs Sandison?'

'Surely. Janet, you and Tom go up and show the policemen where the spoon was.'

I was delighted. It would be long past bedtime before Tom and I got back from away up there. I showed them the exact place, and then this questioning policeman who would speir a hole in your hide asked: 'And did you find anything more, Janet?'

'No, sir.'

'Chust a minute,' Tom said. 'Janet, what more did you and Fly do on your Look Round last evening?'

I told them about the interesting things like the hare and getting our feet wet and paddling up the swamp and seeing the spoon and then the important thing came to me in a flash. 'The cart—Jock's cart! It went west! That way!' and I pointed.

'Dang it!' said Tom with pride. 'I knew she wouldna have missed anything that was in it. How do you know, Janet?'

It was easy to show them the marks at the edges of the swamp below the spring. The policemen were very nice, thanked us and asked us to keep their bicycles at Reachfar for them and they went away west across the Greycairn moor into the bright evening sun which was nearly round to its bed below the Ben, taking with them, though, the spoon present that I had found for my mother. That school jingle about 'Finders keepers, losers weepers' was just a Pack of Lies, I thought.

'If I had found it on *Reachfar*, it would have been mine to keep!' I told Tom.

'Maybe,' he agreed. 'But ye have to be minding that Jock Skinner wouldna have dared to cross Reachfar Moor with it at a-all, though.'

That was true, too. The spoon was irrevocably Not Mine, seemingly.

*   *   *   *   *

One way and another, that summer holidays of 1919, my family gave me cause for a lot of thought. It seemed to me that since the Miss Boyds came, and we had had the Armistice, and I had had my ninth birthday in March, my family was Different in that it was doing things it never used to do. It did not occur to me that I was growing older and might be observing more and differently. It seemed to me that I was just the same, but that my family was Different. Take, for instance, this business of the Miss Boyds. *Last* summer, about this July–August time, my grandmother was calling them all sorts of silly craiturs, Tom was calling them 'hot-arsed-est', and George and even my father would dive into the Plough at the very sight of a Miss Boyd, and now, since their 'trouble', everybody was saying nice things about them and half my holidays were being spent in carrying compliments to them. All right, I told myself. My family usually said nice things about anybody who had trouble, and sent them compliments. But my family, now, if you please, was starting to be nice about Jock Skinner. Jock Skinner, mind you, *that* rascal! As week followed week and an Army spoon was picked up here and a fork in a pawnshop there, my father, my uncle and Tom sat round the supper-table and laughed like anything about 'Jock leading the police and the Army a bonnie dance'. Then, when the police found Bella and the children living 'off the fat o' the land' in a tenement in Inverness, and Bella swore blind that she had been a widow for two years and her husband's name had been Robert Lawrie 'when he was alive, the decent sowl, God rest him' and called Constable Campbell 'a dirty liar she had never seen before, thank God', my *grandmother* started to laugh too, as if it was all just the nicest, grandest thing that had happened in years, and said: 'Aye, Jock and Bella were well met and real fond of one another in their own way. Bella would never *tell* on him, and you have to like her for it, for goodness knows it's not many women that would have been doing with Jock's capers.'

'I wish I had seen Campbell's face when she called him a liar!' said my aunt and gave her joyous ripple of laughter, so that even my mother began to smile too.

In the end I had to have serious speech with Tom on the whole matter and told him I was 'being driven out of my head' with the way my family was changing its mind about things all the time.

'I wouldna like to see you go out o' your head,' said Tom. '*What* things, in parteeclar?'

So I told him about all this laughing about that rascal Jock Skinner.

'Och, weel,' said Tom, 'he is still a rascal and will never be anything else. But you canna but laugh when you think on that wee craitur making a fool of half the police force and them such fine big fellows with their uniforms and a-all. You have to be laughing chust to encourage him, like. Mind you, if he was to come to Reachfar, your granny would stop laughing fast enough. She would be calling him all the rascals in creation again.'

'Why?'

'People only laughs if rascals is making fools of something like the Law which isn't a real person, like a person you *know*, like.'

'Well, I wish they would stop changing their minds all the time,' I said irritably.

'I'll tell you a thing I'll be thinking, whiles,' said Tom. 'It's only fools and daft people that will never be changing their minds. People that's wise will be changing them when they'll be learning something that's new, always.'

I was prepared to consider this at a later date, as I always considered anything that My Friend Tom told me, but at the moment I was busy with Jock Skinner.

'It was Jock Skinner that made the Miss Boyds' trouble!' I said accusingly.

'So they tell me. So they tell me,' said Tom. 'But I'll not always be believing all I am hearing. It takes *two* folk and maybe more to make trouble. Aye. Even if it is only a wee bit lie. Ye canna be telling a lie—not sensible and reasonable-like, whateffer—if you have nobody to tell it *to*. Aye, there's aye more than chust the one person where there is trouble. … Well, I better give the byre a bit muck oot. I didna get at it o' the morning. Ye would give me a bit hand, maybe?'

'Och, surely.'

We set to work in the byre. 'Was I ever telling you about the time Sandy Bawn bought the horsie?' Tom enquired.

The higher philosophy got lost among the cow-dung and the story of the 'dealer' who sold Sandy Bawn a horse which was so old that its hide turned out to be grey after the brown boot polish had worn off. That, dear reader, as I told you in the early pages of this chronicle, is how I was brought up. At one moment I was hearing the wisdom of the ages in the idiom of My Friend Tom, and at the next I was deep in the dung, making the byre fit for our cow-persons to live in, and in other moments there were a million gradations in between.

All too soon, in one way, the summer holidays were over, yet, in another way, I was delighted to be going back to school, for I loved school, and especially this time, for Alasdair and I would be a little class of two, sitting together in the dominie's Big Room, where he was going to start to give us special, different lessons that would help us when we went to the Academy next year. For instance, we were going to start to learn Latin, which was a language that people spoke long, long ago, but the English language that we spoke now was flavoured with it, the way a potato carries some of the distinctive flavour of the particular soil in which it has grown.

In my family Tom was the one who could tell you the most interesting things about the Latin. Tom could read, write and count, which was more than many men of his age and who were ploughmen could do, and he was very proud of all these accomplishments, as well he might be, for they were hard won. Tom read the local newspaper, and everything he could lay his hands on when he had the time, and he had three favourite books, which were, in his order of preference, my father's eight-volume encyclopaedia, my father's big dictionary, and his own Bible. Tom's store of knowledge was literally encyclopaedic, and quite remarkable in another way, for, indeed, the encyclopaedia was all the better for the slanting light which Tom's keen intelligence shed on its dry facts.

'The Latin,' Tom told me, was the tongue invented by a race of people called the Romans, and the thing about the Romans, Tom thought, was that they were called that because they were always roaming about all over the place. Their proper home was in a city called Rome, pronounced Roh-am, in that country called Italy shaped on the map like one of Sir Torquil's riding boots, but they chust would not stop at home in Rome. No. They would be gallivanting all over the place, even up to Inverness one time, long back. Oh yes. Impudent kind of craiturs, they must have been, Tom thought, but very, very clever, and very good soldiers, nearly as good as the Seaforths nowadays. Wherever they went they made a camp for their soldiers, but somehow they had not lasted very long in Scotland— the camps, he meant. Maybe it was the hard winters that did it, especially at Inverness, for after all Tom had nearly had his own nose blown off with the wind in the High Street, even in these days, so what would it be like when the Romans were there? Down in England, though, they had got on better and had stayed there a long while, long enough for towns to get known as Such-and-such-a-Caster, which was their word for a camp. To this day, in England, there was a town called Doncaster, where, Tom understood, there was a fine market, though maybe not up to the standard of the Perth Cattle Sales. In addition to being great hands at the soldiering and making camps, Tom said, the Romans were awful handy at the building trade—making roads and houses and all the like o' that—and their other great speciality was The Law. Now, Tom himself, he would tell you, was not much of a hand for The Law. He could not see, indeed, any need for The Law at all if folk would chust be reasonable, but you had to remember that, in the old days, folk maybe were not so reasonable as they were now—not that some folk was all that reasonable even yet, when you thought of the Chermans and people like that. ... The Romans had not cared for the Chermans either, of course. ... So, anyway, the Romans had The Law, and everywhere they went The Law went with them, chust like Willie MacIntosh taking his kilt to Canada, he said. And the other thing they always took with them, Tom said, was their language, and they just *made* other people speak this language of theirs, for they, the Romans, were danged if they were going to learn any other one.

'And,' said Tom, 'the only people that would chust *not* learn this language of the Romans was the very thrawn people like the Chermans and your granny—but we won't be saying that in the house—and the Chermans stuck to their Cherman and your granny's people stuck to their Gaelic, but *reasonable* people, like you and your father and me, we would be the better of a little of the Latin because it would help us with this English that we are speaking all the time. So chust you listen careful to what the dominie says about the Latin, and come home and tell me, for if it is not too outlandish, I am willing to be learning a little of it myself.'

I promised that I certainly would listen very carefully to everything that the dominie said about the Latin and would be willing to teach Tom everything I knew.

'Indeed,' he said, 'I am knowing a little of it already, and it seems to be a very simple kind of tongue—not near as outlandish as the Gaelic whateffer. It was in a story I was reading once, about a Roman Pope-mannie—Gregory, his name was. It seems it was the way of these Roman soldiers that would be roaming about to be catching prisoners and taking them back to Rome with them and making slaves of them. ... When ye think on that, ye can see why the Romans didn't do so good with your granny's people. Your granny's people would have been making very thrawn kind of slaves, I'm thinking, always supposing the soldiers was fit to catch them in the first of it. ... But it said in this story I was reading that the soldiers had catched a puckle prisoners doonbye in England and took them back to Rome and they was all light o' the hair, like Lady Lydia, most likely. And when the Pope-mannie saw them, he was fair surprised at their light heads, for the Romans, from what I will be reading, was a dark-haired people and he asked who they were, and the soldier that had them said that they were Angle-eye, which is their word for English. And the Pope-mannie said: "Non Angle-eye sed An-jelly". Did you hear me at that? That's the Latin. And it meant "Not English but Angels". Apparently he was thinking that they must be Angels because of their light hair, but, for myself, I think that is foolish. I've never seen right what is to happen to us Highland People in the hereafter if all angels has to have light hair, so I doubt the Pope-mannie had a foolish kind o' notion there. Av coorse, Popes is of the Catholeec releegion, and different releegions has different notions about Heaven. But that's the Latin of it—"Non Angle-eye sed An-jelly". Can you mind that?'

I 'minded' it and told it to My Friend Alasdair on the first morning of school so that he and I would start equal on the Latin. Alasdair had two big brothers at the University in Edinburgh learning to be doctors and they were home for the holidays, and Alasdair had also, apparently, been going into the Latin question with them, for he said: 'I know some too!'

'Tell,' I said.

'Amo, amas, amat—' said Alasdair.

'Away with your capers!' I said. 'That isn't the Latin—that's a song!'

'It's a *Latin* song,' said Alasdair. 'This is it:

Amo, amas, I loved a lass
And she was young and tender;
Amat, alas, she fell on her ass
And hit her head on the fender.

It was a fine song, but after we had repeated it several times we began, somehow, to doubt the true Latinity of it, so that in the end 'Non Angle-eye sed An-jelly' became suspect too, and we decided that when the first Latin lesson came that afternoon we would not 'let on' to the dominie that we knew any Latin at all.

Alasdair and I, this September, became, as the French would have it, 'un peu snob' about the rest of the school and played a lot together at dinner-time, and, in a gallant sort of way, Alasdair would 'see me a bit of the way home' in the evenings. It is a well-known axiom that the distance between two points is shorter or longer according to the company one is in, and although, in the winter terms, the school came out at three, I was seldom home at Reachfar before dark, that September, and having run the last mile or two at that.

There were endless places to play and an infinite number of routes between Achcraggan School and Reachfar, but our favourite place was Jock Skinner's abandoned croft house at the corner of the Seamuir lands. It consisted of a tumbledown 'but and ben', with a decayed thatched roof, an equally tumbledown barn and a little dark wooden shed with a rusty zinc roof. Alasdair had a theory that Jock had buried some treasure in the barn and we spent a lot of time moving the old iron about looking for it. Other evenings we would be pirates or smugglers in their den, and other evenings we would be castaways on a desert island, for the sea came lapping up almost to the back wall of the house. At other times it would be a big and busy hospital, with Alasdair as the surgeon and me as the nurse, and we would 'operate' on a dead rat out of the trap we had found and set, or on a slightly decayed haddock found on the shore near the Fisher Town. Not being 'An-jelly', we had the occasional fight too, usually on some point of protocol or scientific knowledge, like the time Alasdair 'operated' the bit out of the rabbit that he said was a kidney and I said was the heart, with which he said: 'Who's the surgeon here?', picked up the patient by the hind legs and nearly brained me with it. We washed my hair in the sea afterwards, quite amicably, but my mother still gave me a slap on the bottom when I got home because of the smell I had on me.

Alasdair was purely a school companion, however, and on Saturdays and Sundays I reverted to my own solitary Reachfar amusements and did not miss him. Tom, George, Fly and Angus were my earlier companions, and I still preferred them, for I had a vague feeling that Alasdair, being 'village' and the doctor's son and having a big family of brothers and sisters, was basically different from *me*. He was interesting enough in many ways, but not the *same* as George or Tom; and although he was 'quite clever at the school', he was no use at things like making songs at all. Indeed, he was fair foolish at it. I was making a song one day about Miss Tulloch's cat that started:

Miss Tulloch's shop window
Has a big yellow cat ...

and I said to Alasdair: 'Do you know any words like window?'

And he said: 'Surely! There's plenty—there's skylight and door and chimney and—'

I called him a danged fool and we had another fight, but as soon as I came home I asked Tom the same question and he thought for a moment and then said: 'Well, the cattie's name is Belinda—I'm sure it could be Belindow for poetry, like Blow, blow thou winter *wynd*.'

And there you were, you had your song:

Miss Tulloch's shop window
Has a big yellow cat,
Her name is Belindow,
Just fancy that!

I did not play with Alasdair on Friday evenings either, for when I came out of school I had to go straight into the village and find the trap and come home with Dulcie and whoever of my family had come down with her, and I think it was the second Friday of being back at school that I found the trap at the Miss Boyds' and it was my mother and my aunt who were there, for Tom and my grandfather were too busy cutting the corn to come down. And there were four Miss Boyds there—the two old ones and Miss Annie and Miss Violet, who was sitting very quietly in a corner looking down at her hands in her lap. I looked round, but I did not see any cradle with any baby, and she certainly did not have a baby inside her, for you could always tell that, and I decided that the whole thing about that baby was nothing but a Pack of Lies. I was extremely disappointed and annoyed, having an interest in babies whether people had fathers for them or not, so when my aunt was driving us home I said: 'Mother, what happened to Miss Violet's baby?'

'Be quiet, Janet.'

'Mother, did it die?'

'No.'

'Was it all a Pack of Lies about it?'

'Yes. Now, that will do, Janet.'

It was not true. My mother had never told me a lie before, but this was a lie, and she and my aunt were far too quiet—not talking about the new cloth for the winter at Mrs Gilchrist's Drapery Warehouse or anything. Something Awful had been done with that baby. The next morning I asked Tom about it when we were down in the cornfield, but after a lot of questions he got quite nasty and snapped: 'Hold your tongue and stop deaving a man with your ask-ask-asking! I'm telling you I don't know nothing about no baby!'

That was another lie. He *did* know. In the evening I had a go at George when he came home, but he simply became clownish and said: 'Where would a poor hard-worked craitur like me that's got nothing but the Dinchory oats in my head be able to answer a-all your questions? I never even heard there was a baby in it at a-all myself.'

I knew it was all lies, every word of it, so I thought to myself that I would teach them to be going telling a person a Pack of Lies and I would find out about that baby whatever, and *poop* to them; so on Sunday evening, when they were all sitting at the tea-table and I was finished, I asked to be excused and called Fly and went off up to the moor. Then I came round in a long sweep to the east, along the north wall of the house, made Fly lie down at the west gable and crawled along the south wall till I was under the kitchen window. Sure enough, they were 'at it'.

'But, Granny,' my mother was saying in a trembling voice, 'maybe if you went down there to them you could make them see what a sin it is.'

'An orphanage in Glasgow, of all places, Mother!' said my aunt.

'God's sake.' Tom's voice sounded sick. 'There will be all kinds o' mongrel Irish and trash in a place like that!'

'And they have *money*, Granny!' said my mother.

'But listen, lassies,' my father said; 'it's not our *business!* It's all very well Granny trying to help people, but she canna go poking her nose—'

'No,' my granny said. 'That's right.'

'But, Granny, the lassie Violet is breaking her *heart* for the bairn—' said my mother.

'Aye, it must be hard, hard for her,' my granny said. 'But, Elizabeth, lassie, we *canna* go interfering in folks' private business. And what kind of life would she have with the old ones with the baby there, anyway? It's the old ones that have the money, you know. The young ones is dependent on the shoppie, and if the other two in Inverness has put her out, she has nowhere else to go. No. If they are hard enough to have put one of their own to an orphanage-place, what can a stranger like me do with them? I canna see my way clear to do a thing about it, although it is such a sin. No. The best thing we can do is try to forget all about it—that's what they seem to want.' I heard her rise, pick up the poker and make a vicious attack on the fire. 'But, mind you, they'll wait a danged long time before I put Janet down with another pot of jam to them!'

I crawled away along the side of the wall, flicked my fingers at Fly and we both ran away like deer up to the Thinking Place among the tall trees above the well. It was all very sad. And it was all very hopeless, too, for if my grandmother said that she could not do anything, it meant that there was nobody in the Wide World that could do anything, for my grandmother, if not enough in herself to deal with things, would 'speak to' Lady Lydia, Sir Torquil or the minister or anybody who could help her. My grandmother once got old Sir Turk— Sir Torquil's father—to 'speak to' the Member of Parliament, who 'spoke to' Queen Victoria about something that was not pleasing her. My grandmother, if 'she could see her way clear', took a lot of stopping, and now that they had aeroplanes I felt it was possible that even God might find Himself getting 'spoken to' by her in person. But this time 'she could not see her way clear' and that was the end of it. It was hopeless. And there was the poor baby in this orphanage, like the place that we took a penny to school for on a day before Christmas, so that the dominie could send the pennies to buy things for the orphans.

After I had cried a bit I decided that all I could do was take some of my rat-tail money and give the dominie some extra pennies this year, although that was not the same as having the baby down at the Miss Boyds' where I could have gone and seen it sometimes. This baby would never be the same as any other baby now, no matter what you did. It would always be sadly, hopelessly different from other people, for even years and years after this moment, and when it was big and grown up and able to work, people would always talk about it as 'that laddie—or lassie—down at So-and-so, that came to work there a year or two back. That might be who's at the hen-stealing. He was an

orfant, you mind, and you'll not be knowing what's *in* them.'
Even if you had no father, it was different. People would say:
'That laddie that Mary Murdoch had—the father was that wild
young ploughman that was at Dinchory but a fine worker—
he'll be all right.' But when you had nothing but an orphanage behind you, you were quite naked alone and people took
advantage of it to vent on you all the nastiness and suspicion
they had in them, whether you deserved it or not.

*   *   *   *   *

What with Alasdair and playing at pirates at Jock Skinner's and
the Latin, though, I forgot about the baby mostly, especially
now that I was not being sent with any compliments to the Miss
Boyds which might have made me remember. Tom, George
and I, on our side of the table at supper every evening, were
very busy with the Latin, for Tom would say: 'Keep your elbows
off the mensa, George, and you eating in eddicated company!'
and when it was fried haddock after the porridge for supper
George would say: 'Amo a fried haddie, Tom. They are very
bonum'; and my father used to take a fair amount of interest
in the Latin too, although not showing any ambition to speak
it himself. Then, one night after supper, he said: 'Well, we'll
have to be thinking about the seedsman's list for the spring. The
same turnips as usual, Tom?'

'Aye. The Great Purple Tops and the Maggie Borems—you'll
not do better,' Tom said and returned his interest to George and
me and the Latin.

'Janet,' my father said, 'have you ever heard of a Maggie
Borem?'

I looked at him. You would have to be deaf at Reachfar or
anywhere in our district not to have heard of a Maggie Borem,

for everybody grew them. 'Surely, Dad,' I said, 'it's an early yellow turnip.'

'Spell it for me then, till I be writing it on the order for Mr Dickson.'

So I spelled out Maggie Borem for him and he looked at the paper that Mr Dickson sent every year that told you the seed prices, and then he said: 'Well, it's not on the price list. I doubt we're not going to get them the-year.'

'Maggie Borems?' said Tom. 'Who ever heard of Dickson not having the Maggie Borem seed? They *must* be in it!'

'I'm not seeing them. My, that's terrible. Look for yourself, Tom.'

He handed us the list. 'You'd better pick out another early for me.'

Tom, George and I forgot all about the Latin, for this was next year's turnip crop and extremely serious. There were only five turnips listed under 'Yellow, middle-early', so we looked through 'Yellow-early' and 'Yellow-late' too, but there were no Maggie Borems.

'Dickson wouldn't have bothered to write it on the paper,' said George, 'for everybody buys the Maggie Borems whatever.'

And then I saw that look on my father's face that it wore when he was 'taking a rise' out of a person. I took the list from Tom and went over beside the lamp and had a right good look at these turnip seed names. 'Golden Ball,' it started, 'Carse Yellow, Magnum Bonum …' I read the words again, in to myself. 'Magnum Bonum—Maggie Borem!' I shouted.

'Where?' said Tom.

I showed him and George too. 'Dang it!' said George. 'A Maggie Borem is a Latin turnip and me thinking all this time that it was called after Old Cripple Maggie the Tinker!'

This was more or less what I had thought, and George was teasing me too, just like my father. I felt very annoyed, until my father said: 'Well, if you'll all study your Latin you'll not be like *me*, whatever. I don't like to be writing words I don't understand, so I had to be asking the dominie once what this Magnum Bonum was, away back, when I first went to Sir Torquil.'

'What did he say?' I asked.

'He was very nice. He told me it was the Latin for great good, or much good or *very* good, if you like, and that was the only Latin lesson I ever had in my life. But it is very interesting how you will mind on a thing that you like. I have always thought it was a fine name for a turnip.'

I was even more interested in my Latin after that, and so were Tom and George, for as Tom said: 'It was fair remarkable how these old Romans from a long time back was even in among the turnip seed.'

The Latin was also an excellent language for songs, for, indeed, quite a lot of it was a song already without you having to do anything to it at all, and Fly and I could march over a fair bit of the moor to the oft-repeated: 'Bellum, bellum, belli, bello, bello, bella bella, bellorum, bellis, bellis', and there was the additional fascinating corollary knowledge that Jock Skinner's wife Bella must have been called by the name because of her liking for fighting. I thought it a little odd that her parents had christened her in the plural, however, and discussed the matter with Tom, who put forward the very sensible suggestion that probably Bella's parents 'either chust hadn't minded on their Latin very good, or maybe they chust did not know that Bella was the Latin at a-all', and we decided to go on referring to her as Bella and not Bellum, although we were agreed that the latter would be more correct.

About the end of September or early October Fly and I went out early one Saturday morning to pick brambles in the Reachfar Burn, which, in its upper reaches, flowed down from the spring into a deep gully on the softer land of the hill face and this gully was overhung with long trails of thorny, heavy-yielding bramble bushes. There was a tremendous crop this year of big, black berries and we were equipped with a big basket with our 'half-yoking' scones in it to eat when we were hungry, a smaller basket to pick into, which would be emptied into the larger one after we had had our half-yoking, and my father's ashplant with the crooked handle for pulling the long, thorny branches within reach. Fly carried the small basket and I the bigger one, and I was wearing the ashplant over my shoulder like Dick Whittington as we marched to the burn. I had a plan that we must fill the little basket heaped up before we had our half-yoking, told Fly so, and as we began to pick the berries I began to make a song, for berry-picking is a job that is splendid when you first start, but gets very tedious in a very short time. The basket *never* seems to get any fuller.

Bella is a dealer's wife, Bellum is a war,
Magnum Bonum is a turnip growing on Reachfar;
Puella is a girl like me, Homo is a man,
We are picking berries for making bramble jam!

This song went very nicely to the tune of 'Onward, Christian Soldiers' and was a considerable help in the filling of the smaller basket, and Fly and I could sit down, before too long, to have our half-yoking with a clear conscience, for we now needed the big basket before we could pick any more berries. We had finished eating and had tipped the berries into the big basket when

Fly cocked her head and gave a short, low bark. I put my hand over her muzzle to keep her quiet, for it was just about the time for Bill the Post to come this way and we could jump out of the deep gully at him and give him a fright, but it was not Bill the Post. It was somebody else, somebody singing a song like me, but not my kind of song at all. It was a queer eerie song, like the wind in the roof of the barn in a storm, but not lusty or boisterous or mischievous or angry like wind. No. This song was weak, lonely and sad, ineffably sad, but the thing about it that made my neck go stiff as a post and made Fly lay her ears back along her neck and huddle close against me was that it was not a sound that belonged to the world that either of us knew. We huddled, terrified, at the bottom of the gully under the long bramble fronds, beside the friendly, chuckling Reachfar Burn and heard it go past away above us.

Tom had often told me how, in the old days, the 'old people' before the 'eddication came' used to believe in fairies and ghosties and little people and witches and whigmaleeries and all that foolishness, and he told me how, when he first came to work at Reachfar, as a boy long, long ago, he had been to Achcraggan for a message and was coming home by the light of a frosty full moon, by the short, direct way, on a long south-westerly slant across the face of the hill. He had passed through the field below the Smithy, east of which was a hump of ground known as the 'Wee Hillie', and the big frosty moon was at his back and he was coming along whistling when, suddenly, on the ground in front of him there formed a huge, ghastly, black shape, an animal shape, with four legs and a head, but legs so long and a body so big that it blotted out with its blackness the whole frosty silver of Reachfar Hill in front of him. Terrified, Tom turned to run back to the friendly Smithy and safety, and then stopped dead, for, between him and the big moon, on the top of the Wee Hillie, was the Smith's little horsie, which lived out of doors all the year round and had simply woken from sleep and was giving his legs a stretch on the hilltop. 'I never felt so foolish in a-all my life,' Tom said, 'and I thanked the Almighty that nobody was there to be seeing me. I made up my mind then that there was no such thing as ghosties in it, and that's the truth of it for I never saw a ghostie yet.'

But this was not moonlight. This was broad daylight, among the familiar brambles at the friendly Reachfar Burn, and I was not seeing a thing, but *hearing* it, and Fly was hearing it too, and shivering. The old people used to believe too in the 'bodachs', the sad ghosts who 'keened' around the Churchyard over the dead people buried there. That is what this was. It was a 'bodach keening'. I clutched Fly close to me, my right hand sunk in the comforting, strong hair under her neck, my left hand gripping the handle of the berry basket. And then, as suddenly as it had begun, it stopped. We waited for what seemed a long, long time before I decided to climb up the steep bank and go home. I did not know what I was going to say about having picked only the little basket of berries. I did not care. I was Going Home to Reachfar. I put the little basket of berries inside the big one, took my father's ashplant in my hand like a club—or a talisman for battle like King Arthur's Excalibur—and Fly and I climbed up the bank. There was nobody. There was nothing. Only the stubble field under the sun, and a rising covey of startled partridges which had been feeding. Like Tom, I felt a fool and was glad that nobody was there to see Fly and me.

We walked a little way up beside the gully where the burn ran, and there, sitting in a little bay among the brambles, was Miss Violet Boyd, making a daisy chain. I was never so pleased to see anyone in all my Born Days.

'Good morning, Miss Violet,' I said.

She looked up at me, just a glance, smiled without opening her lips, but did not speak and went on busily with her chain. It was not a real daisy chain—it was all sorts of things chained together—a thistle flower, a dandelion and a golden-red bramble leaf or two. Then I noticed that she had a late-blooming wild rose in her hair at one side and a bunch of rowan berries at the other side, and chains on her wrists and several chains of flowers and leaves round her neck already. ...

In the time that has elapsed since that day, I have seen several performances of *Hamlet*, but I have never seen an Ophelia who really broke my heart as an Ophelia should do. I know, now, that this is because, at nine years old, I saw a real, not-being-acted Ophelia. ...

At nine years old, though, I had never seen tragedy and did not recognise its grim face when I found myself in its presence for the first time. The Miss Boyds had always been 'different', and now this one was at this caper of making flower chains. It was a game for little children that I myself had long outgrown, and my aunt, who was about Miss Violet's age, would never indulge in it, but I had known the Miss Boyds to giggle and nudge one another in the street, just like the wee ones in the Baby Class when the minister spoke to them, so the flower chains were not too surprising in a Miss Boyd.

'Did you hear the singing a little while ago?' I asked her in a hushed voice.

She looked at me again with that fleeting glance, smiled again without opening her lips and went back to her concentration on her chain.

She was not wearing her spectacles and her face had a soft,

unprotected look and a stillness that was not usually in the fluttering-glance faces of the Miss Boyds.

'Did you hear it, Miss Violet?' I persisted, but she merely sighed and added another dandelion to her long chain.

Suddenly I knew what was the matter with her. She had had to have her teeth out, and was shy about it, like Mr Dickson, Ironmonger and Seed Merchant's sister had been when her teeth had had to come out, and my mother had told me just to wish Miss Dickson Good Day, not bother if she did not speak to me, and Not To Gawp At Her. I Did As I Was Told, and then, one day, when Tom and I went to buy some nails at the shop, there she was, all smiles, having grown a lot of beautiful white new teeth. When a hen was hatching chickens I knew, you must not chase her off the nest, for the eggs had to be kept warm all the time, and I thought it must be very much like that when you were growing new teeth. I could remember growing some new teeth myself when I was about six and a half and some of them had been sore when they were coming; so if you were grown up they would be bigger teeth and probably sorer still.

Then Miss Violet rose from her seat among the bramble bushes, gave me her soft, closed-mouth smile again, reached forward and hung her chain of flowers round my neck and walked away down the slope of the field in the direction of the County Road and the shore. 'Good day, Miss Violet!' I called after her, but she did not seem to hear me.

I felt better now, though, and Fly was no longer shivering but had her ears cocked up and was poking about around the bushes after rabbits as usual. I began to think that I had never really heard that singing at all, and that my Imagination Had Run Away With Me again, as it had done the night the eagle came in through the skylight of my room to carry me away in its claws to its eyrie up the Ben, tear me apart and feed me to its eaglets. I screamed until the whole house was awake, and my mother told Tom and George to get their guns and have a good look for this eagle, but all they found was a young swallow that had mistaken my skylight for the nest-place under the eaves of the house, and having come into the room could not find its way out. Tom brought it down from the far rafter where it had perched and gave it to me and then held me up to the skylight with it in my hands so that it could fly away. Everybody agreed that a person's Imagination Could Run Away With Them sometimes, and could give a person quite a fright, but you soon Got Over It. I had Got Over It now—it had been lucky meeting Miss Violet, but the thistle in her flower chain was pricking my neck, so I took it off and hid it away far down in a rabbit-hole in the gully so that her feelings might not be hurt by finding it discarded. Then Fly and I filled the little basket three times more with berries before we heard the Poyntdale sawmill away down the burn stop its whining, which told us it was time to go home for dinner.

Tom, my aunt and I came out to the berries again in the afternoon, for you had to catch the bramble crop before the first frost came down and it could come any night now that we were getting into October, which was the real 'backend o' the year', and, while we picked, my grandmother already had the big brass-lined jam pan with the first lot of berries swinging from the crook over a big fire. We picked until it was dark and had three big baskets full, but there were still more, we told my grandmother, when we reached home.

The next day, being Sunday, we went to church as usual in the morning, but after dinner, when my grandfather had gone off for his Sunday sleep, Tom said: 'What about the brambles, mistress?' Tom was very, very fond of bramble jam—not jelly, like the 'fushionless' stuff that the shops sold—but thick black jam with whole berries in it. 'It's going to freeze, mistress. Did you notice the Ben this morning?'

'Aye, and I could count the windows in the train across the Firth yesterday,' my grandmother said. She glanced at the ceiling where my grandfather was moving about above. 'There is frost in it, right enough. Look, take the baskets and be off—don't let Granda hear you. What he doesna know won't be on his conscience and the fruits o' the earth weren't given to us for us to let them get spoiled. … Just put the baskets in the milk-house when you come back and come in and don't say a word. … No, Kate, you canna go. If you're not here for early tea he'll think it funny, but he'll not bother himself about *that* three.'

That Three, of course, was George, Tom and me, so my grandmother gave us a picnic tea to carry and off we went, tiptoeing and giggling just for fun along the yard, for my grandfather would probably already be asleep. I had been sick and tired of picking berries the evening before, but picking them with Tom and George on a Sabbath Day was different. When we reached the gully they made a great to-do of stripping off their second-best jackets and rolling up their shirtsleeves, and Tom said: 'The way to go about a chobbie like this, George, man, is to get started and not be stopping to gawp about you or light your pipe or anything, but chust pick like the devil and when the baskets is full your time is your own.'

'That's chust the way,' George agreed, and reaching up far, far, with his stick he bent down a great big branch, loaded with berries, which spread itself across the grass. 'Would ye be having a staple about ye, Tom?' he asked.

Tom reached into his trousers pocket, produced a big fencing staple and George pegged the branch to the ground with it and put a heavy stone on top of the staple. 'There, Janet,' he said, 'chust you sit down there and fill your little baskety at your ease.'

This was a magnificent way to pick brambles, sitting on the grass, no danger of being scratched or getting your hair caught, simply reaching round you and picking the berries off one big plume after another. This one big branch filled my basket and I tipped it into Tom's and went to take out the staple to release the branch again.

'No, Janet!' George called. 'Come out o' that! We're not needing you stuck up in the air like a bramble.' He took me out of the centre, we stood back and he hit the stone off with his stick. 'Watch for our staple!' he shouted and with a whoosh the released branch went up in the air. I retrieved the staple from where it had flown and we pegged down another big branch. Tıying to be helpful, I placed the staple over the main limb for him, but he said: 'No, not that way—*this* way,' and he set it at a different angle. '*Your* way we'd lose our staple down the gully when we let the branch go. This way, it will fly back out to us.'

'Why?'

'We-ell, it's the angle o' the top o' the staple, like. I canna tell ye the areeth*met*ic of it. … Tom, man, what would be the Latin for bramble, now, think ye?'

'Brambellum, man! I was thinking you would be knowing that. Magnum bonum brambellum!' said Tom, eating a great big crown berry.

'Stop your capers!' I said in my grandmother's voice. 'And put them in your *basket.*'

In spite of all their capers, though, George and Tom with a little help from me had filled four big baskets in no time at all, and then we filled my little basket with Special Select berries to make a tart before sitting down to have tea.

'Well,' said George, 'the frost and the village people can get the rest, but I doubt it will be the frost. Still, there's not many left. My, it's a grand day for the back-end. Now then, Mistress Janet, where's this tea you have for us hardworking men?'

After we had had our tea and scones and butter and jam and the pieces of Sunday cake that my grandmother had put in, wrapped in a special paper bag, Tom and George filled their pipes and sat looking away down the slope to the hills at the other side of the Firth. I took off my shoes and went away to have a paddle in the Burn with Fly. The water was very cold, but it was fun to stay in until you felt you had no feet at all and then hop out on to a warm stone or the warm grass. After a spell at this, and having paid a call on Donald the Trout, I hopped my way in and out of the water upwards again, and suddenly thought of a way of giving Tom and George a good fright. I would creep up the course of the Burn into the gully and see if I could sing like a bodach keening just under the place where they were sitting. So Fly and I made a proper, silent, poacher's approach, and soon we were inside the tunnel of bramble fronds, right below where they were sitting, yarning.

'Aye, it's a terrible thing right enough,' George was saying. 'Clean out of her head, they tell me she is, the poor craitur.'

'Och, fair fearful, man,' Tom was saying. 'You'll often see a cow go that way when they'll be taking the calves away and them moaning like to break your heart. That's the way I am in favour of the hand-feeding from birth with the milking cows— apart altogether from the calves sucking making the teats tough. Aye. A man person canna understand it right, but it is a cruel thing.'

'Aye. It is that.'

There was a silence between them, and into it I put my first keening note, making it as good an imitation of that bodach I thought I had heard as I could. There was a jerky, uneasy movement up above. It was working—I was going to get them on the run. I crouched lower, opened my mouth and had a second, even more artistic go, that made Fly look at me as if she could not believe what she heard, her head on one side, her tan-fringed ears cocked forward above her amber eyes. I had to end a fine, long, ululating trill in order to have a silent giggle.

'God sake, man, George, there's a kelpie in the Burn!' said Tom.

'Michty me! Where's the bairn, Tom? We must be off!— Fly! Fly here!' He gave a long, piercing whistle and I tried to hold Fly, but this was too much. Fly had been trained from my infancy to respond in some way to that whistle which would tell my family where we were and now, even though I tried to hold her muzzle, she jerked her head free and barked.

'Ye danged wee deevil!' said my uncle, peering down through the brambles. 'What a fright to be giving us and us taking our ease on the Sabbath Day!'

'It's me that thought for sure that it was a kelpie that was in it!' said Tom.

It was a grand joke, and they seemed to have had a right good fright, and shortly after that we started for home with our baskets of berries.

'Have you seen anything o' that Miss Boyds this whilie back?' George asked casually of Tom when we were well on the way.

'Not since long, to be speaking to, whatever, George,' Tom replied. 'Why was you asking?'

209

'I was hearing the other day that Doctor Mackay was thinking maybe the youngest one—what's her name now?'

'Miss Violet?' I said.

'Aye—Miss Violet has the measles or something o' that kind. He was saying that people—especially bairns—should keep away from their house for a whilie, for he's not wanting the school full o' the measles. If you get the measles, you have to be stopping out of school for a month or more.'

This was Awful. Imagine missing a whole month of Latin! 'Doctor Mackay is just a foolish mannie!' I said defiantly—defying all measles and all infectious complaints that could keep a person out of school. 'Miss Violet's *not* got measles! Measles is red spots! She's just had her teeth out, that's all!'

'Oh, is that it?' said Tom. 'Was you seeing her, then?'

'Yes, just yesterday, when I was out at the berries, and she had no spots on her. She was fine!'

'Was she now? I'm pleased to hear that. Was she picking berries too?'

'No. She was making flower chains and then she went away.'

'So you was speaking to her?' Tom asked.

'Surely! … But she just sort of smiled, like Miss Dickson before she got her new teeth. She hasn't got measles at all.'

'Still, it's not like Doctor Mackay to make a mistake,' George pursued after a moment. 'He is a very clever man, writing yon medicine papers in the Latin and all. Maybe the measles is in her right enough, although the spotties isn't showing yet. Anyway, it's not *me* that's going near her or to the house or anything.'

'Nor me neither,' said Tom. 'Indeed, if I'll be seeing her, the best thing to do would be to go home and tell Granny. People shouldn't be going about on Reachfar ground with that measles in them.'

'That's quite true, Tom, man. It would be a devil of a chob if Dick or one o' the cows was to get the measles,' said George. 'Tom, man, what would be the Latin for measles?'

'Measlums,' said Tom. 'Measlum, measlum, measli, measlo, measl-oh! That's the way it goes.'

It made a very good song, along the lines of 'There was an old man called Michael Finnegan':

George and Tom each had a measlum,
On their nose and on their chin again.
The wind came out and blew them in again,
Poor old George and Tom. Begin again ...

and we sang it all the way home, but stopped well out of hearing of the house, of course, because of the Sabbath Day, and sneaked quietly to the milkhouse with our baskets.

I came to the conclusion that the Miss Boyds must have the measles in their house right enough, though, for I did not see any of them around the village for the next week or two. I thought of asking Alasdair about it, for he would know, but I decided not to, for I often had a kind of feeling that it was better 'chust to be taking no notice at a-all' of a thing like measles, in case they might hear you and come and land on you, the way the bees would come and settle in a big ball on Danny Maclean's hand when he made a certain noise.

And, of course, I had a great many other things to think about, for, as I mentioned to Tom, the more you became grown-up and the more things you learned about, the more things there still seemed to be that required to be learned about. There seemed to be no end to it, I told him.

'That's so,' Tom agreed. 'That's chust the way of it. It is very interesting. It is chust like the way the more you *have* to do, the more you *will* do. If people has only a little to do, they get lazy and don't want to do even that little.'

'Why is that, Tom?'

'I don't know right. I think it is chust contrariness. Life is very, very contrary, like yon bittie in the Bible that I can never get the hang of, about "from him that hath not shall be taken away". The best a person can do is chust do their best. As the Reverend Roderick will be saying, there is some things that is too wonderful for *me* a-altogether.'

There was a sadness about Tom and George these days. There was a sadness in everyone round Reachfar, indeed, but, naturally, I noticed it more in Tom and George than in the others. It was a bleak, grey sadness, which made them frown and stare away across the Firth to the hills with eyes that seemed to search for some hidden explanation. It was a dumb, closed sadness, as if they were shutting their minds against some injustice which they did not want to recognise, as if, not finding recognition, it would clear away like mist before the sun.

I to the hills will lift mine eyes,
From whence doth come mine aid …

That is what they made me think of when they gazed away to the Ben in that puzzled way, but the aid did not come. The greyness remained, lurking, ready to spread through the air around us like a fog at some chance word or action, as on the day when I said: 'Look here, you two, what about the Harvest Home this year? It will soon be time, won't it?' The greyness came down. 'I don't think there is going to *be* a Harvest Home this year,' George said.

'That's foolishness, George Sandison!' I was indignant. 'There is *always* a Harvest Home!'

'Wheesht! Not so loud,' said Tom, although we were away up in the stackyard where nobody could hear us and it wasn't Badness to talk about the Harvest Home as it was to imitate the minister, anyway.

'*Why* isn't there going to be?'

George leaned on his rake and stared away at the Ben in that searching way, and Tom said: 'Well, ye see, since the War things is not the same. Apples and raisins and things is very, very dear, and your father says that the Laird kind of feels that he canna *afford* it like he used to.'

'But we don't *have* to have raisin dumpling! We could sing and dance—'

'Listen,' George said. 'I don't think we should be speaking about it. If Sir Torquil feels that he canna afford it, to be speaking about it and showing that a person is disappointed will chust make things worse for him. For *me*, I am chust going to go on as usual as if I had never even *heard* o' such a thing as a Harvest Home.'

'But you are disappointed all the same, George?'

'Och, aye, surely. But when a person's disappointed it's better to be disappointed in to yourself and not be bawling about it at people. That only makes it worse. ... Man, Tom, I wish I had a sweetie! You wouldna have a black-strippit ball about you?'

'If it's *my* jar of black-strippit balls that Mr Macintosh gave me that you're hinting at,' I told him, 'Granny has it away on the top shelf of the kitchen press and you know fine that she's in there, baking.'

'If she wasna there you would be willing to give us one, though?'

'Surely.'

'That's fine.' George hung his rake on the nearest stack. 'Come, Tom.'

The two of them clattered away down the yard in their big boots and disappeared round the end of the loosebox. In two minutes my grandmother was in the stackyard.

'Where are they off to?'

'I don't know, Granny. They just took a notion and went off.'

'I'll notion them!' she said.

She too turned eastwards out of the stackyard and went off down the outside yard. I ran swiftly down the west side of the garden, into the house, up on to a chair and extracted a dozen black-strippit balls from the jar. As I ran back up to the stackyard, concealed by the garden hedge, my grandmother was returning along the yard, her apron gathered up in front and a pleased look on her face.

'I knew that speckled hen was hiding her eggs,' she was saying. 'I am real pleased the two of you happened to notice her, the brute!'

It was remarkable what a number of our hens developed this habit of 'laying away', and more remarkable still how it was always George and Tom who could find their hidden nests. I knew at this time that George and Tom 'had the knack' of making a hen lay in some spot that they chose, so that they always had a trump card of eight or nine unexpected eggs up their sleeves to be played as and when required, but in spite of a lot of study of hen habits and all sorts of efforts with decoy eggs in nice-looking places, I never developed this knack myself.

Having seen my grandmother into the house to take the eggs out of her apron, the three of us sat down in the lee of a stack and had four black-strippit balls each, but even now I cannot see these mournful-coloured sweets or smell their sugar-peppermint scent without feeling again that searching, wandering sadness, which was my first knowledge that the world I knew was subject to change and was not, as I had thought, a steady, constant thing created to wait, ready and beautiful, for me to explore it as if it were some treasure-box of bright jewels.

*   *   *   *   *

Near the end of October, on a cold, windy day with sleety showers, Fly and I went out to the East Moor on a Saturday morning to bring the ewes in-bye for Tom, for my grandmother said that, early in the winter as it was, she was smelling snow.

'It's two score that's out east,' said Tom. 'Be sure you have them all, Janet.'

Fly and I set off, while Tom went to the west to get the other flock. The three moors of Reachfar were distinct in character. The West Moor, which Tom had gone to gather, was hillocky and scarred by a deep watercourse like the Reachfar Burn, but more rough and rocky and the sheep would hide in the crannies, which made them difficult to find. The Home Moor was the one with the trees, just above the house, with the high heather, the wild flowers in summer, and was the winter shelter for the sheep. The East Moor, to which I was headed, was a long slope of grassy hill, bleak, stony and unsheltered, and when you emerged on to it from the trees of the Home Moor you could round up the sheep with ease. Its only feature of interest was the spring that was the rise of the Reachfar Burn which, up here, was only a stony trickle among the boulders. The sheep would come in gladly from the East Moor when there was a threat of bad weather, and as they filed through the little gate into the wood, they could be counted easily, for I was not as clever at counting sheep in a packed, moving flock as Tom and George were.

When I reached the little gate the wind came lashing up from the north-east, edged with stinging sleet that poked like needles through my woollen hood and the backs of my woollen gloves, so I crouched behind a juniper bush and sent Fly out over the grey-green hill. She did not waste any time, but gathered the ewes in and brought them to the gate, and they filed past into the shelter, I counting them carefully. Thirty-eight.

'Dang it!' I said to her cocked head. 'Two more!' I waved a hand at the long slope and off she went, down and round by the spring. She came back with only one ewe, chased it through the gate and then began to jump about and bark. I had to follow her out into the teeth of the wind after closing the gate and she led me away down the slope to the moor's edge. The sleet thinned a little and I saw the last ewe, her wool hopelessly entangled in the barbed wire of the fence. Fly lay down while I pulled my coat up against the tearing wind and got out my knife. It did not take a second to free the ewe and she galloped away, gladly and of her own accord, up to the gate, and then, carried on the wind and mingling with it, coming from the little hollow beyond the boulder by the spring, I heard the bodach's sad, keening song. For a moment Fly and I stood rigid in the freezing wind, and then I saw the edge of a blue coat by the boulder. Bodachs did not wear blue coats. Fly and I crept forward and looked over the top of the big stone, and there sat Miss Violet, nursing a dead rabbit which she had wrapped in what looked like a woollen jumper. Her hands were as blue as her coat, and her hair, which was decorated all over with sprigs of withered heather, hung round her face in wet, lank rat-tails.

Measles or no, this was no place for a person to be sitting

when my grandmother was smelling snow.

'Good day, Miss Violet,' I said.

She gave me her queer, closed-mouth smile, looked down at the rabbit and began to sing the bodach's eerie song to it, rocking it a little and patting it with her right hand.

'Baby, baby,' she said then in a funny, high voice and began to sing again.

Some of the girls at school played at 'babies' in the dinner-hour with their rag dolls or even pieces of stick to be the babies, and would be feeding them with their dinner pieces and all that sort of capers. It was funny for a grown-up person to be playing babies, but there you were—you never knew what these Miss Boyds would be at next.

So, 'It needs its dinner,' I said, just to see what would happen.

She nodded at me in a pleased way, sprang to her feet and pushed me roughly in the direction of the gate where the ewe was waiting. I felt a little frightened now, because she looked so odd and wild, and I said in a shaky way: 'It needs milk for its dinner.'

'Home!' she said. 'Milk! Baby!' And gave me another strong, rough push.

I knew now that she was sick or something, and apart from that I wanted my mother, my grandmother and my *family*, so I said: 'Yes, milk for the baby! Come!'

She followed me docilely, carrying the rabbit, stumbling now and then on the rough ground, and after each stumble she would sing a little and pat her 'baby'. The sheep scattered away in the shelter of the trees, and Fly, Miss Violet and I followed the shortest route back to Reachfar.

When I opened the door of the big warm kitchen where my

aunt was baking and my mother and my grandparents were drinking a 'fly cup' of tea, I had never been so pleased to see my family in all my life.

'I brought Miss Violet,' I said, and ran to stand beside my mother.

It was not my Grandmother but my granny who rose slowly from the chair beside the fire, her fine old eyes fixed on the cold, rain-streaked, white face. 'My, it's myself that is pleased to see you, Miss Violet,' she said, and then she looked at the dead rabbit. 'And you brought the baby to see me too! My, that's fine. Come, then, to the fire and be warming yourself.'

'Come, Janet,' my mother said, and took me away through to the parlour where she kneeled down and lit the laid fire although it was only Saturday and not Sunday.

'Mother, is Miss Violet sick?'

'Yes, Janet. She is sick in her mind.'

'Is that why she thinks that rabbit is a baby?'

'Yes. … Now, I am going to get you a drink of milk and a scone, and then you'll have to go to the West Moor and get Tom. We'll have to put a message down to Achcraggan.'

Fly and I found Tom among the hillocks of the West Moor and told him about Miss Violet and her rabbit baby, and we came back to the house, and my mother brought oatcakes and butter and cheese and tea to Tom in the parlour. Then I had to go to his room and get his other working boots and a pair of dry socks for him. It was very funny to see Tom taking his wet, muddy boots off in the parlour—I had never seen such a thing in all my Born Days—and then my mother said: 'And now I am going to put Janet's oilskins on her, Tom, and you will just take her with you for company and to hold Dulcie and things for you.'

'That will be right handy,' said Tom.

I was delighted to go with Tom, for the kitchen was not very nice with poor Miss Violet and her rabbit baby sitting at the fire and I did not want to be left alone in the parlour on a Saturday, either, for that was far too odd a thing for comfort. I would far rather be out in the rain with Dulcie and Tom.

'And, Tom,' my mother said at the door, 'just you stop at Poyntdale and tell Duncan about Miss Violet, just in case you miss the doctor at Achcraggan. If the news gets round that he's wanted at Reachfar somebody will stop him on the road.'

Tom and I went away along the yard to the stable to harness Dulcie, and as we passed the kitchen window we could hear Miss Violet singing another little eerie song to her rabbit baby, and the voice of my grandfather telling her what a bonnie bairn she had.

When we were in the trap, under the cover that was a leopard-skin on one side and leathery, waterproof stuff on the other, I got close to Tom and put my hand in his pocket the way I had not done since I was very, very small and not at school yet, and we drove through the sleet down the hill to Poyntdale.

When we drove into the Square I climbed down and ran to the big threshing barn which was the likeliest place to find my father on a wet winter day, and, sure enough, he was in there talking to Sir Torquil and Lady Lydia and I told them what my mother had said.

'Duncan,' said Lady Lydia, 'ask them to yoke the old brougham.'

My father called a man who was sewing bags of oats and gave the order.

'And she—she's nursing a dead rabbit for a baby, Dad, and—and, since she came in to the fire, it's starting to stink.'

'Wheesht, lassie!' my father said.

'Never mind, Janet,' Lady Lydia told me. 'I'll get a better baby for Miss Violet. You run to Tom now and go on to Achcraggan.'

I ran away into the sleet again and Tom and I went on to the village and the Miss Boyds' house. We had an awful job with the Miss Boyds. They were not people like my family and Lady Lydia and Sir Torquil, who could always tell Tom and me what to do. Oh no. We had to tell *them* what to do, and Tom and I were not used to that. Only the two old ones and Miss Annie were there and I was glad there were no more of them, with the running about and crying and wringing their hands they went in for. At last Tom got quite impatient and rude to them and said: 'For God's sake, stop your fecklessness, leddies! Miss Annie better come with us and you two stop here until we are coming back and get her bed ready and be boiling a kettle or something!'

'Yes, yes!' they said, and one of the old ones grabbed a kettle, the other took it away from her, then they dropped it altogether and ran and got two coats and started to put both of them on Miss Annie, but at last we had her in the trap and we set off for the doctor's house. We could see the doctor and Mrs Mackay and Alasdair at their dinner through the rain-streaming window, and when the doctor saw us he jumped up from the table and ran out to his front porch.

'Something wrong with the Reachfar people, Tom?'

'Well, not ecksactly, Doctor,' said Tom, and then told him about Miss Violet and her rabbit baby.

'Uh-huh! I see. All right. Come in for a minute, the lot of you, till I get my bag.' He went into the hall, bellowing: 'Hey, Dougal! Yoke the trap. Mother, give Tom a dram. God sake, what a day! Alasdair, go up the stair for my big, old water-proof—the fishing one. ... Let me see now...'

He disappeared into his surgery. I stood in the hall eating biscuits while a pool formed round me, while Tom, standing in another pool, drank his big dram of whisky and water.

'Put this on you,' Mrs Mackay said to Miss Annie, and made her put a great big oilskin on top of her own coat. 'It will be cold on the hill today, and you are not like this hardy little Highland garran,' and she patted my wet sou'wester and gave me another biscuit.

The doctor came out of his surgery. 'Expect me when you see me, Mother. Behave yourself, boy! ... Tom, you and Janet go first. You come with me, Miss Boyd.'

This was better. Much relieved, Tom and I got in under our leopard-skin behind Dulcie and set off for home, happy, in a selfish way, that poor Miss Annie, so frightened, was no longer sitting between us, but we did not talk much. The sleet came down in a steady, steely slant, everything was grey and dripping wet, and all the houses were shut tight against the weather, making the out-of-doors lonely and sad.

When we got to Reachfar I ran to the house and let myself quietly into the passage, and my mother came out to help me to take off my wet clothes.

'Miss Violet has been asking to see you,' she said gently. 'Don't be frightened of her, pet. Just talk to her canny and gently as you do when I have a headache. Come.' She opened the kitchen door and said: 'Here's Janet back from school, Miss Violet.'

Miss Violet gave me her beautiful, happy, closed-mouth smile—quite different from her former sad one—and then bent her head with a curious humble pride to the big doll—just like the one Maddy Lou had given me and I had broken—that she was holding in her arms. Then she looked up at me and smiled again. Lady Lydia and my granny were sitting beside her and nodding in the happy way they always nodded when they went to see somebody's new baby.

'Miss Violet!' I said. 'My, what a bonnie baby!'

It was Awful to be talking to a Grown-up Person in this pretending way, but my mother smiled as if it were all right, so I bent towards the doll and talked a bit more, just as if it were real.

'*Everybody* is coming to see the baby,' my granny said, 'Sir Torquil and Doctor Mackay and everybody!'

Blissfully, Miss Violet smiled at us all again and then looked back at the doll. I wanted, dreadfully, to get away back out into the rain with Tom, but just then they all came in—George, my father, Sir Torquil, Tom, the doctor, everybody all in a heap, and my mother held Miss Annie back in the passage.

They all, just as if it were a real baby, admired the doll, and Sir Torquil gave Miss Violet a silver sixpence for it for luck, as he gave to all the new babies, and then my granny said: 'And Annie is here to take you and the baby home.'

The brooding happiness left the face, the head reared up, the eyes flashed wild, and she gathered the doll close with a fierce protectiveness. I was frightened of her, but not my granny. More my granny than ever, she bent close over the doll and said in her soft, West Highland, crooning voice—so different from the voice that issued the endless orders around Reachfar—'Och, come now, Miss Violet, lovie. Let your poor sister see your bonnie, bonnie baby. Annie, did you ever in your life see a baby as bonnie as that?'

'But we must go home, though, and get it to bed,' said Miss

Annie in a frightened, trembling way.

'Och, take your time, woman!' said the sudden voice of my grandmother. 'Sit here beside your sister and see the baby and we'll all have a droppie tea before you go. ... Kate, make a droppie tea. Janet will help you.'

I began to feel that if I did not hold on to all my senses they would have *me* believing that that was a real baby before they were done, but, anyway, the doll was better than that half-rotten rabbit that had been lying in some snare or another for days, most likely. I laid out the cups and saucers, and then Doctor Mackay came over to the table with a little brown bottle in his hand, and my aunt, after he whispered something to her, deliberately took a matching saucer from under a cup and put one that did not match in its place. Then the doctor put something out of the bottle into the cup. He had just put the bottle into his pocket when Miss Violet took one of her funny notions, took a piece of the heather out of her hair and, with a gentle smile, handed it to him. He thanked her, tickled the doll's cheek with his finger and, coming back to the table, put the piece of withered heather in his buttonhole. Then he said something that sounded very beautiful, like the last notes of Danny Maclean's fiddle fading away on a summer evening. I said: 'I beg your pardon?' for I wanted to hear it properly. But he only smiled and said: 'Never mind, Janet. Maybe one day I will tell you, if you will remind me.'

Tom and I had potatoes and meat with our tea because we had missed our dinner, and Miss Violet let my mother hold the doll while she drank her tea and ate her cake, but when Tom and I had not nearly finished eating my father said: 'Come on!' and jerked his head at the passage through to the parlour. Lady Lydia, my aunt and everybody was already filing out, and my

223

mother, my granny and the doctor were standing round Miss Violet. She was leaning back in her chair fast asleep! My father took Miss Annie by the arm and led her to the parlour, and I was just behind them.

'Now, Miss Annie,' Sir Torquil said, planting himself on the rug with his back to the fire, 'what have you and these sisters of yours done with the child, huh?'

My goodness, but Sir Torquil was angry, as angry as he was on the day that the second coachman got drunk and drove the greys against the barbed wire.

'Just you make up your mind, madam, that that child is to be fetched back here to Achcraggan. You understand? We'll all help you and your sisters in every way we can, but that child comes *back.*'

'Sir, I always *wanted* the baby!' wailed Miss Annie. 'It's my sisters—'

'Damn and blast your sisters! I WILL COME DOWN AND SEE THEM MYSELF!'

I think I would have taken root in the parlour carpet with terror if Tom's big hand had not reached in through the door and grabbed me by the back of the neck.

'Come on up the stair!' he hissed. 'I stole the plate o' cake off the table when your granny wasna looking!'

So Tom and I went up and got under the blankets on Tom's bed to keep warm and had a fine picnic on the cake, except that George came up before we had properly started and went off with three big lumps although he had not been to Achcraggan in the rain or anything. However, 'what a friend will be getting is not lost' as Tom said, and by the time the three of us had discussed a few odds and ends of things we just got to the window in time to see the coachman bring the brougham to the door, saw my father lift Miss Violet, still sleeping, into it, then Miss Annie got in with the doll and then Doctor Mackay. Then, oh dear, Sir Torquil got in too and the door closed.

'Poor little craitur,' said George.

'Craiturs, you mean,' I said. 'There's two of these Miss Boyds down there and Sir Torquil is awful wild.'

'Aye, and weel he might be!' said Tom, in just as vicious a voice as I had ever heard My Friend Tom use in all my Born Days.

'George!' my father called up the stairs. 'Would ye drive the doctor's pony back to Achcraggan for him?'

'Aye, surely,' said George.

We three went downstairs and I asked to go in the doctor's trap.

'Not your foot-length!' said my grandmother. 'What would you be doing going away there in the rain?'

Not a word about herding sheep in the rain this morning. Oh no. Not my grandmother. She only noticed the rain when it danged well suited her. 'And take that thrawn look off your face—how you got to be as thrawn as you are, it's me that does *not* know. Tom, you'll have to drive Leddy Lydia down in a little whilie.'

'Thank you, Tom, I'll be grateful.' Lady Lydia turned to my mother. 'Elizabeth, my dear, I wonder if you notice it, but I see Janet getting very like her granny as she gets older.'

'Yes, Lady Lydia. I've noticed it,' said my mother with her secret, gentle smile.

'Like *me?*' said my grandmother. 'Capers and nonsense! She is the spit of her mother!'

'In face, I agree,' Lady Lydia smiled.

My grandmother glared at me. I glared back. 'Please, Granny, can I get to go to Poyntdale, then, with Tom and Lady Lydia?'

I did not see anything to laugh at, but Lady Lydia began to laugh—like a hyena, I would have said, if it wasn't Lady Lydia—and then my mother and my aunt and Tom and George all joined in too. My grandmother looked round sternly at them all, and then at my grandfather in his big chair by the fire.

'Och, aye. Och, aye,' he said peaceably to nobody in particular and went on smoking his pipe.

'Iphm!' said my grandmother, tight-lipped, and turned to me. 'All right, be off to Poyntdale ! It's no use my telling you to do anything or not do it, I see. So I'll tell you no more.' I ran to the door. 'Come back here this minute!' she commanded. 'If you are going to walk back from Poyntdale in this rain put on your moor boots.'

I started to put on my boots and they all sat around laughing as if they were crazy. There were times when I thought that the only two people in the world that had any Real Sense were my grandmother and me—*we* saw nothing to laugh at in the amicable settlement of an ordinary piece of household business.

During the next few days nobody seemed to want to talk very much about Miss Violet thinking that that doll was a real baby, and it was nasty to go to bed at night in my attic bedroom and hear the November wind howling, because it made me remember that eerie song on the East Moor and then finding her there with the dead rabbit, and I wondered if she sat down at the Miss Boyds in Achcraggan and sang like that to the doll. Then, with the wind and the rain on the roof and everything, it would get so that I could *hear* the song, and I would start to think that maybe she was wandering out there on the moor with the doll in her arms in the wet cold. Even reciting all my Latin nouns and verbs and all my school poetry and all my homemade songs did not help—I just could *not* go to sleep because of that eerie song being sung to that unreal baby. After several nights of being very frightened, I held on to my mother when she was going downstairs after seeing me to bed, which was a thing that only little bairns did and Shameful in someone who was nine years old, and I said: 'Mother, what *about* Miss Violet?'

My mother sat down on my bed and said: 'Poor Miss Violet. It is kind of you to be thinking about her, Janet. What were you thinking?'

'Could we not get a *real* baby for her? If she had a real baby, she would have to stop singing that funny song because the baby wouldn't like it.'

'You think not?'

I was positive. 'No *real* baby would like it—like—like a bodach keening.'

'Well, I'll have to find out. Sir Torquil is getting a real baby for her, you know.'

'He *is?* When?'

'Just as soon as he can—he is away in Glasgow now, seeing if he can get one.'

'From the orphanage?'

'Yes.'

'Will he get her own proper one?'

'Likely he will. That is what he wants, and Sir Torquil is a bit of a lad for getting what he wants.'

'That's fine,' I said. 'And you mark my words, Mother, when she gets her own baby it won't let her sing that song to it.'

'Maybe you are right,' my mother said. 'Are you going to sleep now?'

'Yes. Good night, Mother.'

She went away, carrying the candle, and I did not hear the eerie song that night. Indeed, I never heard it again.

* * * * *

That winter was unlike all the winters I had ever known. We had the 'tattie holidays', but there was not to be a coal boat because of some funny reason to do with 'after the war', and the coal came in to Fortavoch (pronounced Fort-*a-ach*, with the accent thrown back) Station, the rail terminus that was twelve miles by road from Poyntdale, and we children did not get a holiday. Dominie Stevenson said that if the engine that pulled the coal in had been there it would have been worth seeing, but it had pulled out again in the middle of the night, and who would go twelve miles to see a few carts like big barrows sitting on rails in a place called a siding? From Reachfar we sent Dick and Betsy to help with the carting, but Dulcie did not go, for she was not strong enough for the big loads and the long hard haul. And none of the people like Johnnie Greycairn and Diamond went—poor Diamond was too small for a worthwhile load and his feet would never have stood twelve miles of hard County Road there and another twelve miles back. Tom did not enjoy it at all. He told me it was not at all like the coal boat and 'chust a long, hard drag day after day and no enchoyment in it for man or beast'.

And it was a terribly wet winter again too, after that first short early snow when we gathered the sheep in. When it melted away there was no frost, no sliding, no more snow—nothing but rain and sleet driving in my face in the morning all the way to Achcraggan, and driving rain and sleet on my back all the way home at night. When we were into December Doctor Mackay arranged for Alasdair to walk with me up as far as the Smithy, then I would walk west to the Poyntdale shepherd's house with John-the-Smith's apprentice and somewhere between there and Reachfar Tom, George or my father would meet me.

There were times when I felt like a travelling tinker, always going along in the lee of the hedges with my shoulders hunched against the driving rain, but I knew I was much better off than the tinkers, really, for I had a lot of places with good sound roofs and good fires where I was welcome. Still, it was a scattered kind of feeling. In this sort of rain you could not keep dry, no matter which route you took. I had a pair of shoes and socks in the dominie's press at school, I had a pair of slippers and socks at Miss Tulloch's where I went to get a hot meal at dinner-times, and I had a pair of 'moor' boots at Doctor Mackay's in case my morning pair were not dry at night. I seemed to spend half my time wriggling into and out of my oilskins and sou'wester and 'changing my feet' as Tom called it. And, also, as Tom said, my grandmother 'was as short in the temper as cat's hair'.

My grandmother was 'awful fond' of my mother, and at no time could 'Ealaisaidh Dhu', as she called her in the Gaelic for 'Dark Elizabeth', do any wrong, and the wet weather did not agree with my mother's delicate health, so my grandmother was anxious. My grandmother did not like feeling anxious, and she did not like the wet weather either, just for its own 'clarty' sake, and the only persons to whom she spoke a civil word these winter days were Dark Elizabeth and my grandfather. The rest of us, it seemed, were not only responsible for the clutter of wet clothes and boots that hung around the house, we were also responsible for the wind, sleet and rain that *made* the clothes and boots wet. We were never happy, she said, unless we were 'clarting about up to our backsides in wet heather' and she had always told us, she said, that 'Sheep were useless brutes that brought nothing but ill to the Highlands' and, she said, 'Why that little bairn has to be walking eight miles in a day in this weather to be learning that outlandish Latin passes my comprehension.' She usually said all this on a Saturday, when the wet clothes for the week were at their peak, and Tom, George and I would take refuge in the barn to be 'out of her road'.

People 'in her road' was the worst feature, for her, of the wet weather. My father and George were at home more days than they were out, for no work could be done at Dinchory or Poyntdale on these days; my grandfather was permanently in his chair at the kitchen fire; my mother was at the parlour fire, sewing, to be 'out of the draughts', and my grandmother had no place where she could move about freely and expend her tremendous energy.

'God, man, George,' said Tom one Saturday when the three of us were sitting in the straw of the barn after a particularly vicious tirade, 'it's the Ould Leddy that doesna like the sheep!'

'She likes fine the money they bring in, the ould harridan!' said George.

'She's not ould enough to be minding on them Clearances I've read about,' said Tom. 'What spite is it that she'll be having at the poor craiturs?'

'Och, it's the Clearances that's in it, right enough, Tom. Folk doesna chust mind on the things that happened in their own lifetime, not among people like us, whatever. The hatred o' the sheep was put into the Ould Leddy as a bairn, by folk that could mind on the burning o' the crofts when *they* were bairns, maybe. You and me is not as Highland as my mother, Tom. This land of Reachfar, although it is not very good, is rich ground compared with the glens o' the West, and the old people out of the West has long, hard, Highland memories. She doesna like the sheep and she doesna like what she calls the Government and she never will. … But she's clever, Tom—she is as fly as a badger.'

'Aye, she is clever enough,' Tom agreed. 'It's a peety though, the way she will not be learning Janet and me the Gaelic. Funny, you will never hear her at it now except when she is that angry that she forgets herself. Yet, when I came here as a boy she used to be at a lot o' the Gaelic words.'

'Aye, but she sees now that it is the tongue o' the poor. She sees that the English tongue is winning, and she is going to see that the like o' Janet here is on the winning side. She can see a long way ahead, Tom.'

'Too danged far, whiles,' Tom agreed. 'Sometimes even myself will be thinking the way Hamish the Tinker does that the Ould Leddy has the Sight.'

I sat brushing the dogs with the stable brush and cutting the lumps of mud out of their coats with the kitchen scissors, and listening to every word, for I was always interested in hearing any member of my family discussed as if they were persons, and especially my grandmother. It was only now, at nine years old, that I was learning that my grandmother was a person at all. Hitherto she had been the Law, a Power as unapproachable as the Mystery that made the earth turn from spring round to winter, a Light as blinding as that which, the Bible said, shone round the Throne of God.

'But she is fair devilish the now,' said George. 'I suppose it is the wet weather, but there is an uneasiness about her. You notice how she will be sitting by her lone at the fire of an evening for a whilie after the rest of us is in bed? I never like to see her at that caper. There is always some bad comes out of it.'

I did not like this. This was Going Too Far. My granny was

my grandmother and an ould harridan, often, and maybe she had the Sight, but no *Bad* ever came out of her.

'That's lies, George Sandison!' I said. 'No bad ever comes out of my granny! And when she is an ould harridan and be *at* you, you'll be needing it!'

They began to laugh. 'Ach, you are as Highland as your granny with the temper that's in you!' George told me. 'But I didna mean that the bad would come out of your granny.'

'What, then, did you mean?'

'That she is *feeling* something bad in the air. Maybe it is chust the weather—goodness knows, *it* is bad enough.'

'What kind of bad, George?'

'It is hard to put words on it. And maybe I am chust being a little Highland myself.' He shifted his big shoulders inside his jacket.

'But I mind, Tom, that the last time she was like this was the time Kennie the Shepherd took seeck and she went to see him when he was getting over it.'

'Poor Kennie!' said Tom.

'You mean, somebody is going to *die?*' I said. They looked startled, both of them, and Tom said: 'What capers is that that you are saying?'

'*You* never knew Kennie the Shepherd!' said George.

'But he died!'

'So does everybody when they get old.'

'Kennie *wasn't* old!'

'Av coorse he was!' said Tom scornfully. 'Ninety if he was a day!'

'No, man, Kennie was nearer the hundred,' said George solemnly. 'The poor ould craitur! Och, aye, he was a terrible ould mannie!'

I had a suspicion that this was a Pack of Lies—Kennie had been young—but I did not want to face it.

'It will be old Granny Macintosh that Granny is seeing about,' I said. 'She is nearly the hundred now and sometimes she will not be knowing Jean when Jean is washing her face for her. My mother says that it's not sad at all when an old, old person like that dies.'

'That is what I will be thinking, too,' said George.

'*And* me, forbye and besides,' said Tom. 'Are ye finding any fleas on that dogs?'

'Not yet.'

'This dirty weather and them in the barn so much is bad for breeding fleas,' Tom said. 'People needs the air about them to keep them right. George, do ye mind on the fleas in Sandy Bawn's hoosie when he was old?'

'Lord, aye! They would be hopping up the whitewash o' the wall like a battalion o' the Seaforths on the march.'

'There was a thing I was reading in the paper,' said Tom next, 'that is that foolish that you'll not know whether to be believing it or not. It seems there is a mannie in America that has a circus o' fleas.'

'Ach away with you, Tom!' George said. 'That *canna* be right. Where could anybody be making a circus o' fleas as if they was wise, like horses?'

'It said it in the paper, whatever—that he has them running races and a-all and that people will be paying him money to see them at it.'

'I'll not believe it,' said George firmly. 'Where would people—even American people—be paying good money to see a puckle fleas loupin'? I *saw* the circus, in Inverness, man, before the war, and it's horses, real bonnie piebalds they were, and clowns and lions in a cage. Dang it! Fleas! They'll put *any* trock in the paper!'

'The Romans had a circus,' I told them.

'Do ye tell me that now?' said Tom. 'Now, that's real inter*est*ing—them old Romans thought o' near everything. Had they horses at it?'

'Oh yes, for their chariot races. And they had men fighting each other and men fighting lions—gladiators, they were calling them.'

'They was cruel booggers in a way, too, the Romans,' George said.

'The men would be getting clawed, whiles, likely?'

'Oh yes, and killed as well, George. And at some of their circuses they even threw the Christian people to the lions to eat because they would not worship the Roman gods.'

Tom took his pipe out of his mouth. 'Now, that is chust near enough putting me clean off that Romans, clever as they was,' he said. 'For I never could abide that kind of narrow-mindedness and interferesomeness. What was it o' *their* business *what* gods people would be worshipping? There is times when I chust take a fair scunder at releegion altogether. It chust makes more trouble than it's worth. Och, I'll be going to the kirk to please the Ould Leddy and the Reverend Roderick is a fine eddicated man with his Latin and Greek and Hebrew and a-all, and to be listening to him speaking for a bit hour in the week canna hurt a body. But dang it if I would be fighting about releegion and feeding lions with people about it, for your common sense tells you that that is chust not *reasonable!*'

I was astonished, for I had never heard Tom be so vehement about anything in all my life, hardly.

'Folk is inclined to think they are far too bliddy clever,' he continued, 'with all their knowing what is right and what is wrong for other people. If they would chust think about their own right and wrong there would be far less bother in the world and fighting and badness and people being driven wrong in the head! And if that Romans with all their cleverness couldna think of a better way of having a circus than feeding people to lions about releegion, they deserved for their place to burn to the ground while that mannie played his fiddle! For myself, I would rather pay a penny to see the American mannie's fleas. —But if it was *me* that was having a circus, I would have Betsy with ribbons in her mane—'

'So *this* is where you are at your blethers!' said my grandmother, sticking her white head in over the half door of the barn. 'You would be too *busy*, the lot of you, no doubt, to notice that the rain was off! What about the horses? Are they to *kick* their way out o' the stable for an airing?'

The two men shot through the passage to the stable. I ducked under my grandmother's arm to open the gate of the Little Fieldie for them, and after the horses were through and running madly round on the wet, muddy turf, Tom looked at the sky and said: 'Aye, there's a change working in the weather, right enough, George.'

'I'm not seeing bliddy much difference in the Ould Leddy's temper, though,' said George.

The weather, in the course of that night and the next day which was a Sunday, took a complete turn, and the snow started to fall early on Sunday morning, so it was decided not to drive down to church. It was a long grey Sunday, which George, Tom and I spent in Tom's attic room, which was next to mine, and the furthest inhabited room in the house from the kitchen which only barely contained my grandmother. We went up there at about seven in the morning and all three of us took off our shoes and got into Tom's bed after being told 'for the love of goodness *sake* to get out from under her feet.'

'You know what the Ould Leddy puts me in mind of, George?' Tom asked.

'What?'

'The horses, the day o' the Ar*mis*tice.'

'Man, you're right. As if she didna know hersel' what is wrong with her.'

'Aye, it's instink-like.'

'Aye. Well, we better chust be stopping up here out of her road. Man, Tom, it's fine and warm up here in this bed o' yours.'

'Aye—chust hand me that boxie with my teebacca. Well, well, we're missing the Reverend Roderick the-day. At the thirtieth chapter off Profferbs—' Tom began, and we had ourselves a fine sermon, for Tom could 'do' the Reverend Roderick to the life and was not stuck now, even, for the odd erudite quotation 'from the Latin'.

It snowed all day long, and I began to grow anxious, for a heavy continuous fall like this could put my going to school in jeopardy, but as the light faded it began to freeze and when we three went out with the lanterns to feed the animals in the evening we could walk dry-shod over the crisp, frozen snow. It snowed again in the night, froze again, and by morning the scullery window—the only window in the house that looked to the north—looked nowhere except into a deep, frozen drift. It was a *fine* day for going to school, and I set off just at first light, but by the time I reached Achcraggan the sun was up and gleaming over the lovely white world.

About ten in the morning, though, a queer thing happened.

Sir Torquil and my father drove up to the school in Sir Torquil's trap with my Fly and Sir Torquil's retriever at their feet, and the dominie told all us Big Ones of the Top Class to put our coats and things on and come out to the playshed. There were about fourteen of us, Alasdair and I being the youngest, and when we were all lined up the dominie said: 'A most serious thing has happened. Miss Violet Boyd is lost and everybody is looking for her. Now, you boys and girls know your countryside, and all the places where you play. She may have fallen over the rocks—Jamie Ross, you and your sister know every hole in the rocks—look in them *all*. She may have fallen into a ditch, she may be buried in a snowdrift. I want you all to go to the places you know best, taking great care of yourselves, and try to find her. The ones that have dogs, go home and get them. Nobody but Janet and Alasdair is to go up Reachfar way and I'll take the cane to any other person who is seen up there. The storm is bad on the hill, and Reachfar and Greycairn have plenty of men out. Now, when you hear the church bell ringing, go home, for that will mean that Miss Violet has been found. And all of you, be home before dark. Mind that now. Before dark. If you find her, run to the nearest place you know or tell the first grown-up person that you meet. That's all. Off you go.'

My father let Fly jump out of the trap and she, Alasdair and I set off. All day we hunted up and down the watercourses, poked sticks into snowdrifts, looked behind every bush and boulder, and we covered the Reachfar Burn from the spring where it rose to the sawmill on Poyntdale, and found no Miss Violet. Periodically we would meet other searchers; the sawyers from Sir Torquil's mill were dragging the dam; the fishermen were sailing round the shore and exploring the beach; Tom, George, Johnnie Greycairn and their dogs were black pinpoints away on the Greycairn moor. When Alasdair and I passed the smithy or any of the cottages we would get scones and a warm drink, for every house had a kettle on the boil and a bed ready, but, somehow, you could not eat, for the short day would soon be hidden in the dark and Miss Violet would be out in it all alone, and still the church bell stayed silent. I gave a sob as Alasdair and I, with Fly ahead of us, beat and poked at the deep drifts on the north side of the march dyke between Greycairn and Reachfar.

'You are not to start that crying!' said Alasdair sternly. 'If you start that we're done!'

'We're *not* done! Dang it, she must be *some*where!'

'Where then?' he bawled belligerently. 'You that always knows everything! Dominie's pet!'

'Clevery clarty yourself! I'll set Fly on you!'

I knew now how my grandmother felt when she felt anxious and told us 'for goodness *sake* to get out of her road'. I could have felled Alasdair with my stick just for *being* there, saying things and asking questions. I hurled the stick ahead of me just to vent my feelings.

'We're not behaving right for an emergency,' said Alasdair, as the stick spun through the air. 'My father says the hardest thing to do in any emergency—'

'*Poop* to your old father and his emergencies!'

'WHAT MY FATHER SAYS IS,' shouted Alasdair, 'is the hardest thing to do is THINK, and that's what we have to do.'

'Think? What about?'

'I don't know. That's what's so hard.'

We sat down side by side on a snowdrift and thought.

'I can't think of anything except Find Miss Violet,' I said at last.

'Neither can I. It's all very fine the dominie saying Find Miss Violet, like that. It's not him that's—'

'He said the places where you *play*,' I said.

'You and me plays over half the parish,' said Alasdair, 'and he said to come up here.'

'You and me plays more between the smiddy and the school,' I said. 'Together, I mean.'

'That's right. Come on back that way—besides, maybe they've found her by now and the bell will ring any minute.'

We followed our 'Robbers' Roadie' from the smithy to the cave in the Seamuir Burn, followed down the course of the burn and came out at last on the shore, east of the village, just beside Jock Skinner's old abandoned croft. Still the bell had not sounded and the white silence and the black sea were on either side of us.

'Dang it!' said Alasdair. 'The hospital will be no good for playing in next year—the roof's falling in.'

'We'll be at the Academy next year, you stupid goat!' I told him.

At the flapping door of the old house Fly barked, then jumped back and raised her nose to the frosty sky in a long terrified, terrifying howling. We ran forward. Alasdair got there first and spun round, his arms extended from lintel to lintel. 'Don't! Don't look!' he said. He was a ruddy, freckly, pink-cheeked boy, but his face now was the colour of pale winter cream with the freckles dark on his nose. Over his shoulder, I saw the blue coat and the feet, as the body swung from the rafter along by the far wall. Alasdair grabbed my hand and the two of us, with Fly in front, ran sobbing to Alasdair's home, where the doctor, with the yoked pony tied to the gate, was marching up and down the front garden in the cold wind. I remember the doctor jumping into the trap, I remember Mrs Mackay gathering Alasdair and me in one panting bundle into her arms. I remember the hot taste of whisky and hearing the long, slow peal of the church bell.

I do not remember any more until I woke up, at home at Reachfar, in my own room, the next morning, and Doctor Mackay was there, holding my wrist, and my whole family was in the room, too. Tom was sitting on the end of my bed and I sat up and said: 'This is a fine to-do, if you like!' The doctor laughed. '*I'm* not sick,' I said.

'Are you hungry, Janet?'

'Yes,' I said, and then I remembered. 'Miss Violet?'

'She died.' The doctor said quietly. 'It was better, Janet. You see, her mind was sick and it would not get better, and being alive and going about singing yon way was no pleasure to her, the poor craitur.'

'And thinking dolls was real babies,' said Tom.

'That's right,' the doctor said. 'A person that has a mind as sick as that can't be happy. You see, Janet?'

'Where is she?'

'Oh, at home at the Miss Boyds.'

'Not at Jock Skinner's?'

'No, no,' said Tom. 'We would never leave her at yon dirty ould place! No, no. She is at her own home.'

'Can I get up?'

'Surely,' the doctor said. 'You slept so long we thought you were sick.' He pulled out his gold watch that could ring chimes like a clock. 'Mercy! Eleven o' the morning. Time I was off!'

'Eleven o' the morning?' I shot out of bed. 'Granny Sandison, are you out of your head? Letting me sleep till eleven o' the morning? What about school?'

'None of the Top Class is at school today—they're all sleeping like you. I've seen the whole boiling lot o' them.'

'Not Alasdair?'

'He was still sleeping when I left home.'

My mother put my jersey on on top of my nightgown. 'Come down and have something before you go, Doctor,' she said.

We all went down to the kitchen. It was fine being at home on a Tuesday at schooltime as long as Alasdair was not getting away from me at the Latin, I thought; and while the doctor and all the men of my family had a dram out of the parlour bottle and the women had tea, I had a big plate of porridge. Then I remembered something, and after waiting for a long time until they were all quiet so that I would not be making an interruption, I said: 'Please, Doctor Mackay, you promised to tell me something.'

'What was that, Janet?' he asked.

'It was the day Miss Violet was here and she thought the doll was a baby and—'

'Och, Janet, lassie, be quiet!' my granny but not my grandmother said. 'With your ask, ask, asking about Miss Violet!'

'That's all right, Granny,' Doctor Mackay said. He often called her 'Granny', especially at times when she was helping him with some sick person or to get somebody's baby born. 'Poor Miss Violet! It's nice to be speaking about her a little. We mustn't forget her too soon, poor craitur. Yes, Janet?'

'It was when she was nursing the doll and she gave you an old bittie heather out of her hair and you put it in your button-hole and said something.'

'Did I?' The doctor's face got funny, as if he were shy, but, of course, I knew it was not that, for how could Doctor Mackay ever be feeling shy?

'I don't remember.'

'It was something bonnie, you said, and you said you would tell me.'

The doctor looked round at us all, and my uncle came up behind him with the parlour bottle, put some whisky in his glass and then some water. The doctor held the glass up between his face and the window and looked through the whisky at the snow outside.

'Can you remember now, Doctor Mackay?' I asked.

'Yes. Yes, I remember now. It was a few words of an old story that I read once, Janet. The story was about a young woman that went out of her mind when her father died. Miss Violet went out of her mind because she thought her baby was dead, you see.'

'What was the name of the person in the story?'

'Ophelia. And she was like Miss Violet, picking flowers and making chains of them—'

'And singing that funny way?'

'Yes. Ophelia sang too. And she would give her flowers to people, just the way Miss Violet gave me the heather.'

'Miss Violet gave me a chain too, down beside the Reachfar Burn.'

'She did, eh?'

'And what were the words? The words you said?'

The doctor held up his glass and looked through the whisky at the white world outside the window again. Then he looked down at me. 'The words, Janet, were: "There's a daisy—I would give you some violets, but they withered all when my father died."'

These were the words, right enough, dying away, sad and

lonely at the end, like the last notes of Danny's fiddle. The doctor swallowed his dram and put the glass on the table beside my porridge plate.

'God rest the poor young craitur,' said my quiet grandfather.

'Aye, Reachfar. … One or two of you will come down for the funeral?'

'All of us except Tom and the bairn, Doctor,' my grandmother said.

'That's very good o' you in this terrible weather.' The doctor pushed his arms into the sleeves of the overcoat that Tom was holding for him. 'School again tomorrow, Janet!'

'Yes, Doctor. Please, what is the name of the story that Ophelia is in?'

'The doctor has to go now to see Granny Fraser's rheumatics,' my mother said.

'It is a story called *Hamlet, Prince of Denmark,* by a man called William Shakespeare. He wrote it long, long ago. You will read it for yourself when you are a little bigger. Good day, now, Janet.'

My uncle went out with him to his trap, and I was told to go upstairs and put my clothes on properly, for it would soon be dinner-time. I Did As I Was Told, but while I did it I was repeating to myself the words that Ophelia said in the story. They had, when you said them, pausing in them as the doctor had paused, some of the quality of Miss Violet's queer little song—they had its eerie, broken sadness—but they made you feel, somehow, that you need not be afraid of the song or of the thought of Miss Violet any more.

*   *   *   *   *

You will realise that that story that I have told you happened long years ago in a world that was quite different from the world of today.

In the thirty years between 1919 and 1949 many things changed, and people and places changed too. My mother died in 1920. I grew up, my grandparents died, and down at Achcraggan Miss Lizzie and Miss Minnie, the two oldest of the Miss Boyds, died too. And the two youngest of the Miss Boyds, Miss Iris and Miss Daisy, getting older, sold their shop in Inverness and came to live at Achcraggan where Miss Annie, as Tom put it, was 'making a right old maid's mess o' bringing up that laddie, Andra'. But let me put it all in chronological order.

By the early 1930s, Andra, as Andrew Boyd, called after his 'unctioneer' grandfather, was known, was the bad boy of the district, but in the eyes of Miss Annie and her two older sisters until they died he could do no wrong. Our district had seen many of what it called 'weecked' loons, notable among them My Uncle George in his time, and, in the next generation, My Friend Alasdair Mackay when he grew a little older than when we last met him in this chronicle. Alasdair, in his time, constructed a spring-mounted ghost that jumped over the churchyard wall when a courting couple up the lane by the Manse leaned against a certain gate which they favoured, and succeeded in scaring the whole parish, including the Reverend Roderick and three policemen, half out of their wits. Alasdair and I, too, at the age of about eighteen, when we happened to meet when I was on my way home from Achcraggan one winter Saturday evening, chanced to see the road-men's tar boiler by the roadside and were inspired to tar the seat of old Lewie the Joiner's outside lavatory, so that his sons had to detach him from it by force in the winter darkness of the next early morning, but that is another story. What Andra Boyd went in for was not 'weeckedness' but 'pure badness', and between the two sins our district draws a distinct line. I suppose it is a laughter line. You could laugh at old Lewie stuck to his lavatory seat, but you could not laugh at the fire in the Seamuir stackyard. At least, our people could not. They could laugh at Marion Innes and Hugh Donaldson running into the bar of the Plough to escape the ghost, but they could not laugh at the gate being opened that let the Reachfar sheep through to eat all old Granny Fraser's young turnips. They *did* laugh, however, at George, this time, arriving in Achcraggan with Sir Torquil's riding crop, and for a long time told how you could have heard 'not only Andra, but his three aunties forbye howling west at Ben Wyvis'. This was probably the only thrashing that Andra ever had in his life, for he did no more damage to Reachfar, and our people at home will tell you that 'that was the only thing that was wrong with him'. He was the child who had the two great deficiencies by their standards—that of being actively spoiled and that of being passively spoiled by having the rod spared as well—and they were not surprised that he was 'as full of badness as a clockan egg is full o' stinkin' meat'.

In the early 1930s I went away to the south of England to earn my living, but every year I came home to Reachfar for long enough to catch up with the major local events. Reachfar was the one unchanging place in a world of constant change. In 1934, I think it was, there was a local tragedy that shook the district as it had not been shaken since the death of my young, gentle mother in 1920, when Master Anthony, the young heir to Poyntdale, was killed in an accident with his car one frosty winter night. Poyntdale was now no longer the place it had been, and the loss of the heir was the one more cruel blow that carried Sir Torquil and Lady Lydia into old age in the space of a night. During the 1920s all the outlying farms and the houses in Achcraggan had had to be sold off, and now even further sales took place, so that the once Great Estate was reduced to the cumbersome 'Big House', a few cottages and the lands of the Home Farm. My father had long ago left the service of Sir Torquil, for Poyntdale no longer needed—nor could it afford— the services of a grieve of my father's calibre, and a younger, less experienced man had taken his place on the sadly reduced estate. The ties between Reachfar and Poyntdale were not breakable, however, and young Master Torquil, who was a year younger than his brother who had been killed, was brought home from the Army in India to train under his father for the taking over of the depleted inheritance, with George and Tom to act as tutors-extraordinary whenever they and Master Torquil could get together. The 1930s, up there, were sad years—the time when, in that backwater, the aftermath of the war that ended in 1918 showed its full destructive force. Only Reachfar, on its rocky hill, and Greycairn above that, managed to weather the long storm and emerge outwardly unscathed. Nearly all the little crofts were submerged in the bigger landholdings, and the sheep that my grandmother had hated—the sheep that took the land from the people—were prowling, grey, over the land that had once carried the fine crops and the fat, black cattle.

Change came to the Miss Boyds, too. The house at Achcraggan was their own, but the 'puckle money that they had among them' had lost value and was losing value steadily every day. Old Miss Lizzie and Miss Minnie, having done their fair share in 'making a ruination of' Andra, gave up and died about 1935, although, as Tom said, 'they were chust in their seventies and had chust made the allotted span of it and not much more'. About a year later Miss Iris and Miss Daisy sold their shop in Inverness and joined the household at Achcraggan, thus consolidating the 'puckle money' in one place. I was at home for a holiday just shortly after this, while it was still the fresh news of the district, and went over it all with Tom and George one Sunday afternoon.

'You canna,' said Tom, 'but be sorry for the craiturs, down there with that rascal of a laddie not doing a thing o' good, although they have put him to the Academy and a-all and chust the old man's bittie money and not a penny coming in.'

'And it's not younger they're getting,' said George.

'How old *are* they?' I asked. 'When I was a bairn, the time Miss Violet died, they all seemed to be about a hundred, except poor Miss Violet, and she seemed to be just about twenty. I can see her yet, sitting at the fire with the heather in her hair and nursing yon damned doll.'

'Aye. Yon was terrible,' said Tom. 'Mind you, Miss Violet *was* young.'

'Aye,' George said. 'She must have been just about the last kick o' that dirty ould boogger Andra when he was on his death-bed.'

'He was a terrible man for the weemen, George, man. A right randy ould boogger—the Bull o' Inverness, they used to be calling him.'

'Aye, that's right—Andra Bull.'

Tom began to laugh. 'Lord, George, man, do ye mind on the time at the Sales that the leddy from the south that was a stranger called him "Mr Bull" to his face?'

'If Miss Minnie and Miss Lizzie were over seventy and Miss Violet would only have been about thirty-five now if she were alive, he must have had a long and productive life,' I agreed.

'Aye, and them six old maids wasna the whole of it by a long chalk,' said Tom. 'Andra Bull's bairns is scattered from Perth to John o' Groats.'

I began to understand, only at this late date, why so many men had taken refuge from the Miss Boyds in the Plough in the old days. People whose lives are closely linked to the breeding of animals have a strong belief in heredity.

'How old will Miss Annie be now?' I asked. 'I always thought she was the best of the bunch.'

'Aye, and so she was,' said Tom. 'And I can put an age on her too, for she is chust about ages with myself. She'll not be less than sixty-four and not more than sixty-seven, for I can mind when they were building the hoosie at Achcraggan and I was at the school and seeing her down there with Ould Andra looking at it. The two old ones was grown-up weemen even then—they were a big bit older than Miss Annie. And, av coorse, the young ones was a lot younger. There was the spell between the two wives, ye see, when Andra was—'

'Free for all?' I suggested.

'Aye. It's well seen the Ould Leddy is in her grave when ye dare to be speaking like that!'

In 1939, just before the newest war broke out, I went home to Reachfar, taking with me all the books and possessions that I wanted to store in a place of safety, and up there the imminence of war had a horror less real for my people than the fact that Andra Boyd, who was now twenty and had been 'put to' this trade and that and had made nothing of anything, had committed the final sin. He had got a girl west the country in the family way, come back to Achcraggan through the night on his motor-bicycle that his aunts had given him, taken all the loose money, jewellery and small saleable articles that he could lay hands on out of the house, and had disappeared as completely as Jock Skinner had done when he crossed the Greycairn moor on that Prize Day long, long ago. By this time Miss Iris was a cripple with rheumatoid arthritis; Miss Daisy, who had always been particularly feckless, was now more so; and Miss Annie, who had always borne most of the family responsibility, celebrated this latest family disgrace by going gently but completely mad. This took the form of a refusal to believe that Andra had done anything wrong and a determination to believe that everything was perfectly normal and that Andra would be home for a meal when he was hungry.

'The poor craiturs,' my father said. 'It would be a kindness to them if you were to go down and see them, Janet.'

'Do that, Janet,' said my aunt, who was now married to Hugh, the young grieve who had taken my father's place at Poyntdale, and who was also mistress of Reachfar. 'I'll put up a basket and you'll go straight and not be gawping about you.'

I laughed back at her. 'Ach, poop to the Miss Boyds! But all right. I'll walk down this afternoon.'

They would not know me, of course, I thought, as I pushed open the broken-down gate to the overgrown garden, for Miss Iris and Miss Daisy had never seen a great deal of me, even as a child. I went round, knocked on the back door and it was opened by Miss Daisy. I was wearing a tweed suit and a white blouse, and at that time I wore my longish dark hair piled in the neo-Edwardian fashion on the top of my head. Miss Daisy stared at me and gave a nervous giggle. 'You—you're Mrs Sandison's—you must be her granddaughter Janet.'

'That's right,' I said. 'How d'you do, Miss Boyd? How clever of you to know me.'

'Anybody would—that ever saw your mother and your granny. But come in, come in.'

I followed her into the kitchen. It had always been a dreary villa-ish kitchen—grey and darkish—not a sunlit, firelit, cheerful place like our kitchen at Reachfar, and it was even more cheerless now. Miss Iris, the joints of her hands and arms knotted, her jawbones curiously distorted by the grotesque work of the arthritis, sat in a corner in an armchair, while, between the dresser and the table, Miss Annie was extremely busy laying a place at the table for one person.

'You know about my sister Annie?' Miss Daisy asked quietly.

I nodded and said: 'Good afternoon, Miss Annie.'

She looked at my face for a moment and then smiled brightly. 'Well, good morning, Janet!' she said. 'So it's yourself with the eggs.' She took a bowl from the dresser. 'Just you unpack them for me till I lay Andra's dinner. And how is your mother today?'

'She is very well, thank you, Miss Annie,' I said and began to take the eggs from the basket and put them in the bowl.

She had a curious dignity as she went about her task, in her long skirt and high-necked blouse of about 1910, with the little grey shawl about her shoulders.

'After he's had his dinner'—she looked at me pleadingly—'maybe you and him and me will go for a wee walk up the town?'

'Yes, Miss Annie,' I said.

She bustled off through to the scullery very busily, and Miss Daisy said: 'She is always wanting to go up the town and I can't let her go alone and I don't like to leave Iris too much.'

'I'll go,' I said. 'That's all right.'

I talked to Miss Iris and Miss Daisy while Miss Annie waited upon the imaginary Andra who had come in and was now eating his dinner while we had our tea, and then Miss Annie and I, with Andra, went up to the village street and walked from the Plough at one end to the doctor's house at the other. All my old friends, Bill the Post, Mrs Gilchrist, Miss Tulloch and the doctor, knew that we had Andra with us, of course, and were punctilious about bidding him the time of day, and then we made our way slowly back to the Miss Boyds, for, of course, Andra had to be going back to his job in Inverness.

'What is Andra's job, Miss Annie?' I asked, after we had seen him safely away on his motorcycle.

'Oh, he's in business and doing very well,' she said and bustled away to take off her hat and coat.

During the war I did not have many leaves that were long enough to allow me to make the journey from Buckinghamshire, where I was stationed for most of the time, all the way to Reachfar, and when I *was* at home time was too precious, or I was too selfish, to give it to walking round Achcraggan with Miss Annie and the imaginary Andra. Of the real Andra not a word had ever been heard.

At the end of 1947, however, I married, and after a short honeymoon by car in Sutherland and Caithness, my husband and I came back to Reachfar for a few days on our way south to Ballydendran, near Glasgow, where our new home was waiting for us. My husband, whose nickname is Twice, is a Scottish Borderer who had never seen the Highlands until I first took him to Reachfar, but he is a great connoisseur of people and was fascinated from the first by the seeming imperviousness to change of the people of my district. Tom's attitude to the wireless set, which I had given him before the war and which sits on the little table that used to hold my 'bitties drawer', is typical of what Twice appreciates with such glee.

'This is my sound boxie that Janet gave me,' Tom told him the first time they met. 'It is a wonderful contrivance, if you'll be minding to get its battery from the garratch at the smiddy on Saturdays. It's a sort of engine, like. You would be knowing about it maybe?'

'A little,' said Twice, who is an engineer by profession.

'When you'll be turning this knobbie, you can hear the mannie as plain as if he was beside you, and him speaking in a roomie away down in London. It is a wonderful thing. But, av coorse, only if you'll be using it for a good purpose. If a person will be using it for badness, like that mannie Hitler was doing, it is a very bad thing indeed. Being chust an engine, like, it has no more sense, and some of the capers and nonsense that will be coming out of it whiles, you chust would hardly believe.'

Twice had heard me speak of Tom often enough—as has everyone who knows me—and of George too, but in spite of all I had said he was not quite prepared for the shock of their outlook. My father and George, a little younger than Tom, had, by 1947, long since accepted the motor car as part of life, but Tom, with magnificent resistance, had never so far set foot in one of the stinking contraptions. He had travelled, as far as Inverness, by train and by motor bus, his theory being that these contrivances were driven by men wearing 'snooted bonnets that had proper control o' the engines', but a car, driven by a 'civilian' as it were, and especially a member of the family, Tom regarded as a lethal weapon put into our hands by the devil for our destruction.

Twice, in the past, had driven my father and George down to the Plough in Achcraggan in the evening, and had greatly enjoyed the conversation that took place there between them and such cronies as Donald Beagle, who still carried the name of the long-defunct family boat, Doctor Mackay, the drunken Captain Robertson of Seamuir and Bill the ex-Post, who sat in a corner with his melodeon.

The Plough was now quite a different place from the dark mystery that I had feared would blow up on Armistice Day. It was owned by an English ex-Air Force officer, with a limp and green corduroy trousers, whose pretty, lipsticked young wife served behind the bar, and it had a steady clientele of 'arty' people who came by car from all sorts of places, especially in summer, for it was no more than a pleasant evening run from Inverness, that crossroads of the North. 'The Cronies', as Twice called the older local men, were vastly entertaining in their comments on the bearded young men who wore velvet trousers and coloured sweaters and on the sprightly young women in their slacks or shorts, and Twice was fired by a burning ambition to get Tom into the Plough of a Saturday evening. After much argument and persuasion, Tom gave way, and was got into the front seat of the car between Twice and me, while my father and George sat in the back. My aunt, a widow since the war, stayed at home, of course, to look after the place.

The road down from Reachfar to Poyntdale was better than it had been in my childhood, but still bumpy, but Tom conceded that the car did not 'loup about' as much as the trap, on the whole.

'Mind the bridgie at the Poyntdale dam, though, lad! Don't let her get away from you!' he warned.

'I wish you would buy me a snooted bonnet, Flash!' Twice said to me.

At ten miles, or less, per hour, we crawled down the Poyntdale road and made the eastward turn on to the County Road at the shore.

'My, but what a rate to be going at!' said Tom. Twice pointed to the speedometer. 'Ten miles an hour, Tom—see it there?'

Tom was fascinated. 'That clockie? That is miles that it is saying on it?'

'Miles an hour,' said Twice.

'Make her go a little harder, lad—chust a little, though, mind!'

The needle of the powerful, though old, Bentley crawled to fifteen.

'I'm not feeling much difference, lad.' The needle crawled on again. By the time we came into the long clear sweep round the bay to the Plough Tom was crowing like a six year-old and shouting: 'Geordie, man, the clockie is saying sixty mile an 'oor—a mile a meenute! Faster than the aeroplanes!'

Inside the Plough there was no holding him. Flown with his wonderful experience, he held forth to the crowded bar about the remarkable age we lived in and ended: 'And a-all you bonnie leddies in here having your dram. Aye. It is myself that likes to see it. There was a time when a-all the leddies would be stopping ootside and only the menfolk would be enchoying themselves.'

I had a vision of the Miss Boyds, sitting in a row on the sea wall, on the grey afternoon of Ar*mis*tice Day.

It was growing dark outside now, but the lounge bar was bright with firelight and the 'bonnie leddies' were very colourful in their bright slacks and brighter sweaters, and as delighted with Tom as he was with them. To him they were visitors from a strange, new world—they might have come from Mars—and to them he was a remarkable survival of an age that they had never known. I have never met a person who did not 'take to' Tom, and the 'bonnie leddies' were no different, in this way, from the women who had been their mothers and their grand-mothers.

We had a very gay evening, but just before closing-time, when the last song was being sung by a young man from Edinburgh who had come in with My Friend Alasdair, to the accompani-ment of Bill the ex-Post's melodeon, the air outside was rent by the sound of a high-powered car, the door swung open, and a short, thin, blue-chinned, flashily-dressed man said: 'Double whisky,' and threw a five-pound note on the bar.

'I'm sorry, sir,' said the landlord's pretty wife. 'I can only let you have a single—the last of tonight's bottle.'

'Hell—all right.'

He took the drink, pushed a half-crown of the change at her, at which she said: 'Thank you, sir,' and turned away about her duties. He then opened his padded-shouldered, dark coat, pushed his black felt hat to the back of his head and, reaching into his inner pocket, brought out a glittering cigarette case of gigantic proportions. Under cover of the singing, Twice whis-pered to me: 'Who is the spiv? Know him?'

I have told you that in 1918 there were old maids. After the 1939–1945 war there were 'spivs', the offal-caters who grew fat on the ugly by-products of war, such as food and clothing shortages, and 'dealing' in surplus stocks that the Government had for disposal. I suddenly felt that the greyness of the long-gone Armistice Day had invaded the cheerful room.

'Let's get the old fellows home, Twice,' I said quietly, as the spiv looked round with shifty eyes from beside the wooden pillar that went from bar to ceiling. Twice collected my father, George and Tom, and the young people bunched round to see them to the car and say goodnight. I summoned the thought of my grandmother and stared through the sneering ferrety face at the bar until, like the face of the Cheshire Cat, it disappeared, first behind the pillar and then out into the darkness beyond the door. Then I rose, thanked the landlord and his wife for their hospitality, said goodnight and went out to join my family.

The next day Twice and I drove my aunt, Tom and George down to Achcraggan for the groceries. Traditionally my father had stayed at home to look after the place, although nowadays there was very little to look after, for much of the land had been let to the surrounding larger farmers. Nor were there butter, eggs and honey to exchange for the groceries now, for my people kept only cows, hens and bees enough for their own household supplies and were living mostly on their savings and their pensions, but the 'marketing' was the same leisurely business that it had always been. My aunt disappeared into Miss Tulloch's, whose niece now helped her aunt in the shop; Tom disappeared into the post office and George into the bank, it being agreed that we would all meet at the Plough at its forenoon opening time.

Twice and I, having provided ourselves with a bottle of the 'Finest Port Wine' from Miss Tulloch, went to pay a call on My Friend Bella Beagle, who was now very old and seldom left her home, which, however, still maintained the clean whitewashed-inside-and-out standards of the old Fisher Town, and had a row of the dark-green glass balls, which were once used as floats for the fishing-nets, sitting on the mantelpiece between the brass candlesticks. After we left her we walked round the back of the Fisher Town and the village, which led us past the ruins of Jock Skinner's croft to the Plough.

'It all seems so terribly long ago,' I said to Twice.

'But this hasn't changed as much as my part of the country. Just after the war, when I went back to my parish in Berwickshire, there was literally nobody left that I knew. They seem to live longer up here.'

'Oh, a lot of them are gone, though. Still, this arty, beauty-spot tourist influx is a good thing, and the electric scheme up the Glen should help when it gets going—except that the whole place will probably change its character.'

'Not as long as George and Tom are alive.' Twice laughed as we went into the pleasant bar-parlour of the Plough. 'What will you have?'

'Beer, I think, please. We'll probably have to wait for hours. Tom and George never had much sense of time, but now they have retired, as they call it, they are worse than ever.'

'An old shepherd I once knew,' said Twice, 'said that the Man Who Made Time made plenty. I just wish more people could remember that.'

We had been sitting for about half an hour when I heard a powerful car stop outside. 'Is that the car that was here last night?' I asked.

'No,' said Twice.

'Are you sure?'

'Certain.' I moved to look out of the window. 'Oh, ye of little faith in my ear for an engine!' He smiled, leaned back in his chair and looked out. 'No. This one has an American registration—'

An old lady, but elegant to the last blue-tinted curl of hair, in a wide-swinging tweed coat above nylon-clad ankles and tiny feet, came into the room, followed by a large, pink-faced, white-haired, distinguished-looking obvious husband. I smiled good morning at them as they went to the bar and turned back to Twice.

'By the way, who *was* the bloke in the big car last night that you didn't like? We never got around to it.'

'Cross my gullet with another beer and I'll give you practically his life story,' I said.

Twice went to the bar for the beer and I sat looking out of the window at the old pier where I could see again the coal boat, the destroyer dashing up the Firth and Betsy's head rise between me and the distant hills on that far-off Ar*mis*tice Day.

'There you are, my dear,' said Twice, and put down the glass half-pint mug in front of me. 'Give.'

But before I could speak the white-haired lady was standing in front of Twice, laughing up at him. 'Young ma-an, is this yo-ah wife?'

'Yes, madam,' he said. 'She is.'

'Ah can tell you two thi-ings about her that every husband oughta know-ow!'

'You can?' Twice smiled. 'Please sit down.' Twice has a great ability for taking things as they come. He turned to the white-haired man. 'Won't you join us, sir?'

We all sat down, the lady laughing at me while my mind went back frantically over the 1939–45 war and my working life before it, as I tried to remember all the Americans I had ever met.

'Ye-es.' She smiled at me with dancing dark eyes under the blue-silver hair and then turned to Twice. 'Yo-ah wife is a poet and she is also pra-ably a wi-itch—but the kind, clever sorta wi-itch!'

'Mrs de Cambre!' I said.

'That's right, honey.'

'But—how in the world did you know me?'

She laughed. 'Did'n' I know your mother and your gran'-mother?'

We talked for a long time, and for another long time after George, Tom and my aunt joined us, and in the end came back to that Harvest Home which, although we did not know it that lovely night, was the last Harvest Home in the old lavish tradition to be held at Poyntdale.

'It's a sha-ame you weren't there, Henry,' Maddy Lou told her husband. 'It was the grandes' party I ever been to.' She then turned to Twice. 'An' the mos' remarkable thi-ing happened. Miz Sandison, Janet's grandmother, tol' my fortune. She said a great happiness would come to me through my son. He was jus' eighteen at the time. Henry's family is an ol' French Southern family and I was very unhappy at that time because we had only this one boy—I was kinda haunted that somethin' would happen to him. We-ell, Miz Sandison said this happiness would come through my son and that it took the form of a three within a three. She was dead certain about it an' tol' me to remember it, and when Ah went back to London I tol' Henry.' Her husband nodded. 'He jus' laughed at the time, but it made us sorta feel better, an' then the queeres' thi-ing happened. Our boy married at twenty—an' when he was jus' twenty-one his wife gave birth to *triplets,* three boys! Can you imagine tha-at?'

'The three within the three years, see?' said Mr de Cambre. 'It certainly was queer.'

'Ach, it was only a lucky shot in the dark!' said George. 'The Ould Leddy was as fly as a badger at that fortune-telling caper. Three within a three could mean nearly anything!'

'Now, now, George, man!' said Tom uneasily, with a look south-easterly over his shoulder in the direction where the churchyard lay. 'There was times when there was no telling with the Ould Leddy. No. There was times when she chust wasn't canny with the things she would be knowing. I think myself that the Sight was in her, right enough.'

'So do I,' said Maddy Lou positively.

'And was Granny a poet too?' Twice enquired.

'No,' said Tom solemnly. 'No, I wouldna say she was a poet. No. Indeed, she had very little time for the poetry. It's George and Janet and me that would be at the poetry, when we was oot aboot, oot o' sight o' the hoose, like. Aye. We had some right fine ones.

From Reachfar and looking east, you see the big North Sea,
And from Reachfar and looking west the Moor of Dinchory.
From Reachfar and looking north, you see the Firth and Ben,
And from Reachfar and looking south, you see the Home
    Moor Glen.
And in between the compass points there's plenty things to see,
Like flowers and birds and animals and George and Tom
    and me.

That's the one we made when we was learning the points of the compass.'

'Ain't that cute, Henry?' said Maddy Lou.

'Och, yes. We was great hands at the poetry,' said Tom. 'Twice, chust ask the chentleman to be bringing us another droppie of what everybody would care for and to be helping himself to one at the same time. ... Mind you, I wouldna be saying but the Ould Leddy would be knowing about the poetry a-all the same. There wasna much that she didna know when you think on it.'

'Not very much,' George agreed. 'Between them, Leddy Lydia and herself knew everything in the parish and further, when I think on it.'

'Aye, they was the terror o' all the weemen in the country-side,' said Tom. 'And how is her leddyship, madam?'

'She is we-ell, but very lame. ... You should come and visit with her a li'l sometimes.'

'Thank you, madam. It's George and me that would be real pleased, and Duncan too, if her leddyship would like it. Av coorse, we a-always call on her at the New Year, but if she would like it George and me being retired now can take a run down to Poyntdale any time.'

'She'd jus' love it! She misses Torquil. She speaks about the ol' days a lot of the time.'

*   *   *   *   *

When we had parted outside the Plough I had in me that remote quiet sadness that comes with nostalgia, that comes with the knowledge that, happy as the past time was, one cannot go back, coupled with the knowledge that one would not go back even if one could. What was past was past, and the happiness or sadness of these past days was now an integral part of all of us, grafted on to us, fed and given its quality by the stock on to which it had grown. As I watched the eternal water of the Firth flowing against the old stone of the long, sloping pier, I was thinking of my own good fortune. All that had stayed with me of those days of which we had spoken was happiness. Those days had come forward through life with me, a permanent background, clearly outlined in the brilliant northern light, that had influenced—and for good, I thought—every new experience that slid on to the stage of life in front of it. The light from that background had, for me, illumined everything; the restful shadows of its 'Thinking Place' had dulled the sharp edges of many harshnesses, and the sunlit songs of the Strip of Herbage had, in the Old Testament words often quoted by the Reverend Roderick, 'made the rough places plain'.

'Deaf as a post, Twice!' said my aunt's voice. 'Gawping about her, as Granny called it. Janet, Twice says we might as well have our dinner here since we are so late, and the hotel gentleman says he can manage us.'

'Oh,' I said. 'Yes. Yes, that's fine—'

'I have to go back up the village afterwards, anyway. I forgot to get that paint your father wanted.'

'George,' I said, as we sat down at the table in the old stable of the Plough which had been turned into a pleasant dining-room, 'how are the Miss Boyds?'

'Ach, much the same as ever, poor craiturs. Iris is terrible cripple and Annie is dafter than ever, still thinking that Andra will be in for his dinner any minute.'

'It's a queer thing that, and him been away for years. Maybe he is dead for a-all anybody knows, but poor Annie will never believe it,' Tom said.

'But I saw him last night!' I said.

'Andra? Where?' my aunt asked.

'Right here in the Plough!'

'Ach away, for God's sake!' said George. 'It's dreaming you were—or else fou'. Andra has never been seen in Achcraggan since back before the war! Besides, how would *you* know him? You hardly ever saw him in your life!'

'I knew him all right,' I said.

'*I* never saw a person here last night that I didna know, and none o' them was Andra Boyd,' said Tom. 'When was you seeing him, Janet?'

'In the bar, just before we left, standing by the pillar.'

'It's the Sight that's in her, like the Ould Leddy!' said Tom.

'The Sight be damned!' I said. 'Twice, *you* saw him! The spiv you asked about.'

'Oh, the spiv? Is he this Andra Boyd? *He* was there all right, George. Drove away in that big green Panther—you know, the car that was beside ours when we came out.'

'Car? Andra Boyd? Away ye go, Janet! You're not right in your head. It *couldna* be Andra. Where would *he* have a big car? … The ould craiturs down in the housie there have all they can do to make ends meet.'

'It was Andrew Boyd,' I persisted. 'Want to bet on it?'

'Not me!' said Tom. 'I'd as soon bet with the Ould Leddy hersel' as bet wi' *you*. But if it *was* Andra you saw, it is a very, very surprising thing indeed, that's what it is.'

'I never thought to see him back.' George was still unbelieving.

'No, nor me neither,' said Tom.

When we had finished our lunch we left the car at the Plough and walked the short distance up the street to the shop of Mr Dickson, Ironmonger and Seed Merchant, where Miss Dickson was still smiling with the teeth she had 'grown' forty years ago and which were rather a loose fit now. She told us, among other things, that we could not buy paint 'without a special Government paper permit-thing since the war', but added: 'Chust go out and round the back, George, and tell Davie what you are needing and that I said to cover it up in a baggie or something for you.' She then turned back to Tom. 'What I will be saying is that what the Government doesna know canna hurt it.'

'Aye and me too, forbye and besides, Miss Dickson,' Tom agreed.

'And was you hearing the news?' she asked next. 'Andra Boyd is back. It seems he has done very well away south about Sheffield or London or some place down that way and him driving in a big car and a-all. Aye. He was at Young Lewie the Joiner the-day to be giving him an estimate to be sorting the roof o' the hoosie for the Miss Boyds. Is that not a wonderful thing when ye think on it?'

'My, it is that,' said Tom.

'I was chust saying to Annie Gilchrist—it was sad about Teenie, the gossiping ould craitur, how she went so sudden in the end, wasn't it?—that I aye knew that Andra wasna a bad laddie at heart. And there he is, minding on his old aunties and a-all they did for him, the craiturs.'

'Old hypocrite!' I said to Twice in the background. 'She and all the rest of them hated the very sight of Andra. As for his *heart*—'

Twice grinned. 'He didn't look as if it took up a lot of room,' he agreed. 'But a spiv has to bury his excess profits somewhere and Achcraggan is nicely out of the way but looks like turning into a tourist resort.'

'That's about it,' I said.

Still, as Tom had said many times in my hearing, 'People is very very peculiar and inter*est*ing craiturs,' and we can never know *all* that is in them, or actuates them or otherwise causes them to 'live and move and have their being', for, when we left Miss Dickson and came out into the street, whom should we meet but three Miss Boyds, accompanied by the spiv, who was more flashily dressed than ever.

'Well, well. Good day! Good day!' said Miss Annie, who was leaning on Andra's arm, while the crippled, bent Miss Daisy was leaning on Miss Iris on one side and on a stick on the other.

'Andra's just had his dinner and then he was for us to come out for a bittie, so—' She turned to me in a most business-like way. 'If you've brought the eggs, Janet, the back door is open and just go in and leave them in the bowl on the dresser for me. That's a clever girl. And how is your mother?'

'She is very well, thank you, Miss Annie.'

'And how are ye yourself, Miss Annie?' George enquired.

'Och, I'm fine, thank you, Mr George. I'm busy, though, with Iris, poor soul, and her so lame, and Daisy is not much use.' The younger sisters let this pass with a smile. 'But we had a drive round in the car with Andra this morning and that makes things brighter for them. You'll come back for a droppie tea with us?'

'Not today, Miss Annie, thank you,' said my aunt firmly. 'We have to get back up the hill.'

'That's so. It is a long way. Och, well, there will be another day.'

Andra, who had not spoken a word, was obviously restive, and Twice, George and Tom were restive too, for they could not think of a word to say to him. He looked as foreign as if a back alley from Soho had been transplanted with him into Achcraggan village street.

'And where are you off to now, Miss Annie?' I asked, feeling that if something was not done we would all be frozen there for all time.

'Mercy! I was nearly forgetting—my memory isn't what it was. We are going to Teenie Gilchrist's, the Draper, and she'll be away to her tea if we don't look smart. Yes. Andra is going to buy hats for us, for a present. We'll have to go now. Good day! Good day!' They moved slowly away from us up the uneven pavement. There seemed to me to be in the air a faint echo of a giggling, a nudging and a fluttering, a small stirring of a fidgeting with ghostly frills, as they passed on, the three old women, and the flashily dressed man in the dark overcoat that was too wide at the shoulders and too narrow at the hips.

'I don't know how you knew him, Janet,' George said. 'He's quite different from when he was a laddie.'

'And you never saw much of him then, whateffer,' Tom accused.

'By Jock Skinner,' I said.

'He's no more like Jock Skinner than *I* am!' said my aunt scornfully.

'It must be the Sight,' Twice said mischievously.

I did not say anything, because it would have been too difficult to explain my belief that we all have our own 'Sight', which is conditioned by the things we have seen in the past. *They* had not seen, through my eyes, the things I had seen forty years ago. *They* had not been in the Miss Boyds' kitchen that first morning when Jock Skinner pushed his ferrety face with its sharp little eyes round the lintel of the door and announced: 'I'm always glad to oblige the leddies,' and I had stared at the spot where the face was until it disappeared like the face of the Cheshire Cat. *They* had not been sitting in the bar of the Plough last night, precisely where I was sitting; *They* had not seen, with my eyes, influenced by my memory, the ferrety face by the pillar at the bar; *They* had not seen it fade away from sight like the face of the Cheshire Cat.

While I had been thinking of these things, my family had been giving Twice the history of Andra in so far as they knew it, and it was Tom who spoke the final sentence as the car pulled in to Reachfar: 'Och, aye. Quite a time of it, George and I had with them ould maids one way and another in the ould days.'

My father came out of the house and opened the door of the car: 'Well, you had a right day of it the-day, Tom! Had your dinner?'

'Och, yes, man—a grand dinner in the stable at the Plough.'

'And who was you seeing in Achcraggan City?'

'Man, Duncan, you will chust be hard put to it to be believing it! Andra Boyd is back!'

'No!' said my father.

'Aye, but *so!* We was speaking to him in the street, him and his aunties—Janet's friends, the Miss Boyds!'

THE END

Afterword

Jane Duncan Remembered

by her niece and nephews

SHONA

My early memories of Aunty Bet are around the blue airmail letters with exotic stamps and distinctive handwriting which regularly arrived for my parents from Jamaica. I also recall visits by Aunty Bet and Uncle Sandy, who I remember as quite a glamorous couple, descending on our small village in rural Aberdeenshire. From the visits came Neil's toy sit-on tractor which he used to service his imaginary farm, and my favourite book, *Tales of Scotland*, which I still have.

After Aunty Bet came back from Jamaica after Uncle Sandy's death, the memories are much clearer and centre on our long, apparently sun-filled summer holidays in Jemimaville. I do, of course, remember Rose Cottage from my earlier years and suddenly the cottage was brighter. Gone were the heavy velvet curtains, the clutter of old-fashioned furniture, the pine-clad lean-to kitchen and the outside toilet with its smell of Jeyes Fluid, and in came the pink-and-white striped wallpaper in the west room (Aunty Bet's bedroom) with the bookshelves lining two walls and filled with the fascination of all kind of books. No longer had we only the books we brought, Edward Lear's verse and a book about Victorian and Edwardian water cures! There was a bathroom too.

All day we played on the shore, in the orchard and around the village, stopping only to eat, and in the evenings, we played cards or Scrabble with Dad and Aunty Bet. For someone so skilled with words, I don't recall her being that good a Scrabble player.

I don't remember if it was Aunty Bet or Mum who cooked, but quantities of food arrived and were consumed—always with lots of vegetables and potatoes grown by Uncle George, and later Fraser, in the productive Rose Cottage garden.

Aunty Bet and Uncle George then moved to the Old Store—it had a 'modern' look, with views right on to the Firth. I remember how I loved staying there in the spare bedroom with the stripy woollen blankets and the slippery green quilt. The food was always wonderful and if I stayed on my own, I relished the quiet and the adult attention away from our hectic household and noisy brothers. It was always good to get back to them, though, to resume my big-sister role. Uncle George, both before and after his disabling stroke, was the centre of the Old Store world and life there was warm and calm.

Aunty Bet did occasionally write—on her knee, in long-hand, leaning on her old atlas, and sitting by the log fire—but usually she put her fountain pen aside while we were around. If questioned, she would tell me about her life experiences, but she wore her fame lightly and I had little idea how well-known as a writer she was at that time.

I saw her as emotionally strong, capable, clever, practical, very intuitive and caring. She was quiet and modest and helped look after the people around her in the village—she relieved the village shopkeeper, taking over the Post Office function to let her have a holiday.

She was funny and witty, sharing Dad's sense of fun. They were very close and she must have been devastated when he died.

When I got married, she was the one who took me aside from all the fuss and presents and listened to my apprehension and excitement.

Sadly, she died when I was six months pregnant with my eldest child, Sarah, and when we were on our way north to visit her. She would have been very happy to know the next generation of the family—another 'Hungry Generation'.

Shona Hollands
Bridgnorth, January 2010

NEIL

This is Neil. I was Neil in the *Camerons* books, Duncan in the *Hungry Generation*. I remember meeting Aunty Bet that first time when she came to visit us at the schoolhouse in Aberdeenshire. That was over fifty years ago now.

I think I was about seven years old and a very shy child indeed. Almost everything frightened me then, until I understood that it would not, or could not, harm me. I knew she would not harm me but I was very frightened of meeting Aunty Bet and she always frightened me a little bit right through my childhood. Why? I knew she loved us Cameron children.

I think it was because she was a shy person herself and a very private person too. For that reason, perhaps, she came across as somewhat remote and reserved. It seems to come through in *My Friends the Hungry Generation* that she had the same fear of us children as I had of her. I think that she had had little contact with children and did not know how to communicate with them. I certainly had no experience of tall, fierce-looking women who had come from Jamaica and were so incredibly clever that they actually wrote books. So when I was seven and she was forty-nine, we were frightened of each other, I think.

All through my childhood, our long summer holidays in Jemimaville and lots of other visits 'up North' were very special.

For a few years all crowded into the quite tiny Rose Cottage. We children ran wild all day on the shore of the Firth and were summoned for food or bedtime by the loud ringing of a bell. Aunty Bet and Uncle George moved down to the Old Store at the bottom of the garden in 1961 and slowly the holidays changed as we teenagers began to do other things. We continued to visit, of course, but I don't think we saw enough of her for our relationships to be very close.

We had to be careful when we visited. As I remember, she wrote furiously from early January to March. I know my parents worried about her in these dark winter months as they thought she did nothing but write and did not eat well or rest enough. By Easter, usually, the latest manuscript would have been sent off to the publisher and she was free to get into the garden, and welcome some company. She had many friends locally and all round the world but they all knew that there were times when she had to be left alone. I remember her saying to me once that she had a miserable time between sending off her manuscript and getting word from Macmillan confirming that they would publish. Even at the height of her powers and her undoubted popularity with her readers, she never lost the fear of failing to get her latest work accepted.

When she died suddenly in 1976, I was no longer frightened of Aunty Bet and was developing a new relationship with her. I was 24 by then. I had started work and was within a few months of qualifying as an architect and heading out to practise my profession and explore the world. For me, the new relationship we were building was about me drawing on her vast knowledge of literature and philosophy. It was also about me accessing her great store of wisdom and understanding of life and of people. My father died before I could learn 'grown up' stuff from him and now a second wise teacher had gone from my life much too soon. I felt cheated.

But at least Aunty Bet had written things down and the wisdom and perceptions are there on the page. Written in her books and articles, of course, and also in a few treasured letters. Like many authors, she was a prolific letter writer. For many years, she replied religiously to the many fans who wrote to her. Eventually, the volume became too much, even for her, and she wrote *Letter from Reachfar* in which she related much of her 'real' story and answered many of the questions people asked in their letters to her.

I know that my father and she corresponded regularly during the war, when he served in the Royal Navy and she was a WAAF officer working in photo-intelligence, and as a child I remember my mother nagging my father to write to her in Jamaica. When she came home to Jemimaville, the phone call replaced the letter for my Dad but my mother and she continued to write regularly. None of these letters survive, to my knowledge. I had never been much of a letter writer but after my father died in 1973 something made me want to make more contact with my Aunty Bet. So we wrote to each other from time to time. I still have some of her letters from our sporadic correspondence in the early seventies and splendid letters they are, full of wisdom and written with the intensity and clarity that any reader of her books would expect.

In one of them she advises me that whatever I did, professionally or for fun or the most mundane of chores, I should do to the best of my ability, 'whether it is frying fish or writing a novel' as she put it and she continued: '… I don't want to fry fish or write novels better than anybody else. I don't recognise any best except my own.' Simple advice perhaps, and unremarkable, but the way she expressed this simple and ubiquitous message to me in a personal letter changed me and changed my attitude from then on. As I re-read this particular letter nearly 35 years on, I could hear her voice. For me, that is the power of the personal letter in the hands of a professional wordsmith. Truly wise people are rare. Truly wise people who can communicate vividly in the written word are much rarer. My Aunty Bet was one of these.

We still have Rose Cottage in the family. My wife Christine and I took our children 'up North' all through their childhoods and we all still love Jemimaville and the Black Isle. There are portraits of Aunty Bet and George on the wall and most of her extensive personal library is there still in the bookcases. The world has changed so much in the 100 years since Aunty Bet was born. Her beloved Black Isle hasn't changed much and her work is as fresh and vibrant as the day it was written. Some things never change, I am very happy to say.

Neil Cameron
Sheffield, January 2010

DONALD

In my earliest recollections my Aunty Bet was living in Rose Cottage with Uncle George while the Old Store was being converted. In my eyes she was no different to my other aunties, Anne and Mary. Like them she was kind and generous to my sister, brothers and me. We had the privilege of being the only children in the immediate family. We had no cousins and we were spoiled rotten by all three of them.

When we were on holiday in Jemimaville, usually in August, we had the freedom to go out unaccompanied and the village was our playground. We would climb trees, paddle in streams or at the edge of the Firth and when Aunty Bet rang the brass hand bell we would run back for lunch or tea, or dawdle back for bed. For years she had no television so if the weather was bad we played cards or board games, or read.

I remember her in the lean-to kitchen preparing meals for eight while my father sat outside, on a stool by the rainwater barrel, peeling potatoes, a glass of bottled beer by his side. I remember Uncle George working in the big garden which sloped down towards the sea, hoeing the vegetable patch or trimming the topiary animals, straight-backed in his collarless shirt and waistcoat.

It is this humble domestic activity I remember most clearly, I suppose because food, fun and affection are more important to a five year-old than celebrity or faintly exotic personal histories. But as I grew older I became more aware of this other person called Jane Duncan (and the more mysterious 'Mrs Clapperton' who had returned from the colonies). When she moved to the Old Store with Uncle George (and the two dogs Dram and Macduff) there was more room for Jane Duncan, the big writing desk, the endless rows of books. I began to think of her as more than an aunt. In my world she was rich and famous.

She seemed to pull off the trick of being both the 'lady' in the big house and a true member of the community. She established the Friendly Shop tearoom in Cromarty, three tables, twelve chairs, home baking, homemade jams and sweets. The group of friends who cooked and baked and the teenage girls who served in the shop would also sell bric-à-brac collected from around the Black Isle by tradesmen. On reflection, this was probably carefully worked out. Fans of the *Friends* books would be diverted from her private space at Jemimaville but would still be able to meet and chat with her at the shop. And Cromarty's economy gained from the number of visitors who came the extra five miles to see the shop, and the village she had represented as Achcraggan in her writing. Although Aunty Bet seemed to enjoy her own company and writing is a solitary business, she was far from antisocial and I'm sure she enjoyed being at the centre of the bustle in the Friendly Shop while the queues for tables stretched down the street.

Back in Jemimaville she would entertain a series of guests in the summer months: family such as ourselves and my mother's relatives, old friends from Jamaica, new friends and colleagues from England she had met since becoming a publishing sensation, favoured enthusiasts for her writing, such as Professor Russell Hart from Boston. Often these guests would stay in Rose Cottage.

Not long after she moved into the Old Store with Uncle George, he suffered a stroke and became paralysed down one side. She cared for him, in the Store, for the rest of his life. He would sit in a chair by the stone fireplace, his back to a big window which looked out over Udale Bay. His bed was in the corner of her large open-plan living area. She had help, regular visits from the district nurse, a cleaner, a gardener. But she did quite a lot herself around the house and garden and enjoyed cooking, particularly for the summer guests.

Within a few years of returning from Jamaica she had established for herself a new life as a successful author. I'm sure she felt she had come 'home', even though the Black Isle had never been her true home. She had built a house and garden to her own design. She was within a few miles of the family croft, the Colony, where my father, her brother, had lived as a child with their paternal grandparents and where she had spent school holidays. In many ways her life was as she had dreamed it and planned it after the sad circumstances of her return. For me, the cover illustration of her last novel *My Friends George and Tom* captures the essence of that life. She had also, it seemed, established a pattern of working at her writing in the winter and welcoming family, friends and fans in the summer.

I have no doubt that what brought her back to the Black Isle (and after the early success of the *Friends* books she could have chosen to live almost anywhere) was the strong attachment of place and people. Her two closest relatives were her Uncle George and my father. So it must have hurt her deeply when both died within a few years of each other, my father in 1973 after he had moved back to Easter Ross with my mother, my younger brother Iain and myself.

I had spent the last two years of my schooldays at Dingwall, around fifteen miles from Jemimaville, but left for university in Edinburgh shortly after my father's death. We all continued to visit Aunty Bet until her sudden death in the autumn of 1976. She is buried, near my father and mother, in the graveyard of Kirkmichael. From the graveyard, you can look across the bay to the Old Store on the shore and to Jemimaville just above it. Much higher on the ridge of the Black Isle you can see the ruin of the Colony.

I still have much to remind me of her, the large photographs of her parents (my grandparents), the carver chair on which she sat at the dining table. More importantly, I have kept a part of her own book collection. This includes some of the best known novel sequences, *romans fleuves*—Anthony Powell, C P Snow, Proust. This was a format which suited her style and approach. Her effective description of people and places attracted loyal readers and she was able to address bigger themes in the natural flow of her characters' lives. I think that to some extent the perception of *My Friends the Miss Boyds* suffers as a result. People who have read their way though the series of *Friends* books may see it as a scene-setter, an introduction to Janet Sandison and her world, an introduction to some of the other characters, the beginning of a long story of one woman's life. But, leaving the other books aside, the *Miss Boyds* is still a fine novel. It treats some challenging issues in a human and funny way, and presents a convincing picture of how lives were led in the north of Scotland. And I think it hints at why she returned to the Black Isle in search of contentment. As a child she was probably happier on summer holiday at the Colony than going to school in dark, damp winters on the outskirts of Glasgow, and more secure in the care of loving (and loved) relatives before the stresses and risks of adult life as a young, independent-minded woman.

So, oddly perhaps, the books which give me the clearest impression of my own memories of Aunty Bet are the Janet Reachfar books for young children. To me they represent both a rosy recollection of her childhood holidays (which seem much like my own childhood holidays that she helped create) and a blueprint for the world she tried to establish in Jemimaville: the kindly and wise woman running house and home from the kitchen, the practical men with good advice and fascinating tales, the dogs, and the drama and excitement of life coming not from imperfect relationships with imperfect people, but from nature and the imagination.

Donald Cameron
London, January 2010

Acknowledgement

Millrace would like to thank Shona Hollands, Neil Cameron and Donald Cameron for their kind permission to publish this edition of *My Friends the Miss Boyds*. We hope that it will help to introduce Jane Duncan to a new generation of readers.

Other books by Jane Duncan

My Friend Muriel
My Friend Monica
My Friend Annie
My Friend Sandy
My Friend Martha's Aunt
My Friend Flora
My Friend Madame Zora
My Friend Rose
My Friend Cousin Emmie
My Friends the Mrs Millers
My Friends from Cairnton
My Friend my Father
My Friends the Macleans
My Friends the Hungry Generation
My Friend the Swallow
My Friend Sashie
My Friends the Misses Kindness
My Friends George and Tom
Letter from Reachfar

for children
Camerons Ahoy
Camerons at the Castle
Camerons Calling
Camerons on the Hills
Camerons on the Train
Herself and Janet Reachfar
Janet Reachfar and Chickabird
Janet Reachfar and the Kelpie

writing as Janet Sandison
Jean in the Morning
Jean at Night
Jean in the Twilight
Jean Towards Another Day